NO
GOING
BACK

BOOKS BY CASEY KELLEHER

NO GOING BACK

CASEY KELLEHER

bookouture

Published by Bookouture in 2021

An imprint of Storyfire Ltd.
Carmelite House
50 Victoria Embankment
London EC4Y 0DZ

www.bookouture.com

ISBN: 978-1-80019-525-7
eBook ISBN: 978-1-80019-524-0

For Joy
My favourite mother-in-law
X

PROLOGUE

Her eyes gradually adjust to the pitch-black darkness of Richmond Park as she shines her phone torch down on to the footpath, focusing on where she is walking, instantly regretting taking the shortcut through the park now that she's alone.

It's too quiet, and she feels vulnerable now that no one else is around. It's just her, here in the dead of night. She turns constantly as she walks, scanning the pathway behind her to check that she is actually alone, convinced she keeps hearing small sounds behind her. No one is there.

Even so, she walks faster, eager to reach the park's exit at the other side. Looking up ahead of her, she can see the familiar, faint red-lighted towers of London, looming just off in the distance, peeping through the mass of woodland that stands between them. Yet somehow, in the midst of these trees, the City of London seems worlds away.

A noise, then, behind her again. She turns once more, but this time, before she has the chance to convince herself that she's just being paranoid, that she's being stupid, there's a figure right there, pressing up against her. Grabbing her tightly, a gloved hand concealing her mouth to stop the scream that she tries to force out, as she realises the danger that she's in.

Her attacker is strong. They force her down on the ground, and she struggles under their weight, fruitlessly trying to fend them off. Her attacker fights back, harder and stronger, in a bid to overpower her. She kicks out and the shunt of her foot catches her assailant off-guard, making them double over in pain and giving her a few seconds to scramble back up.

Which is no easy feat, with the roundness of her bump and the extra weight of her baby that she is carrying.

She stares through the darkness, working out the quickest escape route – through the woods ahead of her, or back the way she came, down the pathway to the park's entrance? She has a few seconds but she knows it's futile. Whichever way she chooses, she won't get away. She won't be able to outrun her attacker. So, she does the only thing she can do and screams out – a blood-curdling screech for help that echoes across the park, magnified by the silence. All the while praying that someone will hear her cries or that, at least, her attacker will retreat.

But her hopes are short-lived: she catches the sliver of light gleaming from the serrated edge of the knife's blade as it strikes her. It all happens so quickly, so unexpectedly, that she doesn't even register the cut at first. That her stomach has been slashed in a single movement, from just above her navel, down to the bottom of her belly. She feels winded, as if she's been punched, and instinctively she moves her hand to her stomach, pressing against the fabric of her woollen jumper, protective of her unborn child beneath it.

She feels the warm liquid spilling out of her before she sees it. In shock, she brings her hand back up and strains to see the blood that covers her palm. Her blood. So much blood. Pumping out of her.

'Help me!' She manages to scream as loud as she can, hysterical, before the dizziness overcomes her and she falls to the ground.

Her attacker retreats now, alarmed, either by her continuing screams or the sight of the growing pool of blood, turning on their heel and making a run for it and leaving her splayed out on the cold, damp footpath, cradling her stomach underneath the blanket of darkness that stretches out over Richmond Park.

She stares up at the night sky, focusing on the cluster of stars above her. And bleeds out.

CHAPTER ONE

Staring at the television screen as his horse galloped towards the finishing line, as if it had a rocket shoved up its arse, Ashley Cooke couldn't believe his luck. The tip he'd had on Dark Horse was proving to be a winner. As soon as Ashley had heard its name, he'd known it was a sign and meant for him, because he'd always liked to think of himself as exactly that: a dark horse. Underestimated and undervalued by most of those around him. Still, he'd been told by very reliable sources that Dark Horse was set to win hands down. Which was why he'd borrowed the obscene amount of money that he had from the Boland brothers. Because there was no way he could lose.

Rubbing his hands with glee, Ashley downed his pint in anticipation of the celebration that was soon to come. He was still embracing the immediate effects of the line of coke he'd snorted in the men's toilets, just moments before, as the gear surged around his blood, keeping him fired up – alert and full of energy. He was on top of the world. Today was his day. Today he was set to win big, finally.

Ashley couldn't wait to see Shelby's face when he told her that he'd managed to come up with the deposit for a place down at the river. One of those posh apartments that he knew she had her eye on. And, even more importantly, he couldn't wait to wipe the sanctimonious look off his father-in-law, Pete's, face when he finally proved to the man that he and Shelby didn't need his handouts. That he was more than capable of providing for his new wife.

Ashley scoffed to himself. He was high as a kite and the beer was going down well too. His eyes fixed on the screen, he remembered how he'd once so desperately wanted an in with Pete Baker.

When he'd found out that Shelby was the man's daughter, he'd bent over backwards to get her to go out with him, dying for a chance of an introduction to one of London's once most notorious gangsters. Ashley had been desperate to get on the man's payroll and earn some decent money. Because Pete Baker was still respected. He had years of clout and reputation behind him and had earned some serious money over the years. And Ashley had wanted a piece of that too. And now look at him.

He'd stupidly managed to get Shelby pregnant within just weeks of starting to date her. And the irony wasn't lost on him that, although Pete Baker couldn't stand the sight of Ashley from the first second they'd met, he'd soon changed his tune once he'd realised what Ashley had done to his daughter.

Wanting Ashley to do the right thing and stand by Shelby, Old Pete and Janey Baker hadn't been able to get the two marched up the aisle quickly enough. They had put on the over-the-top, glitzy, extravagant wedding of Shelby's dreams, all bought and paid for, of course, by Daddy Dearest. And Ashley had had no choice but to just go along with it all.

The biggest insult of all, though, had been the wedding gift: a deposit for their first house together. Because Ashley had known what Pete Baker was thinking. It was the same reason that Pete had finally given in and offered Ashley a job. Of course, he had; how else was his precious Shelby going to get on in life without someone supporting her? And it was clear he didn't think Ashley could do that without his help.

Though even giving him a job hadn't panned out the way that Ashley had hoped. Pete treated him like a dogsbody, giving him all the shitty jobs that no one else wanted to do, and the wage, though regular, was pretty basic.

The one thing Ashley had refused point-blank, though, had been the gift of the house deposit. Putting his foot down, he'd told Shelby in no uncertain terms that he drew the line at being beholden to his mother and father-in-law for the rest of his days. He'd made her a promise that he'd get the money himself. Until then, they were living in his flat on the Griffin Estate. But he knew that Shelby hated it there. That she wanted to get out.

And today was that day. It was the last few tense minutes now, but his horse was still up there in the lead, steadfast and running at a blistering speed. The horse at his rear, Victory Call, was gaining. But Dark Horse could do it. He was set to win. Ashley had every faith. He'd got this tip from someone on the inside, someone with the know. This was his lucky day.

Only Dark Horse was starting to lag, head-to-head with Victory Call now. The loud cheering in the pub started to blur into one loud, white noise, until all Ashley could hear was the whooshing sound inside his ears. His heart sinking as he forced himself to keep watching as Victory Call took the lead. Charging across the finish line ahead of Dark Horse. It was over. The race done.

He stared at the screen in complete dismay. Ashley Cooke had just lost a small fortune that wasn't even his to lose.

CHAPTER TWO

'Which hospital are you taking him to?' Stepping aside as the two paramedics guided the trolley that cocooned the critical patient onto the ambulance, DC Lucy Murphy stared down at the victim, noting the straps holding the patient down and the neck brace. His body had no doubt suffered from numerous breaks and who knows what kind of internal injuries, after being hit head-on by a speeding car.

'St George's Hospital.'

'Okay, I'll meet you there,' Lucy said, turning and making her way back to her own vehicle further up the street.

The man was critical and would no doubt end up with life-altering injuries. But he was alive, and from what Lucy had learned so far about the incident, since she'd arrived on the scene, she was surprised that the man had survived the horrific ordeal at all – small mercies.

Despite the fact that it had just gone midnight, people from the street were out in their droves now, she noted as she made her way back to her car. All taking in the chaos and commotion of the aftermath. No doubt in shock that something so sinister and horrific had taken place on what was normally a quiet, residential Wandsworth street.

Reaching her car, Lucy stopped as DS Morgan pulled up beside her and wound down his window for an update.

'What are we looking at? A hit and run?'

'It's looking more like attempted murder, Sarge,' Lucy said, jumping as the ambulance siren echoed loudly behind her and turning briefly to watch the vehicle pull away. 'It appears to have been a targeted attack. Deliberate. There was a verbal altercation first. Then the attacker got back in his car and purposely drove at the victim before driving off again. The patient is critical, Sarge, they're taking him to St George's Hospital. I'm going to meet them there and see if I can get a statement from him once he's able to talk.'

'And the attacker? Is there any news on him? Did we get a number plate or any vehicle details?' DS Morgan said, mapping out in his head the resources that they would need in order to track down the perpetrator.

'We've already got him.' Lucy pointed further up the other end of the street, to where one of the patrol cars was parked next to a second ambulance. 'He didn't make it further than the end of the road. Lost control of the car in his bid to make a quick getaway and smashed head-on into a garden wall. His car's a mess, probably a write-off, but somehow, luckily for him, it looks like he only suffered a few minor scrapes and bruises. Claims he's got whiplash though, so a paramedic is just giving him a quick once-over before our lot take him in. Though, if anything, the whiplash was probably caused afterwards by the "helpful" resident who caught up with him.'

DS Morgan raised his eyes questioningly as Lucy nodded discreetly over to where a group of residents stood on the edge of the footpath nearby, having an animated and intense-looking conversation with a couple of uniformed officers.

'That guy there gave chase and he caught up with the assailant once he'd crashed. When our lot turned up, he had him in a headlock!'

'Yeah, that would do it!' DS Morgan said as Lucy suppressed her grin in agreement. Her sentiments exactly.

Her boss gave the burly looking man a once-over – all six foot six of him, and he was almost as wide as he was tall. His muscular body was covered in tattoos, and he had a permanent disgruntled look on his face.

'I think I'd rather take my chances with the wall than get detained by him. Still, we've got him, so that's a result, regardless of how we actually got there.'

'Oh, it gets better, Sarge. We've got it all on camera too. The man's wife…' Lucy nodded to the petite lady, with bright yellow bleached hair, standing beside the big burly man and talking animatedly over her husband every time he tried to get a word in. She was clearly used to being centre of attention. 'She managed to film the entire incident on her mobile phone. From up there.' Lucy turned and pointed up to the open bedroom window directly across the street from where the incident happened. 'She got the lot. Zoomed in on the attack, got close-ups of the attacker's face and the number plate of the vehicle he was driving. She even filmed her husband giving chase to the car before it had reached the end of the road.'

'A couple of modern-day heroes by all accounts.'

'Yeah, only it may have backfired on them. And us. They wanted the whole world and his wife to know that they'd caught the guy red-handed, Sarge. When we first turned up, they were doing a Facebook Live. They clocked up a fair few views too. It went viral. We managed to get it taken down, but now the assailant is claiming he's been assaulted and is a victim of a crime. And that his whiplash has been made worse. No doubt he'll use the footage to his advantage.'

DS Morgan rolled his eyes at that, imagining the backlash that the police would get.

'Another quiet night on the job…' Lucy said with a grin. Policing could be frustrating at times, but she was doing her best to not let it get to her.

'If only.'

'SARGE!' A voice behind them shouted, making Lucy turn quickly, just in time to see a man hurtling towards her at speed.

'Oh shit!' Lucy said, recognising the attacker and realising that he was attempting to do a runner from the police officers and the paramedic who had been giving him a once-over.

'STOP. POLICE,' Lucy shouted loudly, and instinctively charged towards the man in a bid to stop him.

The impact of his full weight as it slammed against her caused them both to collide and fall in a heap onto the pavement. Lucy felt her back thud against the concrete, temporarily winding her. But the man was scrambling back up onto his feet – she had to move quickly.

She grabbed his arm, pulling him back with every bit of strength she had in her.

Desperate now in his bid to escape, the man threw a punch, his closed fist locking with Lucy's jaw. An acute pain exploded in her head. Impulsively, she wanted to reach up and touch where the pain radiated in her skull, but for now she had to ignore her own injuries and keep hold of the suspect with all her strength. DS Morgan was at her side now, helping her to cuff the suspect as he continued to lash out.

Now Lucy, her face burning, her back aching, had had enough. Clambering to her knees, she twisted the man's arm behind his back before pinning him down to the floor, pressing his face down on the cold concrete as he screamed out in pain.

'You're breaking my arms,' he yelled.

'Oh, I'm sorry. Here, let me adjust my hold for you, sir!' Lucy said sarcastically, making sure that the pressure she was placing on the man was no more than needed and that he was, in fact, comfortable. Though she had no intention of releasing her grip. It was obvious to her that he was clearly still trying it on and doing his best to cause as much drama and controversy as possible to avoid being detained.

But Lucy and Morgan had him now. Sitting straddled across the assailant's back, Lucy waited as the original arresting officer finally managed to reach them all.

'I take it your whiplash has miraculously disappeared then?' Lucy said as the detainee started to butt his head back and forth in a bid to try and crack Lucy with his skull. 'You just added assaulting a police officer to your already long list of offences. You do not have to say anything, but it may harm your defence…' Lucy said, taking great satisfaction in the fact that she'd just taught the man a very valuable lesson in underestimating the strength and force of female police officers, as she read him his rights before handing him back to her colleague.

CHAPTER THREE

'Ashley! I've been calling you all night and don't make out you haven't seen my calls; you're normally surgically attached to that bloody phone of yours,' Shelby spat furiously down the phone. She was leaving her seventh voicemail message for her husband tonight. To say that she was beyond annoyed was an understatement.

It had gone midnight now, and Shelby knew from bitter experience that if Ashley had gone on a bender straight from work again, the chances were he'd be on the missing list all night.

God knows what – or worse, who – he'd be up to. Shelby didn't even want to think about it. Her mind was already in overdrive as it was. How dare he keep doing this to her? Fobbing her off and treating her as if she wasn't a priority in his life? She was his wife. She was carrying his baby. And what did she get in return? A lying, cheating, no-mark of a husband. That was what. Lording it up all over London, spunking his wages at every bar and club instead of coming home to her.

And she knew why he wasn't coming home to her: because she was fat. At eight months pregnant, she felt like a beached whale. Her bump huge and swollen, the rest of her carrying more weight than usual too. Because she'd indulged with her pregnancy. And why shouldn't she?

If she wanted some cake, she'd earned it. It wasn't as if she was able to knock back her favourite Chardonnay every night now. Shelby had let herself go. She knew it. What man would fancy her at eight months pregnant? Not even her husband any more it would seem. Well, she'd had enough. She hadn't signed up for this blatant disrespect from Ashley, and there was no way that she was just going to sit back and keep putting up with it.

'You're a pig, Ashley. Doing this to me yet again. You're out of order. You knew that I was cooking us a nice dinner tonight. I've been sat here on my lonesome all evening like I'm the last thought on your mind…' Shelby said, fighting to hold back her tears now. Because she wasn't upset. She was furious. 'Well, I'm sick of this, Ashley, and I'm not doing it any more.' Shelby pouted angrily, though she knew her words would fall upon deaf ears. Ashley would do as he pleased, regardless. Then he'd pick up the pieces afterwards. After he'd spent the night shagging some skanky little tart in the meantime, no doubt.

If she didn't take drastic action and teach Ashley a lesson he wouldn't forget in a hurry, he would only keep on doing this to her. Or he'd get worse. And Shelby didn't want this life for her or her baby.

'I'm leaving you, Ashley. I'm going to go back to my parents. Tonight. Right now,' she said resolutely as she pressed the phone to loud speaker, before dragging her suitcase out from under the bed. 'And this time, I'm not messing about. It's for good. Me and this baby deserve better than this. We deserve better than you,' Shelby said dramatically.

Feeling victorious now, she hung up the mobile phone and slung it down on the bed before throwing some of her clothes inside the case. If her words didn't have the desired effect on the man the minute he replayed them, then maybe coming home to an empty flat would do the trick.

A few days at her parents' house would be just the remedy she needed. Let Ashley sit here and fester all on his own. Let him make his own dinners for a change. Maybe then, when he realised how much he needed her, he'd learn to appreciate her a bit more and stop taking advantage of her all the time.

Ashley would be screwing once he realised that she'd involved her parents in their latest domestic again, too. Because it wasn't any secret that her father barely tolerated Ashley.

Shelby smirked as she zipped up her case and put her coat on, relishing the thought of the revenge she'd reap, using that knowledge to her advantage. Ashley needed a proper wake-up call once and for all, and if she wasn't capable of making him see the error of his ways, then maybe her dad would.

Her parents would, of course, welcome her home with open arms, and she was looking forward to having someone run around after her again for a change. She'd get her mum to make her favourite curry that she liked. And maybe some of that homemade soup that she always whipped up for her when she was feeling down in the dumps.

About to call a cab, Shelby had a change of heart. She'd walk it. Their house was only five minutes away if she cut across Wandsworth Common. And turning up in the middle of the night, having walked there on her own because she was beside herself at Ashley not coming home yet again, would be sure to send her father into a frenzy of rage.

Giving the flat one last look-over, Shelby switched all the lights off before shutting the front door behind her.

CHAPTER FOUR

Stepping into the dark alleyway that ran alongside Smokes nightclub, Ashley Cooke was glad of the peace and quiet. The music inside the club had been so loud that he'd felt the heavy thud of the bass pulsating right through him. Combined with the copious amounts of beer he'd managed to knock back tonight, he'd started to feel queasy.

Shit, I'm getting old! He laughed to himself at how pathetic he was as he pulled out the cigarette box from his jacket pocket and sparked up, before breathing out a long plume of smoke into the cold night sky.

He needed to pace himself, he mused, grinning at the thought of Kate, one of the young hostesses he'd been plying with drinks all night, finishing her shift shortly. He'd pulled, and he was going to need every bit of stamina he had if he wanted to keep that one on her toes. Ashley knew the score. He wasn't completely stupid; he knew what the hostesses were all about. They were paid generously to keep the men dangling, clutching to the belief that these women wanted to spend time with them. Stroking the men's egos and anything else that helped in order to keep the men spending their money. And Ashley had spent out all right.

But Ashley knew that Kate wasn't using him. She was different. He could sense it. They'd been flirting with each other for weeks, and it was getting more and more intense each time he saw her. She had been doing more than just her job tonight. She wanted him as much as he wanted her. The chemistry between them had been palpable, almost electric. And she'd made her intentions blatantly obvious when she'd invited him back to hers tonight, after her shift finished.

She should be out soon.

Glancing at his mobile and seeing the first of many missed calls from Shelby, Ashley groaned inwardly before switching it off and shoving the phone back inside his pocket. Tonight, finally, after a whole week of feeling sorry for himself since losing his big bet on the horses, his luck was well and truly in. This time he'd cracked it, he was certain. And Ashley needed this more than he realised.

Craving the thrill of the chase and much-needed boost to his ego.

Nothing, not even his nagging wife would ruin that for him.

'That was quick…' Hearing a noise behind him, Ashley grinned as he turned, expecting to see Kate standing there. Only his smile was knocked from his face just as quickly as he was knocked off his own two feet.

The force of the unexpected blow sent an almighty explosion of pain through the side of his skull as he slammed backwards onto the ground.

'What the fuck?' he managed to say as he lay on the cold, damp pavement and stared up at the two men who loomed over him menacingly.

'Sam. Russ,' Ashley said, gulping down the bile in the back of his mouth. A wave of pure fear engulfed him as he recognised the faces of the notorious Boland brothers.

'Ashley, mate!' Sam sneered. 'Long time no see! Anyone would think you've been avoiding us.' The two men didn't wait for Ashley's reply. Instead they set upon him. Unleashing their pent-up fury as they dished out countless kicks and punches.

'Please, Sam. Russ,' Ashley begged, gasping for breath as he curled up into a ball on the pavement and tried to shield his head with his hands as the blows kept coming.

Though even that didn't help. The men were fierce and brutal with their reprisal, as Ashley had known they would be once they finally caught up with him.

He'd let his guard down tonight, being out in public and flashing his cash around inside the club. The alcohol and promise of spending the night with Kate had made him lose his head.

He'd known that the Boland brothers would catch up with him eventually. He was stupid to think that someone inside wouldn't have tipped them off.

Of course, they had.

Everyone was out for themselves. On a mission to make their own earn and Ashley had made enough enemies in his time.

He screamed out as an explosive punt of a boot caught him under the chin. Ashley felt his jaw crack before the metallic tang of blood trickled down his throat, along with a jagged piece of a broken tooth. He was scared but he knew if he didn't at least try and speak up for himself, these two monsters would kill him.

'Lads, please. I'm about to be a dad, Sam. Please, don't do this...' Ashley begged. But the truth be known, he knew that this had been coming to him. Sam was right. Ashley had been avoiding the brothers like the plague all week. Because he didn't have their money, and he knew that you couldn't bargain with the likes of the Boland brothers.

Tonight, stupidly, he'd been too busy thinking about getting his leg over with a pretty hostess, after weeks of flirting had made him forget for a few minutes to keep his wits about him. The brothers must have been waiting outside the club for him in their motor. They must have seen him here, lurking alone in the alleyway, hidden away from any passers-by, and taken their golden opportunity to set upon him.

And Ashley was under no illusion that anyone would intervene and help him. Even the doormen at the club wouldn't come to his aid. Because if they'd spotted the Boland brothers making their way down here, they would have known that it was in their best interests to turn a blind eye. Anyone with half a brain cell knew that interfering with the brothers going about their business would cause more trouble than it was worth. Everyone except Ashley, that is.

He'd stupidly believed that he'd be able to pay the men back somehow, and now he realised how naive he'd been. He'd pissed these men off big time, and the ultimate reprisal would be to pay with his life.

'That's enough, Russ!' Sam Boland ordered, seeing the stream of blood pouring from Ashley's nose. He put his hand on his brother's arm, a signal to rein it in.

Russ needed telling. His temper was colossal and, when it got the better of him, there was no telling what damage he could cause. Sam was glad that this time Russ listened. He knew they needed to be smarter than that. Putting the man in a wheelchair or killing the bloke wouldn't get them back the money he owed them.

'We said a week, Ashley. We agreed. It's time to pay up; only suddenly you've disappeared off the radar. Not to be seen or heard from by any fucker. Not answering my calls. It doesn't look good, Ashley, does it? The fact I'm having to chase you for what's mine…' Sam shook his head to emphasise his disappointment. 'In fact, it almost looks as if you're purposely mugging us off. Making us out to be a couple of cunts.'

Ashley shook his head, finally realising the enormity of the situation and the real danger he'd put himself in. The brothers were capable of murder, and the only thing stopping Russ from beating him to death was Sam's instruction. Ashley needed to try and keep Sam onside and explain.

'No, Sam. I'm not. Honest… I was sorting it.' He cradled his head; the pain inside his skull was excruciating. The truth was Ashley had no way of getting his hands on that kind of money. Only he wasn't going to admit that out loud. Right now, he needed to focus on making these two men believe that he could get it. Otherwise they'd set upon him again, and Ashley wasn't sure that he could take much more. They'd end up killing him.

'I've had a lot going on. My missus is about to drop our firstborn…'

'Yeah, we heard. Shame you left your missus on her own tonight. Be a real shame if one of our boys was on his way round to yours to dish out a little warning to you. Guess he'll have to leave her a message for you,' Russ taunted.

'Please. There's no need to drag them into this. I will get your money. I swear. I just need a bit more time,' Ashley begged.

As sick and twisted as these two were, even they wouldn't stoop as low as to hurt a pregnant woman, surely?

'It's out of our hands now, mate,' Russ sneered, enjoying the look of terror on Ashley's face as the man winced.

'Fuck!' Ashley said, screwing his eyes shut in despair at the thought of these animals hurting Shelby.

And even if this was just a veiled threat to scare him, the last thing he needed was the Bolands paying Shelby a visit full stop. Because she'd go running straight to her old man the first chance she got. Then he'd really be in the shit. Pete would kill him for dragging his precious daughter into this mess.

'You've got forty-eight hours, Ashley! Do you understand?' Sam said now, looming over Ashley and glaring down at him closely, his words concise and loaded with intent so that Ashley understood.

'H-h-how am I going to get that k-k-kind of money, Sam, in two days?' Ashley said, glad that for now the beating had stopped. Only his dilemma was far from over. There was no way that Ashley would be able to get his hands on the £20k he owed the brothers in such a short time. Otherwise, he would have done so already and saved himself the kicking.

'That ain't our fucking problem, mate, and I think the words you are looking for are "thank you"! We're doing you a favour, mate!' Russ interjected then, narrowing his eyes as he continued to glare at Ashley with disdain.

Russ had come across a lot of men like Ashley over the years. Chancers. Ponces. Men that, when it came down to it, wouldn't know what integrity was if it hit them full force in the face with a bat.

'Thanks… Thank you.'

'Forty-eight hours, Ashley. No more, no less, so you do what needs to be done. Beg. Borrow. Fucking steal. Just make sure you get every last penny to us.'

'This is yet *another* lifeline, Ashley,' Sam said. 'Because trust me, my brother could happily finish you off right now.'

Ashley nodded as he tried to sit up. Crouching awkwardly on the wet ground, he winced as his head throbbed at the sudden movement. Aware that Russ was capable of committing his murder and grateful for the lifeline that Sam was throwing him. That he wasn't going to die. Not tonight, at least.

'I'll get it. You have my word…'

'Oh, fucking behave!' Russ roared with laughter. 'This spineless, gutless, poncing little weasel has given us his word, Sam.' Russ shook his head before spitting out a gob of phlegm in Ashley's face. 'You're so full of shit, mate. It wouldn't surprise me if you were conceived by your mother taking it up the arse. Your word don't mean shit to us. We want our money.'

Nodding profusely, Ashley let the two men know that he heard and understood them completely, then watched as they turned and walked back down the alleyway before he collapsed back down onto the cold, wet floor and stared up at the black night sky.

His clothes were torn and covered in blood. His whole body was burning in pain. Closing his eyes, desperate to fight back the tears that threatened, he was grateful for the small mercy of being alive. But he was well aware that there wouldn't be any more chances after this. Somehow, he was going to have to get the Boland brothers their money.

He thought of Shelby then.

He grabbed his phone from his pocket; he needed to warn her.

Though seeing all the missed calls, Ashley's finger hovered over the voicemail button instead. Wincing as he listened to the newest message. The usual barrage of abuse as Shelby screamed down the phone at him, calling him every name under the sun.

Only this time she said that she'd had enough. That she was going to her parents' house.

Ashley hung up. Part of him felt relieved; despite the inevitable fallout from his disgruntled in-laws that was to come, at least Shelby would be safe.

She wouldn't be home to open the door if any unexpected visitors turned up at the flat tonight.

Because Ashley knew that Sam and Russ meant it when they said they'd send someone to pay Shelby a visit, and if they did that then all hell would break loose. Not only would he end up with those two nutters on his back, but he'd have to deal with Pete Baker too. And Ashley really wasn't sure who was worse.

CHAPTER FIVE

Clamping his hand over his nose and mouth, John-James Andrews, or Jay-Jay as he liked to be called, recoiled at the stench of ammonia from the puddles of piss that soaked the floor of the lift on the Griffin Estate. He decided to take the stairs instead.

Though in fairness, the stairwell wasn't much better, he thought, taking the concrete steps two at a time. The acrid stench of piss was just as strong out here, if not worse. And spotting the trails of what looked like phlegm that had been gobbed all up the walls, Jay-Jay shook his head in disgust. The place was a shithole. And that was really saying something coming from him.

Having finished serving time at Her Majesty's pleasure only ten days ago, on the notorious B-Wing at HMP Wandsworth, Jay-Jay had recently swapped the four monotonous, grey walls of his cell for something even worse – if that was at all possible.

Remembering the hole in the windowpane of his cell that he'd jammed an old pillowcase into, in a bid to keep out the cold, the irony wasn't lost on him that prison had been like a palace in comparison to the damp, musty old sofa he was currently bedding down on, in a derelict squat he was sharing with a couple of druggie wasters.

At least inside he'd had a warm bed to sleep in and three semi-decent meals each day, as well as access to a gym and a TV. The only real downside was the place had been full of cunts. Hundreds of men locked away like lions prowling their steely barred cages.

Full of testosterone and attitude and looking for any easy target to take out their pent-up anger on. Wannabe gangsters and bad men. All trying to prove themselves to be top dog.

The violence was a much-needed release inside, helping to alleviate the never-ending boredom. Jay-Jay was no stranger to that, having spent his whole life fighting for survival. Because he'd had to. He'd had no other choice.

And that's exactly what he'd been forced to do when Younus Abbas had stood over him, grinning like a lunatic, and slammed a cosh down over his head in front of everyone in the prison canteen: he'd been forced to fight to survive. The man had taken Jay-Jay's rejection of his offer to join his religious cult and army of foot soldiers inside as a personal insult.

'You think you're better than us? You think you are special? Well I'm here to show you what happens when you think you're too good for us,' Younus had said as he continued to beat Jay-Jay with the leather-covered makeshift baton.

Jay-Jay had had no choice but to repeat a habit of a lifetime and fight back. Forced from a young age to live in the fucked-up care system, as a small child he'd been systemically verbally and physically abused by the very people who were supposed to be looking after him, only to be spat back out onto the rough London streets the minute he'd turned sixteen. He could more than handle himself if he needed to; he had nothing to prove to anyone in there, including himself.

Grabbing Younus by his throat, a sea of red mist clouding Jay-Jay's vision, he'd squeezed the man's windpipe, before he grabbed the weapon from him and beat Younus repeatedly with it, mashing his features to a pulp until an officer dragged him away.

Later, when a prison officer had entered his cell and Jay-Jay had been expecting some form of reprisal, instead he'd been handed a mobile phone. Sam Boland's voice had been at the other end of it, and the man had made Jay-Jay an offer that he couldn't refuse. Protection from Younus, following the vicious attack, in return for Jay-Jay's services once he was released.

All Jay-Jay had wanted more than anything was to serve his time without any aggro and get back out. Because that was the thing with prison. Once the system managed to suck you in, it was hard to claw your way back out. But it was too late for that now. So, Jay-Jay had accepted the offer.

And now here he was. On his very first job working for the Boland brothers. Sam Boland had been true to his word. He'd offered him a decent wage and more opportunities after this, provided he did a good job. And the work was easy. All Jay-Jay had to do was throw his weight around a bit and dish out a few slaps if anyone tried it on with any funny business. If anything, he'd enjoy it.

Reaching the top landing of the flats, Jay-Jay eyed the sign listing the door numbers, making sure he was at the right place, grimacing as he stepped over what looked like a used condom discarded in the middle of the floor. He made his way down the balcony towards the targeted flat and glanced up and down the passage to make sure no one was watching him.

There was only silence now, apart from the downpour as the rain pelted past the balcony's wall. The yellow glare of the odd streetlamp shone from below in the communal garden. The flats all sat in darkness, and Jay-Jay guessed most residents would be sleeping now. Reaching the door, he took his tools out from his pocket and got to work on picking the lock.

He held the PVC door carefully as the latch clicked open, to stop it from swinging inwards and banging off the hallway wall. Jay-Jay crept inside, scanning each room that he passed, making sure that it was empty. Until he reached the last room, right at the back of the flat. The bedroom, he guessed as he eyed the closed door and imagined Shelby Cooke asleep on the other side of it.

Oblivious to him being inside her home.

He was relying on the element of surprise to really shake things up and add that extra layer of fear. He reached for the handle and brought it down slowly. The door creaked open. Staring at the silhouette on the bed through the darkness, he crept towards it. Only, as he got nearer, he realised it was a mound of clothes. There was no one here. *Shit!* No job meant no money, and Jay-Jay had been counting on tonight's earn.

Switching the light on, pissed off now, he scanned the room, wondering if Shelby had been tipped off about his visit, as he noted the drawers and cupboards all left open and the pile of clothes spread out on the floor.

He saw the cup on the side and placed his hand on it. The tea inside was still warm. Which only meant one thing: Shelby Cooke had only just left.

Jay-Jay moved fast, back out of the flat, to race back down the stairwell. Because if he'd only just missed her, she might still be nearby.

CHAPTER SIX

Turning and glancing behind her again, Shelby scanned the communal gardens of the Griffin Estate, cursing herself for being so stupid as to come out so late on her own, as she cast her gaze into each far corner of the run-down courtyard. She was convinced she'd heard a movement behind her, but her mind must be playing tricks on her because there was no one there.

It had gone midnight now, and the heavy showers this evening had left the estate deserted. There was no one here but her.

Stepping down the side walkway that led out to the common, Shelby did one final sweep of the gardens before hurrying her way along the passageway. Paranoid now, she cursed Ashley's name over and over as she walked. It was all his fault that she was out here on her own at this time of night. Getting soaked and freezing her bits off. Well, she hoped that her dad crucified him for this once she turned up at the house at this time of the morning.

She heard the noise again. Footsteps this time. Slapping loudly against the puddles behind her. *You're imagining things*, she told herself. She'd worked herself up into such a rage about Ashley that now she was hearing things. Still, she turned again anyway, just to be sure. But as soon as she did, she wished she hadn't. Because she hadn't imagined the noise at all.

There was a man. Further back at the beginning of the walkway, gaining speed as he walked towards her. Shelby could just about make out his face, despite it being dark and his hood being pulled up tightly. She could sense the air of menace around him. Swallowing down the feeling of dread that consumed her, she turned quickly and picked up her own pace, desperate to make it to the other side of the walkway and out into the open.

As she hurried along, she told herself that it was probably nothing. A coincidence. Just another person making their way home. Hurrying like her to get out of the miserable rain.

But she couldn't control the surge of adrenaline that rushed through her as she quickly made her way down the secluded alleyway. Nor could she ignore the feeling in the pit of her gut that told her she was in great danger.

She moved faster now, hearing the sound of feet smacking loudly against the wet pavement in the haste to keep up with her. Her pace impressive even to her. This far on in her pregnancy meant that she was naturally slower on her feet. She'd practically waddled from the lift and across the communal gardens, dragging her small suitcase behind her, subconsciously distributing the excess weight of her bowling-ball-shaped stomach that swamped her tiny frame.

But now fear had lent her speed. She scanned the length of the alleyway that still loomed ahead of her, gripped with terror that this would be the perfect place for the attacker to strike. Because they were completely alone here.

If she could just make it to the common, where it was open, vast. Someone might be around to help her.

Only the footsteps were louder now.

Whoever was following closely behind was gaining on her.

Just a few feet away. Close enough for her to hear their short, stilted pants of breath. Close enough to observe her body language and sense the fear that rippled through her, how rigid she looked now fully alert that someone was walking so closely, directly behind her.

She sensed the real danger before it happened.

Before the hand grabbed her shoulder and the rope twisted tightly around her neck in one flowing movement.

Shelby screamed out, the noise piercing and loud, echoing the length of the dimly lit alleyway. The sheer volume of the sound momentarily stunning them both.

The pause in the attack giving her a few seconds' advantage, but instead of pulling away as her attacker had no doubt expected, she launched herself towards her assailant. Her quick movement caused the rope to slacken around her throat as she clawed at the attacker's face with her nails.

Then she looked down and saw a knife and realised with horror the attacker's intentions.

Reaching inside the hood, she dug her fingers into her assailant's face, hoping that she found his eye sockets, because she needed to hurt him badly if she wanted to escape.

And she fought now with a ferocity and strength that the attacker hadn't anticipated. Fight or flight. Live or die. For herself and her unborn child. And all the while she was still screaming. Her voice high-pitched and loud enough to have woken half the estate up.

Leaving her attacker no choice now but to punch out. To silence her. A fist connected with Shelby's cheekbone, snapping her head backwards as she fell to the ground.

A voice shouted out from the distance.

The attack was flawed. Messed up. Not willing to get caught, the attacker ran.

CHAPTER SEVEN

'Shelby! It's the middle of the night,' Janey Baker said, pulling open the front door and staring at her daughter questioningly, wondering why she hadn't used her key instead of knocking so loudly. And why she was here so late, full stop.

Janey would never normally have opened the door so late, or to such a furious banging, but she'd checked the security camera's monitors first, and had been shocked to see her daughter's image staring back at her. 'Your father's asleep. At least he was…'

She could hear Pete now, awake and no doubt wondering what all the commotion was.

'Mum! He tried to kill me.'

'What? My god, Shelby, what on earth has happened to you?' Janey shrieked, realising the state Shelby was in as she stepped closer to the doorway, the light from the hallway highlighting her daughter's sobbing face. Dishevelled and shaken, her lip was cut and bleeding and her clothes were wet and covered in mud. 'Come in. Come in,' she instructed, ushering her distraught girl inside to the warmth and safety of their home. Pete padded down the stairs behind them, reaching the hallway just as Shelby threw herself into her mother's arms, sobbing loudly.

'Shelby?' Pete said, taking in the scene of his hysterical daughter, turning up alone at this time of the night and hugging her mother to her as if her life depended on it. 'What the fuck's happened this time? Seriously, you've been married all of five minutes, you shouldn't be fighting as much as you are.' It wasn't the first time Shelby had turned up here in the middle of the night, crying her eyes out and moaning about the useless moron of a man she'd stupidly been lumped with. And Pete guessed this wouldn't be the last time either. Shelby and Ashley had barely been together for five minutes before Shelby had fallen pregnant.

It was never going to be the fairy-tale ending.

Ashley Cooke was the bane of his life. Not only had he managed to get his daughter knocked up in record time, but the untrustworthy weasel had managed to worm his way in to the family business too.

It had been Janey's idea originally, and Pete had agreed at the time that it made sense. That if Ashley worked for Pete, it meant that Pete would be able to keep an eye on the lad. That he could keep him in some kind of check. All the while making sure that Ashley was earning his way and paying for that child of his and giving his Shelby a decent life. Only Ashley seemed to be a law unto himself: he still seemed to do whatever it was he liked and didn't seem to care that he was constantly upsetting Shelby with his actions.

It was pay day, so Pete guessed that the man was AWOL as per and drinking away the bulk of his earnings. Pete could happily kill the bastard.

'It's not Ashley, Dad. Well, not really. I've been attacked...' Shelby said through her sobs, stepping back and looking her dad in the eye. Her cries became more frantic when she saw the concerned look on her dad's face as he took in the sight of her injuries.

'Jesus Christ, Shelby! Attacked by who?' Pete exclaimed in horror, instantly riled that someone had dared to deliberately hurt his precious daughter. 'Did Ashley do this to you? I'll fucking bury that bastard...' Not waiting for an answer as he grabbed his coat from the hook on the wall. 'Where is he?'

'No, Dad, please. It wasn't Ashley,' Shelby said quickly, sensing her father's fury and fighting for breaths between her sobs, so that she could find her words before he went out looking for Ashley. 'We did have a row. Well, sort of.' Shelby thought back to the threatening voicemails she'd left her husband. Screaming down the phone and calling him every name under the sun. 'He didn't come home tonight. He stayed out and he hasn't answered his phone. And I was angry with him, so I told him I was leaving him.'

She wiped a stream of snot from her nose.

'I just wanted to scare him a bit. I want him to be a good husband and to come home to me at the end of the day. Is that too much to ask?' Shelby said, shaking her head sadly now, remembering why she'd come here in the first place: to get Ashley in trouble with her father. Well, he'd be well and truly in trouble now, because this was all his fault. If he'd just come home like he was supposed to none of this would have happened. She'd be at home in her bed, instead of here, battered and crying in her parents' hallway.

'I shouldn't have walked here. I should have got a cab, but you're only the other side of the common,' Shelby said, physically shaking as she thought about her ordeal. She was lucky to even be here right now. 'That's when he attacked me. He was going to kill me; he had a knife.'

'Oh my god. Did he hurt you, Shelby? Did he do anything to you?' Janey sobbed, thinking the worst – that her heavily pregnant daughter might have been raped.

'No, Mum, I fought him off. That's when he punched me.' Shelby held her face then. Her jaw was throbbing.

'Right, I'm calling the police,' Janey said, not waiting for her husband to give her permission as she picked up the phone and frantically dialled the numbers.

'Who was it? Did you get a good look at them? What did he look like?' Pete said now, practically foaming at the mouth as he grabbed his keys. 'I'm going to go and look for him. I'm not waiting for that lot to finally pull their finger out their arses. He'll be long gone.'

'I don't know, Dad. It was dark. He had his hood up. I managed to get a glimpse of his face, but I didn't recognise him,' Shelby said, throwing herself into her father's arms again as a fresh wave of sobs welled up in her chest.

She'd planned to put on an Oscar worthy act when she'd got here. Wanting to seem distressed to get her father onside so that he would have a word with Ashley. Only she wasn't acting now. She was in shock and genuinely terrified that she had almost been killed. Pete could sense it too. The way her whole body shook in his arms. His precious daughter was traumatised.

'That fucking estate. I knew something like this would happen. It's not safe, and it's no place for my daughter. But, of course, Ashley wouldn't listen to me, would he?' Pete said. 'Too busy trying to prove a point that he can stand on his own two feet than to take my offer of a deposit to get you both out of there. Somewhere better, decent, somewhere you belong…' Pete was furious now. The Griffin Estate was notorious for its crime. Riddled with gangs and drug dealers, it was the last place on earth his daughter and grandchild should be. 'The place is a shithole. The dregs of the earth live there,' Pete spat. 'I should never have let you move in with him. I should have put my foot down.'

'I know, Dad!' Shelby said, nodding in agreement. She hadn't been overly happy about moving in with Ashley over at that decrepit estate either. She'd begged Ashley to take the offer of a deposit on one of the fancy new Riverside Quarter apartments on the river, overlooking Hurlingham Park, which her parents had offered to pay as a wedding gift.

Only Ashley had insisted that he'd get them out of the Griffin Estate himself.

And Shelby had felt she had no choice but to at least show willing and support her new husband's decision.

Only so far, his great escape from their dingy flat hadn't materialised. Shelby hated it over there.

But maybe now Ashley would be forced to listen to her father. Maybe now he'd agree to taking the money and starting afresh somewhere better. A tiny part of her felt calmer then, praying that something good would come from tonight and Ashley's actions after all.

'And where is he now? Where is that useless excuse of a husband while all this is going on?' Pete said through gritted teeth, guessing he was up to his usual tricks of being up to no good. 'Because I'm holding that man personally responsible for putting your life in danger. When I get my hands on him...' Pete's words were interrupted as Shelby suddenly doubled over on the floor and cried out in pain.

'Ouch! Mum! Oh God...' She clutched her stomach. 'Something's wrong with the baby.' A sudden wave of agony left her breathless, the pain so acute that she felt as if she was going to pass out.

Rushing to her daughter's side, Janey wrapped her arms around Shelby and helped her to sit on the bottom step of the stairs.

'What's happening to me?' Shelby cried as she stared down at her trousers in horror and eyed the puddle of water at her feet. 'I've wet myself, Mum!'

'Pete, get the car!' Janey instructed knowingly, taking control of the situation as Shelby continued to sob and Pete looked fit to murder somebody.

Recognising that her daughter's waters had broken, the last thing Janey wanted was to panic her daughter any further. 'Pete! The car, now!' Janey ordered, grabbing her own coat.

'Listen to me, Shelby. You're going to be okay. It's probably just the nasty shock you've had but I think your waters may have broken. Let's get you to the hospital, yeah, and get them to check you over. Make sure everything's okay,' Janey said, doing her best to stay calm and composed as she followed behind Pete, leading Shelby out to the car on the driveway.

'Oh, Christ, Mum. The baby can't be coming. Not yet. I've still got another month,' Shelby said as another pain ripped through her.

'Let's just get you to the hospital, my darling, we'll know more then,' Janey said, helping to ease her daughter into the back seat of the car and giving Shelby a reassuring smile.

Though secretly Janey was fearing the worst. Shelby had been through a horrifically traumatic ordeal this evening, and the baby wasn't due for weeks. Time was of the essence. They needed to get Shelby and the baby to the hospital, fast.

CHAPTER EIGHT

'I hear you just took down Usain Bolt?' Detective Constable Ben Holder grinned as Lucy walked into CID's briefing room, her face still blazing red from where she'd taken a punch.

'Fancied himself as a bit of a boxer on all accounts too,' Lucy said, playing her heroics down in front of her colleague. 'I managed to get a clump for my efforts.' She laughed, holding her aching jaw.

'Boxer, athlete and a racing driver too. Busy boy!'

'Not so busy now for the foreseeable with any luck.' Lucy grinned, glad of the result tonight. 'Providing the judge does his job and gives him what he's due.'

'Yeah well, we all know how that one can play out,' Holder said, unable to hide the bitterness to his tone.

He knew as well as Lucy that they could both do their job to their best ability, but at the end of the day it wasn't down to them what justice would be dished out to each criminal. And sometimes no matter what evidence they managed to gather or how much of a case they built, the criminals still managed to walk free. To get off on a technicality or to plead some kind of ignorance or mental health issue.

Still. They had more pressing things to think about now.

'Right, everyone gather round. We've just had an urgent incident come in,' DS Morgan announced, standing at the front of the room and gaining his team's attention. The fractious expression on his face told them all that what he was about to say wasn't going to be pleasant.

'An attempted knife attack, at the Griffin Estate…'

'Gang related?' Lucy said, recalling the recent case they'd cracked a few months back at the estate, regarding a county lines gang.

But DS Morgan shook his head apprehensively. 'The motive isn't yet known; the victim, Shelby Cooke, is female and heavily pregnant,' he said cautiously. He knew how close to home this case would be for his young detective, given the childhood trauma she'd endured, witnessing her own pregnant mother's murder on the very same estate. 'She was followed and attacked. Luckily, she managed to get away almost unscathed. She managed to fend off her attacker, but she is currently in hospital. She was punched and suffered a nasty fall. The doctors suspect the shock of the attack has brought on the onset of early labour. So, for now, we need to focus on looking for her attacker until Shelby is free to make a formal statement.'

'Attempted knife attack, Sarge?' Holder interrupted to voice what the rest of the team were thinking. 'So, if the victim wasn't actually stabbed, shouldn't uniform take this one?'

'We believe that this may not have been an isolated attack,' Morgan said. He'd been getting to this bit. 'It appears it might be a bit more complex than that. We've had intel from some of our MET colleagues over at the Operation Command Unit at Richmond Park, about a murder that took place there last week. The victim was of similar age and also pregnant. She'd been stabbed in the stomach.'

'A serial attacker? Great. So much for knocking off early!' Holder muttered, guessing that this wasn't going to be a simple investigation, completely unaware of Lucy's discomfort as she stood deadly still beside him, trying to keep her composure as she learned the details of this next investigation.

'The attacker left a rucksack at the scene of Shelby's attack, which we've sent off to be tested for any traces of DNA. There was also some DNA left on a small length of rope that was found near the victim's body at the Richmond Park murder. We won't know if the attacks are linked for certain until we get the results back. However, in light of the similarities between the attacks I've asked for a forensic psychologist to come on board and talk us through the suspect's profile, but they won't be available until the morning. Until then, we'll follow all lines of enquiry and wait for news on when Shelby Cooke is able to see us for that statement. That's it for now, everyone. We've all got more than enough to carry on with,' Morgan said, dismissing his team before making a beeline towards Lucy.

'Are you okay?' Morgan kept his voice down, watching as most of the team busied themselves now at their desks. He could see Holder hovering nearby, trying to listen in, but the officer wasn't close enough to hear. 'Off the record, Lucy, if we have any further developments and you want me to keep you off this case, I can…' He paused, knowing how strong-willed and capable Lucy was as an officer – the last thing he wanted to do was single her out or imply that she couldn't deal with this investigation.

She'd made it perfectly clear, when they'd discussed her mum's cold case previously, that the last thing she wanted was special treatment or sympathy. But Morgan knew that this wouldn't be an easy case. It was too similar to what had happened to her mother.

'I just want you to feel comfortable, Lucy. It's your call.'

'Shit! No. It's fine,' Lucy said, shaking her head, trying her hardest to compose herself. She was grateful that her boss was being so considerate.

But she'd known the risks when she'd signed up for this job. She'd known that she was going to have to deal with things that might drag her own demons back up to the surface, and that one way or another she was going to have to face them.

'You're sure?' Morgan said, giving Lucy one final opportunity to change her mind. If she decided to take a step back from the case, if it was too much for her to handle, he wouldn't blame her.

'Honestly, Sarge. It's fine. I'm in for this one.'

'Good. Why don't you go home? Get a few hours' sleep and get back here for the briefing first thing. We've got a long couple of days ahead of us,' Morgan said, before noting that Holder was still hovering around behind them. He turned to him.

'You may as well call it a night too. Get your head down for a few hours and be back here for 7 am,' he said, before going to his office to make some calls.

'You don't have to tell me twice, Sarge,' Holder said, walking back over to where Lucy sat and noting the pained expression on her face as she tried to focus on her computer screen.

'You okay? What was all that about?'

'Oh, nothing. I think the sarge was just checking that I'm okay. You know…' Lucy said, putting her hand to her face. 'After the whack I got earlier.'

Holder nodded, not convinced that Lucy was telling the truth but knowing not to push her on it.

'Cool. Well, as long as you are?'

Lucy nodded, turning away and placing her attention back onto the case file on the computer, as she mentally prepared herself for what lay ahead.

The words swarmed before her eyes as she thought of a pregnant woman being attacked with a knife – such familiar details – twenty years after the case that haunted her dreams. It felt like history was in some ways repeating itself.

Part of her wondered why it still shocked her, the depravity of the monsters that they were forced to deal with in their line of work. Because she'd dealt with sick individuals like this before, first-hand. And it looked like she had to do it all over again.

CHAPTER NINE

Opening his eyes, Ashley Cooke flinched at the brightness of the room. Perplexed for a few seconds at the unfamiliarity of his surroundings, he took in the sights. Brightly painted yellow walls. A purple velvet chair in the corner of the room. A dressing table next to it laden with expensive-looking make-up and perfume bottles. And a half-finished bottle of vodka tipped on its side. He wondered for a few seconds where he was. He wasn't at home, that was for sure. This place looked much plusher than his place back at the Griffin Estate. Scanning the floor, he followed the trail of clothing that had been discarded on the sanded floorboards, till his gaze finally rested on the red lace bra hanging from the door handle, at the same time as he felt a movement behind him.

Kate. He grinned then, his mouth feeling cracked and dry with the small movement. The bitter taste of alcohol he'd consumed last night, stale now, lingering on his tongue. His head was pounding, his whole body on fire. Instantly he recalled the beating that he'd taken last night – this wasn't simply just the hangover kicking in.

Kate had found him sprawled out in the alleyway after she'd finished her shift. Ashley had stuck to his story of getting jumped by a gang of kids. He'd said that they'd tried to steal his wallet and phone, but Ashley had managed to fight them all off. Beside herself with concern and sympathy, Kate had insisted that he come home with her so she could look after him. And she had looked after him. Spectacularly. He could feel her behind him. Still asleep in the bed. Her warm skin pressed against his.

Turning, Ashley grimaced as the pain took over. Still, it was worth it, he thought as he lifted the covers, his grin widening as he took in the sight of Kate in all her naked glory. The subtle curve of the woman's soft, tanned lower back, her bare buttocks pressing against his thighs. Even now, he could feel himself stirring, turned on by the sight of her. He'd surpassed himself this time; this woman was a solid ten out of ten.

Shelby. Shit. He wondered what the time was. Wincing in pain, he reached down to where his jeans lay discarded on the floor next to the bed, and picked up his mobile phone, switching it on and was instantly irritated to see he had thirty missed calls from Shelby. Which he'd been expecting, if he was honest. What he hadn't been expecting, however, were the numerous missed calls from Pete and Janey too.

Ashley closed his eyes, recalling the Boland brothers' threat. That they had sent someone around to his flat to dish out a warning. Ashley could only hope and pray that Shelby had stuck to her word and gone to her parents' house, like she'd said.

She'd sounded sincere enough, from what he could make out between the loaded threats and the stream of abuse that had followed, which had only reinforced his decision to go home with Kate in the end.

Having been beaten to within an inch of his life last night and feeling very sorry for himself, it was no contest in picking between going home to an empty flat or back here with Kate.

Kate had been horrified at the sight of him and had gone out of her way to make a fuss over him and look after him.

What if Shelby was just running her mouth? What if she stayed at the flat after all?

They wouldn't have hurt a woman, would they? They'd been calling his bluff. He'd been certain of it. Only if that really were the case, why were there so many missed calls?

Noting the nearly empty battery symbol in the corner of the screen, Ashley decided that he'd use that to his advantage later when he finally went home with his tail between his legs. He'd tell Shelby that he was attacked. That a gang had set upon him last night and left him for dead all night in the alleyway that ran alongside the club. That he couldn't call her because his phone had died. That he hadn't seen any of her missed calls. It was a weak and obvious bullshit excuse, but it was all that Ashley had – he just didn't have the energy for Shelby's melodramatics about him staying out all night yet again. Getting beaten up would be his perfect cover. She'd soon forgive him this time when she realised that he was hurt. The hard-faced-cow persona that Shelby put on was all just an act.

And Pete and Janey would get over it too, eventually. What else could they do? They couldn't have a go at him for getting beaten up. And it wasn't as if Ashley was going anywhere any time soon; they'd both made sure of that.

'Oh, you're awake?' Kate said, turning over and eyeing Ashley with a wry grin. 'I can't believe that you're actually here. In my bed. I didn't think it would happen, what with your wife being pregnant and all…'

'Shh, don't.' Ashley said, not wanting Kate to mention Shelby by name and break the spell. 'Let's not talk about any of that now.' He suddenly realised that it hadn't been his imagination. That Kate really was into him in a big way.

He'd made it clear from the start weeks ago, that he was going to be a dad soon and that he wasn't looking for anything serious. He just wanted to have a bit of fun. Part of him had been laying it all out there and testing Kate, to see if that would put her off.

Only to his relief, the fact that he was about to become a new dad seemed to have the opposite effect on her completely.

Kate always asked about the baby. And he'd found himself confiding in her more and more lately.

'How are you feeling? Your face looks so sore.'

'It looks worse than it is,' Ashley lied. 'And I'm all the better for waking up next to you, let me tell you.' Ashley smiled then, not missing a trick at sweet talking Kate.

'In that case… don't worry, I'll be gentle with you.' Kate laughed before taking her cue and disappearing down underneath the covers, intent on finishing what they'd started last night.

Ashley closed his eyes and shut all thoughts of his nagging wife and his agony from the beating he'd taken out of his mind, as Kate took him expertly in her mouth.

He was already in for the earbashing of his life when he got home. He may as well make it worth it while he was here.

*

'Where is he? And don't bullshit me, I know he's here. Nicky, the doorman at the club, told us he saw you both leaving together last night.'

Ashley was up on his feet then, wincing in pain as he frantically grabbed at his clothes that were still strewn all over Kate's bedroom floor. He recognised the familiar voice of his father-in-law. And Pete sounded vexed. The fact that he was here at all spoke absolute volumes. Ashley was in a whole world of shit.

Ignoring the pain he was in as he rushed to get dressed, Ashley glanced at the bedroom window, wondering whether, if he was quick enough, he'd have time to fling himself out of it and do a runner.

Only there was no chance of escape, he realised, unsteady on his feet as he slipped them into his jeans, as seconds later Pete marched into the room, closely followed by his second-in-command, Carl Rangers. Another man who couldn't stand the sight of Ashley.

'Pete, mate! What are you doing here?' Ashley said, scrambling to pull the duvet back up around him to cover up his nakedness. He'd forgotten to put on his pants, his jeans still tangled around his feet. His penis wilted on sight of his psychotic father-in-law's angry glare.

Ashley was caught red-handed, quite literally with his pants down. The look on both men's faces told Ashley all he needed to know. He was royally in the shit.

'What the fuck happened to you?' Pete said, eyeing the bruising all over Ashley's body, his face battered, sporting a fat lip and a swollen right eye.

Someone had recently dished out a hell of a kicking, though for some reason that didn't really surprise Pete. Ashley had that effect on people.

'Oh, nothing. It was just some kids outside Smokes last night,' Ashley started as Kate came back into the room, dressed in her flimsy silk nightie. Both men looked her up and down.

'It ain't how it looks, Pete. I swear. I was beaten up last night, and Kate was looking after me. She insisted that I come back here with her. Nothing happened…'

'That true, is it? That nothing happened?' Pete asked, throwing Kate a look of disdain as she self-consciously pulled her robe tightly around her. An expression of guilt was written all over her face, but at least she had the good grace not to give him a lie as an answer. Instead, she diverted her gaze to the floor, her silence speaking volumes.

'Thought as much,' Pete scoffed before looking back at Ashley and shaking his head. 'This one here thinks he's a fucking charmer.

Don't you, Ashley? Thinks he's fucking untouchable. That he can do as he pleases. Only you lost that right when you married my daughter!' Pete bellowed, glaring at Ashley, unwavering hate radiating from him.

Pete had taken an instant dislike to Ashley Cooke on first sight, from the first encounter that Shelby had brought the bloke home to meet them. Not wanting to upset his Shelby, he had plastered a fake smile to his face and done his best at dishing out the pleasantries the entire time that the four of them sat around the dinner table and ate one of Janey's epic Sunday roasts.

But in all honesty, he'd been glad when the meal was over and Ashley had finally gone home. Because as perfect as his Shelby was, she had one flaw: she had bloody awful taste in men. And when she fell, she fell hard. Arse over head.

And Ashley Cooke was the worst of the lot. Nothing more than a cocky wide boy. Only much to Pete's dismay, unlike the other boyfriends that didn't stick around long enough to ever become a problem, Ashley had lasted longer than just a few dates. He'd somehow managed to worm his way into his daughter's affections and, before they all knew it, a few weeks in Shelby was pregnant.

Pete had begrudgingly taken his wife's advice and offered Ashley a job with his firm, on the understanding that the condition would be that Ashley was to do the right thing and marry Shelby: a quick, but extremely lavish wedding that Pete had been forced to fork out on.

At least with Ashley working for Pete, it meant that Pete would be able to keep a firm eye on the man. Only it seemed that Ashley wasn't particularly worried about the repercussions of getting caught out, because here he was yet again brazenly disrespecting Shelby and him.

'Do you remember that, Ashley? The promise you made to Shelby to love and fucking honour her?' Pete sneered, aware that

Ashley was a different breed completely. Pete could tell that from the second he'd first clocked eyes on the lad.

He'd had indiscretions over the years, of course he had. He was a red-blooded male, after all. He had his needs, but he was always respectful to his Janey when it came to his infidelities. Discreet. Never one to rub it in her face. Which is why their marriage of almost twenty-five years had worked. Ashley didn't think about anyone but himself, and Pete wouldn't see his daughter so publicly disrespected in this way.

'Get your fucking clothes on and get out to the car. Or the only thing you'll be honouring is the death us do part bit, when I fucking bury you six feet under.'

'I'm sorry, Pete…' Ashley began; only, Pete didn't want to hear the man worm his way out of this with his pathetic excuses. After the night he'd had, he really wasn't in the mood.

'Save your bullshit excuses, Ashley. Shelby's in hospital. She was attacked last night,' Pete said bluntly, glad to see the look of shock spread across Ashley's face.

He was rendered silent for a few seconds as he tried to make sense of what Pete was telling him.

'Attacked?' Finally, he spoke. 'What do you mean attacked? By who?'

Ashley felt his legs go weak beneath him as he slumped back down on the bed, a sinking feeling in his stomach as he thought about the Boland brothers' threat last night.

'I mean, if you had been at home instead of here, getting your end away, you cheating, fucking waste of space, none of this would have happened. She came to ours last night, upset because you didn't come home. Again. And someone attacked her near the common. She's gone into labour, Ashley. And for some unknown reason, she still wants you to be there.'

'But she's not due for another four weeks…'

'Oh, I'm sorry. Bit inconvenient for you, is it?' Pete sneered. 'Now, you might not give two shits about my daughter, but I do. And I'm not missing the birth of my first grandchild because of you. Now move your arse. And not a word of this,' he jerked his head towards Kate, 'to Shelby. We found you out cold outside Smokes.'

He knew it would break Shelby's heart if she found out Ashley was dipping his wick where he shouldn't be while she was in hospital having their baby.

'Thanks, Pete…' Ashley started, dressed now and following Pete and Carl out to the car, glad of the lifeline his father-in-law was throwing him. But Pete shook his head gravely.

'Don't thank me, Ashley. I'm doing this for Shelby, not you. I told you once and I'll tell you only once more: you break my daughter's heart again and I'll personally break every single bone in your body. Let this be your final fucking warning.'

CHAPTER TEN

'Where the bloody hell is he, Mum? Typical bloody Ashley. He should be here,' Shelby screeched loudly, gripping her mother's hand tightly as she pushed herself back in the hospital bed, as the wave of pain tore through her once more.

'And why won't you lot give me a bloody epidural? It hurts!' Shelby moaned at the midwife, Tracey Flynn, once the pain had subsided enough for her to catch her breath and string a few words together.

'There's no time now, Shelby,' Tracey said, trying her hardest to keep her tone friendly and positive – a hard task when all the patient had done since she'd arrived at the hospital was bark orders at everyone around her; and the way she spoke to her mother was truly disgusting.

'What do you mean it's too late?' Shelby spat her words through gritted teeth as another rush of pain ripped through her. The contractions were coming fast now, each one starting almost immediately after the last wave had finished. 'You should have done this earlier. I knew I should have insisted on going private, bloody incompetent… ARGH!'

'Sorry, Shelby, but there's no time. It looks like this baby of yours is coming. Take another big gulp of gas and air,' Tracey said, keeping her eyes on the monitor as Shelby let out another shriek.

She'd never admit it out loud to a living soul, but part of her was actually glad that this woman was suffering a little bit. She was so rude and up her own arse that maybe a little bit of pain would be the wake-up call the girl needed to keep her humble.

'One last gulp? She's almost drained the entire canister!' Janey said now, concerned at the queasy look on Shelby's face as she greedily sucked in as much pain relief as she could possibly pull down into her lungs.

'I don't feel very well,' Shelby declared, leaning over the side of the bed and emptying the contents of her stomach onto the floor before the midwife had time to get her a bowl.

Tracey didn't have time to clean up the mess now. Placing a towel down on top of it, to stop anyone slipping over and to mask the smell, she swiftly moved to the foot of the bed.

'Okay, we need to concentrate on the baby now, Shelby,' Tracey said, manoeuvring herself so that she could examine Shelby properly. Her suspicions were confirmed as she noted that Shelby was now fully dilated.

'This is it, Shelby. A few pushes and your baby will be here.'

'Did you hear that, Shelby? The baby is almost here. A few more pushes and it will all be over,' Janey said, knowing that she had to step up now and try and get her daughter through the hardest part of her labour. Shelby was emotionally and physically exhausted.

She needed her now more than ever. Even more so, seeing as there was still no sign of her useless husband. And Janey had a feeling that was what Shelby was holding out for.

'No! I can't, not yet. This isn't right, Mum! Ashley should be here. Where the fuck is he? He should be here. This is his child too. Why should I be the one doing all the work?' Shelby winced, gritting her teeth and bearing down on the bed, almost willing the baby to stay inside her for just a while longer. Why should he get off scot-free in all of this? So far, all he'd done was have his fun and sow his seed, and since then she'd been left to do all the hard graft. She was the one who suffered heartburn and morning sickness and watched in horror as her perfect size eight figure was stretched into a doughy, round fourteen. And she didn't even want to think about the stretch marks that lined her stomach and breasts now. This pregnancy had all but ruined her body. And if Ashley didn't get his arse in here soon, she'd ruin him too.

Janey nodded in understanding, knowing her daughter better than anyone. Shelby wanted Ashley to be here to see his child being born into the world; she wanted him to have that bond with their child. But more than that: she wanted him here so he could see how much she was suffering. How much pain she was in, now that this child that had wrecked her body was ready to come bursting out of it. And she wanted him to suffer too.

'I know, darling! And I'm sure he's on his way. Something important must have come up, with work,' Janey said, hoping to sound convincing and not let on to an already suspicious Shelby that her unreliable husband had been doing his usual, and been up to no good as per. 'I'm sure he'll be here soon.'

She didn't want to let on that Pete had already sent her a text and filled her in on what their darling son-in-law had been up to last night: now wasn't the time to be putting ideas into Shelby's head. Pete could deal with Ashley. Shelby needed to focus on her baby.

'But I'm here, darling. Every step of the way. And I know that you can do this,' Janey said, before biting down on her lip as her daughter crushed her hand, gripped in the throes of agony that labour brought.

Shelby didn't do well with any form of pain at the best of times. Even a slight headache made her daughter skulk about, telling everyone who'd listen about how much she was suffering. She had always been the same. That selfish part of her personality, even when she was a small child. If she was suffering, she wanted everyone around her to suffer too. The fact that Shelby had made it this far in the labour without any pain relief was a miracle as far as Janey was concerned.

'Ouch! Mum, I can't do this. I can't…' Shelby groaned loudly, digging her long, fake nails into Janey's hand and scraping off a layer of her mother's skin as a wave of almighty pain spread through her. She felt as if her insides were being ripped in two. 'Please, Mum, make it stop.'

'Okay, Shelby, I need you to listen to me now,' Tracey said, her tone authoritative. 'The baby's head is crowning. The next wave of pain you feel is going to be the one. I need you to take a deep breath and muster up all of your strength now. And when I say push, you are going to give me the biggest push that you can. Right down into your bottom. Give it everything you've got.'

'I can't!' Shelby looked at her mother then for help as she shook her head, terrified of what was happening to her. Of being in so much pain and feeling as if she had no control. The fear on her face evidence that she knew that this baby was coming out, right now. Whether she was ready for it or not.

'You can do it, Shelby. And you must. Now breathe,' Janey said, used to using her matter-of-fact tone with her daughter. She'd spent a lifetime not pandering to the girl's constant wants and needs.

Unlike her husband, Janey knew to stand firm with Shelby and not give in. The girl had always needed a firm hand, which is where Pete had failed miserably. He was a great father, and he'd always had good intentions, but he'd loved Shelby so much that he had wanted to give her the world. And in doing so, he had unwittingly created a monster. With her every want or demand given in to, Shelby had become spoiled and bratty. And even now, at twenty-four years of age, and about to be a mother herself, Shelby still depended on her parents more than anything.

As she watched Shelby close her eyes and push with all her might, Janey squeezed her hand gently for encouragement. This baby was going to be the shock that Shelby needed to make her finally have some responsibility of her own. Janey hoped that it would somehow be the making of her daughter too. Something that would give Shelby a purpose. Shelby needed to grow up and, like every other woman before her had discovered, having your own child soon put paid to any grand notions that your life was truly your own.

'Push, darling, push!'

Letting out one last almighty animalistic groan from somewhere deep down inside of her, Shelby collapsed back onto the bed with relief as the room was filled with the most enchanting sound of a baby crying that she and Janey had ever heard.

Just then the door opened and Pete and Ashley rushed into the room.

'Oh, Shelby, love. You did it,' Janey said. Tears filled her eyes as she looked down at her firstborn grandchild cocooned in the midwife's arms, before turning to where her husband stood, his face full of emotion.

'She did it, Pete. Look.'

'Congratulations, Shelby, darling,' Pete said then, his voice thick with pride, as the reality of his grandchild being born hit him.

'Would you like to cut the cord?' Tracey asked, looking at the younger of the two men and guessing that he was the AWOL father.

Ashley stepped forward, searching Shelby's face for permission and anticipating a mouthful of anger. Only Shelby smiled back at him and nodded, overcome with emotion now that her ordeal was over. Ashley had made it just in time.

Ashley cut the cord, and the nurse handed him the baby.

'Congratulations, mummy and daddy. You have a beautiful baby boy.'

'He's perfect, Shelby. Just perfect. He looks just like you,' Ashley cooed, staring down at his tiny son before passing the child to Shelby.

'Have you decided on his name?' the midwife asked.

'Riley.' Shelby nodded, taking her son in her arms and staring down at the tiny boy.

She'd done it. She'd given birth to her son. And he'd been worth every second of pain, she thought as she stared down, transfixed, on his tiny, perfect features and the lock of dark hair on his head.

'Hello, my darling, Riley, I'm your mummy,' she whispered as she looked down at her baby.

Overcome with a rush of love that she'd never experienced in her life before, she felt a lone tear of happiness escape down her cheek. 'I'm going to look after you, always. I promise.'

CHAPTER ELEVEN

'Okay! If everyone can please gather round again. We've had some developments on Operation Maple.' DS Morgan's voice carried across the CID room. 'I'm sure everyone here is aware that we wanted to rule out any connection with the knife attack on Shelby Cooke, which happened just after midnight last night over at the Griffin Estate, and the murders that happened last week over in Richmond Park,' DS Morgan continued.

As his colleagues gathered round in front of his desk for this morning's briefing, he was met with a sea of faces. All detecting the seriousness of his tone: what he was about to deliver to them wasn't going to be good news.

Originally, the Operational Command Unit over at Richmond Park thought that the attacker might have been known to the victim. A jilted lover or boyfriend perhaps. The father of the child? A jealous acquaintance.' Morgan paused, looking around the room and making sure that he had the team's full attention. 'At least at the earlier stages of the investigation, they were treating those murders as a domestic-related incident. However, the investigating sergeant has informed me that all of those lines of enquiry have been exhausted. And given the evidence that we now have, and in light of this second attack last night, we do now believe that these incidents are both linked. And that Shelby Cooke's assault wasn't an isolated attack.'

The room was silent then. Every officer in the room giving their superior their full attention. Because this information changed everything. It confirmed what they'd all been dreading.

'So, you think it's a serial killer, Sarge?' Holder asked now, wondering if this morning's victim had been his next target until she'd managed to get away.

'It's not quite that simple… we don't think his motive was to kill. At least, not for killing's sake.' DS Morgan shook his head and then gestured to the man standing to the right of him, clearly deciding to let his colleague explain further.

Dressed in crumpled grey trousers and a plain white T-shirt, the stranger's casual attire was in stark contrast to the stern expression he wore on his face.

'Some of you are familiar with my good friend here, Zack,' Morgan said, introducing the man. 'And for those who aren't, Zack Lownrey is a forensic psychologist. He has been working on profiling the murderer since last week, and he's been fully briefed on last night's developments too. So, I thought it would be a good idea to let Zack give you a run-down of his thoughts from here on in,' DS Morgan said, stepping back and letting Zack take the floor.

'Hi everyone,' Zack said, clearing his throat before continuing. 'As DS Morgan just explained, we had already ruled out that the attacker was known to their victim, and in light of this second attack we did consider the attacks to have been targeted and to be some kind of deranged fetish perhaps, or acting out on a feeling of hate and repulsion towards women. However, further to some evidence that was left at the scene of the crimes, we now have reason to believe that there is an even more sinister motive behind these attacks…'

'What's more sinister than stabbing a pregnant woman?' Holder muttered under his breath loud enough for Lucy to hear.

Though Lucy didn't respond. She couldn't. All she could think about was the sight of her mother. Sprawled out on the bed. Covered in blood. *Focus!* she told herself.

Trying to stay calm and not react to the news, she stared intently ahead. Only by doing so, she'd unwittingly caught Zack's eye. Holding his gaze as he looked back at her and continued talking, she hoped that he couldn't tell just by looking at her that she was struggling to control her quick and raspy breath as she fought the onslaught of a panic attack.

Breathe, Lucy. Breathe.

'This bag was retrieved from the scene of last night's attack.' Stepping forward to the desk, Zack held up a photo of a plastic evidence bag, containing a black rucksack. He looked at Morgan then, giving the sergeant his cue to fill his team on what the two men had already privately discussed.

'It was dropped on the ground after the victim fought the attacker off and before the offender fled. We found some disturbing items inside.'

Zack held up the other photos of two smaller evidence bags as DS Morgan continued.

'The bag contained some surgical implements such as a pair of operating scissors and a scalpel, alongside a baby blanket and a large bath towel.'

The two men paused then, letting that information sink in and hoping that the team understood where they were going with this. Though they knew that the reality of this crime would be a tough conclusion to come to even for these experienced officers.

'We now believe that the attacker was attempting a foetal abduction…' Zack said finally.

'A foetal abduction?' Lucy muttered quietly, shaking her head as if unable to comprehend what the forensic psychologist was telling them. She glanced over at Holder, hoping to gauge his reaction to this news. But the look of genuine horror on her colleague's face, and the fact that Holder was now rendered completely silent like the rest of the team in the room, only reiterated to Lucy how messed up this attacker's attentions had been.

'What do you mean by a foetal abduction?' Lucy said, her voice coming out louder than she'd intended. Unable to comprehend her worst fears. It couldn't mean what she thought it did, surely?

'I don't understand. He didn't mean to kill the first victims. Is that what you are saying? That it was a kidnapping gone wrong?'

Lucy shifted uncomfortably as the room full of her colleagues all turned to look at her, sensing her distress.

'No. Not a kidnapping,' Zack confirmed with a rueful shake of his head. 'Kidnappers' motives are usually money or power. This appears like something else altogether. We believe that the assailant had intended to steal the woman's child. To cut the baby from her womb. We think that his first attempt, last week, went terribly wrong. And that he tried to commit a second foetal abduction last night; only this time his victim fought back.'

Lucy could hear her colleagues all around her discussing their thoughts on the heinous crime, but all she could do was focus on herself.

'What sort of a sick fuck goes around cutting babies from women's stomachs?'

Holder's voice. His words penetrating her brain. She felt her chest constrict. Her heart was beating wildly now, and she could feel beads of sweat forming on the back of her neck and panic rising up inside of her. Heat rocketed upwards from her feet.

One pregnant woman and her baby murdered, and another woman attacked. This time at the Griffin Estate. The same estate that Lucy grew up on. The same estate where her mother had been murdered so brutally over twenty years ago. She'd been pregnant too. *Breathe.*

When DS Morgan had first told her about the case, when he'd asked her if she wanted him to take her off the investigation, she'd thought she could cope. That she could deal with the investigation professionally and not let her emotions get the better of her. Only this new information changed everything. This wasn't just a one off. They were looking for a depraved murderer who hunted pregnant women down while they were alone at night and butchered them. This wasn't going to be a shut and close case. Still, Lucy was adamant that she wanted to work on the case with her team. Not just for the first victim's sake, so that she could help bring this depraved killer to justice, but for her own sake too. She wanted to finally lay her demons to rest. To deal with this head-on once and for all.

'I mean, I've heard of it. Womb raiding, they call it in the States. But I've never known of it happening over here.'

Lucy could hear Holder still talking. She could hear Zack's voice too, but their voices were faint, faded out, as an incessant, high-pitched ringing filled her ears, drowning out the rest of the noise in the room. She felt as if the room was slowly closing in on her.

'There could be a number of reasons behind the attacks,' Zack intervened, sensing the tension in the room now. How hard it was for these good, decent officers to get their head around what they were dealing with. 'But you're right. It's a very rare crime and, because of that, there's no real study for us to compare the motives and methods behind these attacks or last night's attack. Foetal abduction is not exclusively linked to mental illness, but we mustn't completely rule it out.'

'Yeah, I mean you'd have to be completely gone in the head to even think about attempting something so messed up,' Holder voiced loudly before Zach could continue.

'Predominately, yes. There have been a small number of these types of attacks carried out in America. Mainly by women, I will add. But our attacker is a male. We know this because the second victim managed to get a good look at him.' Zack exchanged a look with DS Morgan to confirm this fact.

'Yes. Thankfully, Shelby Cooke managed to get a good look at the attacker and is willing to give a description to our Facial Imaging Officer, once she's able to. Hopefully, we will have something more to go on then. But we need to move fast with this.'

Zack Lownrey nodded in agreement. 'It's a race against the clock. The attacker is an extremely dangerous and volatile man. He's attempted this attack twice now, and he isn't deterred by the fact that these women and their babies may lose their lives in the process. So, it's safe to assume that he'll try it again. And more than likely, soon.'

Lucy felt the room spin around her and closed her eyes to try and shut out the images that were flooding her mind now. Her mother's body, wrapped in a white dressing gown, sprawled out on her bed. A pool of blood all around her. So much blood. Her vision blurred; tiny white spots fluttered in the air around her as darkness closed in.

'Lucy, are you okay?'

Holder. She tried to find her voice and speak. To tell him, that no, she wasn't all right. She needed to sit down. She needed air. Only her throat felt as if it was closing up and she couldn't find her words. Reaching for a chair that sat just a few centimetres from where she stood, she felt her legs give way beneath her. Falling, she expected to hit the floor, instead she felt a pair of arms wrap themselves tightly around her. With no other choice than to give in to the darkness. She was gone.

CHAPTER TWELVE

Opening her eyes, Lucy flinched as the three male faces stared down at her. She was lying on the floor and a jumper had been placed underneath her head. Sitting up, her face flushed with embarrassment as she realised that her entire team had stopped what they were doing and were looking at her.

'Sleeping on the job, huh!' Holder said, staring down at Lucy as she opened her eyes. 'I mean, I get it, we're all knackered.'

Holder grinned, hoping to make Lucy smile and make light of the fact that she'd just fainted in front of their entire team.

'Okay, everyone. Take five. Grab a coffee. We'll resume the brief in a minute,' DS Morgan said, sensing Lucy's discomfort and dismissing his team.

'Are you okay, Lucy?' DS Morgan said, the concern in his voice evident for them all to hear.

Lucy nodded, still dazed.

'You fainted,' Zack said, seeing how disorientated Lucy appeared. 'It's very warm in here. Do you want me to get you some water?'

'Please,' Lucy said, accepting the offer graciously, mainly because she didn't want all three men staring down over her and fussing.

'I caught you,' Holder said with a grin. 'Prevented you from getting into any more bumps and scraps this morning. Do you think it was because of the whack you got from that idiot last night? Should we get her seen by someone?' Holder said, addressing DS Morgan now.

'No, honestly. I'm fine. Like Zack said, it's hot in here. I didn't have any breakfast. I'm fine really,' Lucy insisted as Zack came back with a glass of water.

Taking it, Lucy tried to hide the tremor of her hand. Hoping her colleagues hadn't seen it.

She knew why she'd fainted. It was all too much. All too close to home, and as much as Lucy had thought she could hold herself together and work on this investigation, it was already proving too hard for her. But she didn't want to let DS Morgan and the rest of the team down. This was a big case; they'd all be needed.

'Are you really okay?' DS Morgan said then, an undercurrent to his question which only he and Lucy understood. Though Holder picked up on it too.

There was definitely something going on here. Something Lucy wasn't saying. And whatever it was, it seemed that their sergeant was aware of it too.

Lucy nodded.

'If you are completely sure?' DS Morgan raised his brows questioningly. Getting that Lucy didn't want to draw any more attention to herself, he lowered his voice. 'Because my offer still stands. If it's too much, I can pull you from the case.'

'No need. I'm fine,' Lucy said with finality as she started to get up.

Zack held out his hand to help Lucy to her feet. Only Holder stepped around the man and placed his arm around Lucy's back to steady her.

'It's all right, mate. We're partners. I've got her,' Holder said, walking Lucy over to the nearest chair.

'No problem,' Zack said, holding up his hands and shooting Holder a curt smile, not wanting to step on anyone's toes. He made his way back to the desk at the front of the room to let Lucy have a minute before they continued with the early morning brief.

'Sarge, there's a call just come in for you.' One of the uniformed officers poked their head around the door and interrupted then.

Excusing himself, DS Morgan left Holder and Lucy alone.

'Jesus! How embarrassing,' Lucy muttered, trying to pull herself together again, mortified that she'd just lost control like that in front of everyone.

'It happens. Don't worry about it. Like you say, it's hot in here and you probably just overheated. We've all been working every hour God sends this week. The job's intense. I get it,' Holder said. Then taking his opportunity while they were alone, he added: 'What was all that about with the sarge? Why did he offer to take you off the case?'

'Oh, it's nothing. Really. The victim is pregnant… That's pretty grim, isn't it?' Lucy began. Trying to convey her upset without giving too much away about just why this case had affected her. Only she still couldn't find the right words. 'I dunno… I've just a lot going on right now. At home. I guess he was just making sure that I don't take on too much.'

Ben held Lucy's gaze.

'Oh! You're not…?' Narrowing his eyes, he tried to slot the missing piece of the puzzle together.

'Pregnant? Oh, God no! It would have to be the Immaculate Conception if I was. I haven't got time for a boyfriend, let alone a baby.' Lucy laughed then, realising how Holder had done his maths and come up with the completely wrong answer. Though she could see how he could have got there.

'Oh good.' Holder laughed too, blushing, as he realised how relieved he sounded. 'I mean good, I'm glad that you're okay. You know. Not good, you're not pregnant… I mean if you were, it's none of my business.'

Lucy laughed again, despite herself. She'd never seen Holder look so awkward before and, if she was honest, she found it endearing to see that he did, in fact, have a serious side. He just hid it well most of the time.

'I'm sure you wouldn't be short on offers if you did want a boyfriend. He'd probably be the first one queuing up,' Holder said, changing the subject and nodding towards Zack, who stood at the front of the room. His tone was full of dislike. 'No one moves that fast on his feet. Apart from me, but then I've got good reflexes and you were standing right next to me. But I reckon he was keeping a beady eye on you, because the second you fell, he made a beeline. Bit creepy if you ask me.'

'Who, Zack?' Lucy laughed, convinced that Holder was making it up. She glanced over in Zack's direction, only to catch his eye and see him smile back at her. It was Lucy's turn to blush then, realising that Holder might actually be right.

'See. Told ya. I've got the sixth sense for these kinds of things,' Holder said. 'Though he doesn't really seem your type.'

'Oh, yeah?' Lucy laughed. 'And what's my type then?'

'Well, I dunno. But he seems a bit pompous to me.'

'Really? I thought he seemed nice.'

'You say nice. I stay stuck up his own arse.' Holder grinned just as DS Morgan's voice filled the room again. Their sergeant walked back into the room and summoned the attention of his team, interrupting Lucy and Holder's chat.

'Okay, everyone. I've just taken a call from the hospital. Shelby Cooke has had her baby. Mother and baby are both doing well. Holder and Murphy, I want you both down at the hospital, taking a witness statement from her immediately,' DS Morgan said, holding Lucy's gaze as she nodded back at him, discreetly letting him know that she was happy to continue working on the case.

'I'll see if I can get the Facial Imaging Officer to attend and draw up the E-fit, so that we can put out a press appeal later this afternoon,' DS Morgan continued, looking around the room and making sure that every officer knew the urgency of this investigation now. 'And as for the rest of you, I want you all on this. Every lead, every enquiry, I want it all followed up and thoroughly. Because I'm sure I don't have to tell you that if these attacks are linked, once this is out there, we're going to have every media outlet, every newspaper and reporter hot on our heels. This case is high profile and there's going to be a huge amount of pressure on us to find this man, and fast.'

CHAPTER THIRTEEN

'And you're happy that this is a close likeness of your attacker?' Lucy asked, getting the Facial Imaging Officer to angle the laptop towards Shelby one more time, to make sure that Shelby was happy with the image he'd created, just as the rest of Shelby's family were shown back into the private room of the postnatal ward. Shelby stared at the screen, scrutinising the image before nodding at Lucy.

'It's him, isn't it? That's what you think. The man that killed that woman last week over at Richmond Park?' Shelby said, realising now how lucky she'd been last night. She was overcome with emotion then as she stared over towards the hospital cot and eyed her new son, cocooned inside, sleeping. Things could have been so different if she hadn't fought back. She and little Riley might not be here now.

'You think he was going to try and kill me too?'

'What's she talking about? What murder?' Janey asked the officers as she reached for her daughter's hand and gave her a supportive squeeze of reassurance, sensing the distress she was in. Making a formal statement must have brought the whole terrible ordeal to the forefront of her mind. 'Hey, you're safe now, Shelby. Riley is safe now.'

'The murder over at Richmond Park. I've been following it on the news. Well, because I was pregnant too, I guess. It just really got to me.'

'Is that true? Is that what you think this is? Someone is attacking pregnant women. That this wasn't just a random attack?' Janey said now, panic in her voice at the thought that last night's attack had been premeditated, and that her daughter had been in danger of losing her life.

'I can assure you all that we are doing everything in our power to catch this man,' Lucy answered with conviction. 'As yet, it's too early to say if it's the same attacker, but we can't yet rule out the possibility that the incidents may indeed be linked. It's certainly a line of enquiry that we are investigating.'

'Jesus Christ!' It was Pete's turn to talk then, pacing the room and feeling completely helpless that there wasn't more he could do. He could see by the look on the officer's face that she was purposely holding something back. 'A possibility that the two attacks may be linked. Are you having a laugh? You'd have to be Helen-fucking-Keller not to see it. One pregnant woman gets murdered. A week later, another pregnant woman gets attacked. The bloke had a knife for fuck's sake. Of course, it was him.'

'As I said, we are doing everything in our power to catch this man, Mr Baker,' Lucy said cautiously. Trying to calm the situation and Pete Baker down. Aware of how heightened emotions were right now; but her main priority was Shelby. The woman had already suffered enough and Lucy didn't want her traumatised further, if she could help it, by her family getting riled up.

'So, what's happening next? Where do you lot go from here?' Pete spat, his words loaded, as if he wasn't holding out much hope for this lot to do their job properly and catch the man.

'We are waiting for some DNA results to come back, which will confirm whether or not the attacks are linked and, in the meantime, our sergeant is organising a press conference for this afternoon. So, things should move on this very quickly now that Shelby's given us such a good description of the attacker,' Lucy said, knowing that there was only so much protection she could offer Shelby. Once the press got wind of this story, nothing would be sacred. The papers would have a field day with this one, and Shelby and her family would no doubt be dragged through the mill along with it.

'Let me look again,' Shelby said, a moment of doubt creeping in as she examined the screen once more, studying the man's sharp, pointed features. His eyes close together and beady. His crooked, thin mouth. She was feeling the pressure now that she realised that her witness statement was all the police really had to go on. 'I mean, it was dark and he had his hood pulled up. And I only really got a glance at him. But I'm almost certain that's him. But what if I've made a mistake? What if we don't catch him? It will be all my fault.'

'It won't be your fault, Shelby. None of this is your fault. You've done really well with your statement, and if you're happy with the E-fit image, then there's a chance someone else will recognise him too. Even if it's only a vague likeness. It's amazing what can trigger someone's memory. You've done really well.'

'Let me see,' Pete insisted, drinking in the image of his daughter's attacker too, committing the man's features to memory, because he had no intentions of letting this go. 'Looks like a flaming nonce to me.' Someone had attacked his daughter, and someone was going to pay. Prison would be too good for this piece of scum.

'I hope you find the bastard before me, because I'll bloody well murder him when I get my hands on him.'

'Pete!' Janey warned. Knowing that her husband was capable of doing such a thing, and the state he was in now, he wouldn't be doing himself any favours by admitting so in front of the police.

'Well, someone's got to look out for her, haven't they?!' Pete said, glaring at his son-in-law, who was sitting slumped in the corner of the room, looking extremely sorry for himself, and as per was being about as useful as a chocolate teapot. Pete was raging with the lad.

'Where's your concern? Where's your need for vengeance? It's just you don't look too fucking bothered to me, Ashley.'

'Dad, leave it, yeah?' Shelby said, sensing her father's fury and feeling guilty herself now that her actions and words last night had only added to the growing friction between the two men. 'None of this is Ashley's fault. He had a bad night too. Christ, what are the chances of us both getting attacked on the same night, huh?'

'You were both attacked?' Holder said now, eyeing Ashley closely – both officers seeing the bruising on the man's swollen eye. His lip was cut and bulging too.

Up until now, Ashley had sat so silently in the corner of the room that Lucy and Holder had barely even glanced at the man. Now he shifted uncomfortably in his chair.

'Are you okay, Ashley?' Lucy said then. The genuine concern in her voice hit a nerve with Ashley. No one else in the room seemed to give a shit that he was attacked last night too. None of them had a clue about the world of shit he was in right now. And he couldn't let on.

'Yeah, I'm fine,' Ashley said, grateful that DC Lucy Murphy seemed to actually care. 'It was nothing. It wasn't an attack as such. Not like this. It was just kids messing about. Trying it on. It wasn't anything major.' He tried to shrug the whole incident off, not wanting to draw attention to himself.

'Ash! Dad said that he found you in the alley down the side of Smokes. He said that you'd been left for dead. You could have died from pneumonia being left outside all night, unconscious,' Shelby said then, incredulously, knowing that Ashley was only playing it down for her sake. She felt guilty now; she hadn't even noticed the state he was in when he'd first walked into the delivery room. She'd been so caught up in Riley that she hadn't even properly looked at him. She had just assumed he'd been up to no good last night. She realised now that she'd overreacted when she should have just stayed at home, instead of traipsing over to her parents' house in the middle of the night, just to make a point. None of this would have happened if she'd just had a little more faith in her husband.

'My dad went out looking for him in the early hours this morning so that he wouldn't miss Riley's birth. And found him, thankfully. I guess we're both lucky, huh!' Shelby informed the officers, oblivious to the heated look the two men exchanged now that she was distracted.

'Hmm, lucky!' Pete snorted, shaking his head and glaring at Ashley, doing everything in his power not to lose control and blurt out the truth to Shelby once and for all. That Ashley might have had a kicking last night, but he'd actually been found tucked up with some hostess tart's bed. It would break his daughter's heart.

'I'm going to need to take a statement from you as well,' Lucy said to Ashley, after seeing the dubious look on her colleague's face which mirrored her own thoughts.

As much as they both knew that coincidences did happen and sometimes the truth was stranger than fiction, they could also sense that something was going on here. Ashley Cooke was acting cagey, as if he had something to hide. And the fact that he was barely reacting to his wife being attacked last night spoke volumes too.

'Why do you need a statement from me? I told you. It was nothing, just kids.'

'We need to rule everything out, Ashley. Just in case the assaults are linked in some way. Someone might have a grudge against you. They might have then taken the grudge out on Shelby,' Holder intervened. 'Smokes nightclub did you say? We can always take a look at the security footage.'

'There's no need. You'd just be wasting your time. You're wasting your time with all of this. Even Shelby's attack. People get away with stuff all the time. Whoever it was, you won't find him.'

'How can you be so sure? Do you recognise him?' Pete interrupted, forcing Ashley to get up and take a proper look at the image on the screen.

'Why would I?' Ashley shook his head, flustered, as everyone in the room turned their attention on him then. He could feel the heat of his face, burning. His voice cracking as he tried to speak. He knew what his father-in-law was thinking when he glared at him. That Ashley was wracked with guilt about what happened last night – only the man didn't know the half of it.

'Because you've lived on that poxy estate for years. Does he look familiar? You might recognise the sick fucker,' Pete bellowed, incensed again at how unhelpful and unconcerned Ashley was being. He couldn't understand how Ashley could just sit there so calmly when his wife and child had been put in such danger.

'No. I don't know him. I've never seen him before.'

All Ashley could think about was the threat that the Boland brothers had made last night. That they'd been sending someone round to his, to dish out a warning to Shelby. Only this was a whole other level.

If they'd do this to him as a warning, what would they do when he didn't pay up? Because unless he came clean to Pete about the money he owed and begged the man for a loan, there was no other way that he could get his hands on that kind of money by tomorrow. The clock was ticking, and time was rapidly running out.

But he knew that the second he owned up that it was his fault Shelby had been attacked, he'd be a dead man anyway. The fact that he'd gone back with Kate when he'd known that someone was paying Shelby a visit, spoke volumes about his priorities. Pete wouldn't believe that Ashley really didn't think it would be anything more than a threat that was being dished out. Not going by the state he'd been left in. Ashley knew the Boland brothers meant business, and that they were capable of causing real harm.

'Did you actually even look at him properly?' Pete said with disdain. Janey stood beside him, her hand on his arm, as if to calm him down and remind him there were police officers present.

But Pete didn't care. 'Do you actually give two shits, Ashley? Your wife and child could have been killed last night. You do realise that, don't you?'

'Course I do,' Ashley said. 'But you think it might be linked to this other attack? The murder over in Richmond? Because that means that it wasn't personal? It wasn't someone with a grudge?' Ashley asked the officers, needing the clarification. 'Did he say anything to you, Shelby? Anything at all?' Ashley willed his wife to remember.

'No, nothing. It all happened so quickly,' Shelby said, picking up on the desperation in her husband's tone for answers now. Finally, he was showing some kind of reaction.

'I need some air,' Ashley said, feeling the walls closing in on him. 'I'm going to go and make a few calls and let my parents know that you've had Riley.' He looked for permission from Shelby, relieved when she nodded.

Remembering that his phone was dead, he grabbed Shelby's phone from the bedside cabinet and left the room quickly, before he said something to Pete that he'd regret. Because the man was purposely pushing his buttons now, and it was taking everything Ashley had in him not to crack. 'I won't be long.'

Shelby turned her attention back to Lucy and Holder.

'You will catch him, won't you?'

'As I said, we'll hopefully know more very soon now we have this E-fit,' Lucy said, getting up and indicating to Holder and the Facial Imaging Officer that this was their cue to leave. 'Right, well I think we're all done here for now; you look as if you could use some rest, Shelby.' Lucy hoped the girl's family would take the hint and leave her to get some sleep, instead of spending the afternoon all cramped inside this little room, arguing with each other.

'Thank you so much for your time, Shelby. And honestly, you've been really helpful. I'll of course keep you up-to-date with any updates going forward.'

'I want every officer on this,' Pete Baker chimed in again. 'I want this bastard found.'

'We will be doing everything in our power, Mr Baker,' Lucy assured the man, before leaving the room with the E-fit artist and Holder close behind her.

*

'Well, what did you make of that?' Lucy said to Holder as they made their way towards the lift, guessing that Holder was in the same mind as her.

'I'd say that Ashley Cooke was acting shifty as fuck. He was definitely hiding something. The bloke couldn't get out of the room fast enough once all eyes were on him,' Holder said, confirming what Lucy had been hinting at.

'Yeah, I got that too. Do you think it would be worth checking out the CCTV of that club on the way back to the station? Just to see if his story matches up?'

'Oh, a hundred per cent. That's what I like the most about you, Lucy.' Holder nodded his head and grinned. 'You're on the same page as me. We don't suffer fools gladly.'

CHAPTER FOURTEEN

'Pick up. Pick up!' Gritting his teeth, Ashley impatiently paced up and down the hospital corridor, pressing Shelby's mobile phone to his ear with one hand, running his fingers frantically through his hair with the other. All the while praying that Sam Boland would answer his phone. Because Ashley needed to put a stop to this madness once and for all, and the only way that he could do that was to make sure that they knew he'd meant it when he said he'd get them their money. No matter what. But only if they promised to leave Shelby and Riley out of it.

'Hello?'

Finally, a voice.

'Sam? It's Ashley. Ashley Cooke,' Ashley said, his words tumbling from his mouth.

'Fucking hell, mate! Don't tell me that you managed to get your hands on the cash already. It must have finally sunk in that we ain't fucking messing about, eh?!' Sam said, sounding mildly amused.

'You gave me your word,' Ashley said, feeling a wave of humiliation wash over him as he tried to stop the tears that threatened now. He could almost hear the smirk on Sam's face. Wiping a stray tear then, ashamed that this was what the Boland brothers were capable of lowering him to. Nothing more than a quivering wreck of a man who was forced to beg and plead with his wife's attackers to leave them alone.

'You said I had forty-eight hours. You said that Shelby wouldn't get hurt. That it was just going to be a warning,' Ashley said, fighting to keep the panic and fear from his voice.

'Ashley, what the fuck are you talking about? If you ain't calling to tell me that you've got my money, why are you calling me?' Sam said, the boredom in his tone evident to them both.

'Shelby's in hospital, Sam.' Ashley lowered his voice. 'The bloke you said you were sending around to my flat attacked her. He had a fucking knife, Sam!' Ashley was unable to control the tremor in his voice now as he spoke; fear mixed with anger taking over. He knew from bitter experience that there was no reasoning with the likes of the Boland brothers. Their vicious reputations preceded them, as he'd learned first-hand last night. Thank God Shelby had been able to fend off her attacker, or who knows what would have happened? Ashley would have lost everything.

He hadn't realised until today, until he'd seen his newborn son nestled in Shelby's arms, how much he actually did love her. Shelby and Riley were his. His very own little family.

And just the thought of either of them getting hurt, or worse, losing them both made him feel sick to his stomach.

They deserved better than he'd given them up until now.

They deserved better than him full stop.

'She's had the baby early, Sam. It must have been the shock that set her labour off. Your guy punched her. What sort of a sicko attacks a pregnant woman with a knife and punches her in the face? The police are crawling all over the place, Sam. They are saying that he attacked another pregnant woman too, over in Richmond Park last week. That he murdered her. He could have killed my wife and child too.' He lowered his voice as a nurse walked past him, aware of the concerned look she flashed him as she recognised the distress he was in. Ashley realised that he was crying uncontrollably, distraught now. The enormity of

what he'd got involved in had hit him with full force. Making
his way around the corner, he ducked into the men's toilets for
some privacy.

'Ashley. I don't know what the fuck you're talking about, mate,
but whatever happened to Shelby had fuck all to do with us. I
don't know anything about an attack or a knife.' Sam sounded
vexed at Ashley, curt, as if trying his hardest to control his temper
as he gave Ashley his last and final warning. 'We have a business
arrangement, Ashley. I gave you a very generous extra forty-eight
hours to find what you owe me, and I'm a man of my word.'

'And I'll get it. I will. One hundred per cent. Just please promise
me you won't involve Shelby. She's been through enough,' Ashley
said, unable to stop his plea turning into a strained whine.

'That's down to you, mate. The clock's ticking, Ashley. So, I
suggest you stop chucking out false allegations that could get you
a serious clump and get your arse into gear to get me my money.'

Staring down at the phone in disbelief then as the phone went
silent, Ashley realised that Sam Boland had hung up on him.
He felt sick. Weak and unsteady, he grabbed on to the sink in
a bid to steady himself as his legs shook violently beneath him.
Of course, Sam would deny all involvement in Shelby's attack. It
wouldn't be in the man's favour to admit anything over the phone,
especially after Ashley had mentioned the police swarming all over
the hospital. Sam wasn't stupid; he probably thought that Ashley
calling him was some kind of a set-up. That the police were listening in on their conversation. Worse than that, he knew now that
the Bolands weren't going to back down anytime soon. And they
didn't care what had happened to Shelby or Riley in the fallout.

Staring at the sickly-looking reflection that glared back at him
in the dirty, smeared mirror, he took in the sight of his battered,
bruised face, his pale, greying skin, barely recognising the broken,
desperate man that glared back at him. He shook his head then,

defeated, and shoved the phone back into his pocket before punching the wall. *Fuck!*

The pain from the impact of his fist locking with the brickwork cracked his knuckles and radiated all the way up his forearm. All he wanted to do was go home and crawl into bed and pretend that none of this was happening. Just close his eyes for a bit and make it all go away.

Only he had Shelby and little Riley to think about now. He needed to get back to them.

Splashing his face with cold water to disguise the fact that he'd been crying, Ashley took a deep breath and tried to pull himself together. The last thing he wanted to do was draw any more attention to himself. Because people would get suspicious, and it wouldn't take much to piece everything together and work out that Shelby was attacked because of Ashley's selfish actions.

And God help him if Pete got wind of any of this.

*

Hearing the main door slam, Pete Baker stepped out of the toilet cubicle where he'd been standing, silently listening in on the end of Ashley's phone call.

He'd only caught the tail end of the conversation, but it was enough to know that his hunch that his degenerate son-in-law was somehow linked to Shelby's attack was right. He'd known to trust his gut about the bloke, and it hadn't let him down since he'd first clapped eyes on the loser. Ashley was a wrong 'un, and by the sounds of it, he was up to his neck in shit as per usual. He'd do anything to save his own arse. Not only that, but the man seemed to have a way with sweet talking Shelby into believing the constant stream of bullshit that flowed from his mouth.

If Pete was to remove Ashley from his daughter's life for good, then he needed to play this smart. He needed to get some proof that Ashley was involved in something bad, so that there was no way that the man could blag his way out of it. Shelby needed to see him for exactly who he really was. Pulling his mobile phone from his pocket, he made a call.

'Carl? Are you still outside in the car? I want you to go back down to Smokes nightclub and I want you to check out the security footage from last night. Give them a bung, threaten them. Whatever you need to do, just get it done.' Pete clenched his fists with anger as he spoke. 'I want to know who Ashley has pissed off.'

Pete hung up. He'd thought that Ashley couldn't stoop any lower than cheating on his daughter while she was in hospital giving birth to their child. But this. This was something else entirely. If his gut was right about this, then he was certain that Ashley had somehow put his daughter's and grandson's lives at risk. And Pete was determined to get to the bottom of it, if it was the very last thing he did. And then he was going to take great pleasure in annihilating Ashley Cooke once and for all.

CHAPTER FIFTEEN

'Well, that took a little longer than I'd hoped but I've managed to get a press conference set up. It's going ahead shortly,' DS Morgan said as DC Murphy and DC Holder arrived back at CID. 'How's Shelby and the baby doing?'

'Good, Sarge. Considering.' Lucy smiled, glad that on this occasion there was a happy outcome. 'She had a little boy. Riley. We've left her to get some rest. She seems pretty shaken up, which is to be expected. But other than that mother and baby are doing just fine.'

'And she managed to give the Facial Imaging Officer a good description for the E-fit?'

'Yes, Sarge. She was a bit worried about some of the details, but I believe she gave us a very accurate description of the attacker.'

'Good,' DS Morgan said, sensing that there was something the two officers were holding back on. 'Is there something else?'

'Her husband was attacked last night too, Sarge. Ashley Cooke. And he was acting a bit cagey while we were at the hospital. Too quiet and subdued for a man whose wife had just been attacked. The father-in-law picked up on it. Something isn't right there,' Holder said.

'Hmm. The husband was attacked too. Yes, that's a hell of a coincidence.' DS Morgan nodded, instantly suspicious.

'He told us that he was attacked by kids outside Smokes nightclub. Only Lucy and I decided to call in there on the way back from the hospital, and guess what? Ashley was bullshitting us. Because it wasn't kids that beat him up. It was two grown men.'

Holder had DS Morgan's attention now.

Ashley Cooke was lying. Why?

DS Morgan and his team were convinced that their attacker was linked to the previous murder in Richmond Park. What were the chances that the attack on Ashley Cooke on the same night as his wife was a coincidence? They needed to be vigilant and rule out any connection with this latest intel; otherwise they'd be leaving themselves wide open to criticism if this investigation turned into some kind of shitshow once it all went public. Which it inevitably would, and soon, in light of this new information.

DS Morgan had endured enough investigations in his career to know first-hand how quickly things could flip back around on them. They needed to be thorough and rule everything out and cover their backs at all times.

'We're going to run some checks through the system, Sarge, and see if the E-fit Shelby gave us has any similarities on either of the men. See if we can get a match,' Holder said, feeling confident that there was more to this than they'd all been led to believe, and wanting to at least try and rule it out. 'There was a lot of tension between Ashley Cooke and his father-in-law too. You might remember him. Pete Baker? I looked him up, and it appears he did a stretch about twenty years ago, but he's managed to keep his nose clean since then.'

'The name rings a bell.' DS Morgan nodded, vaguely recalling the man's name from when he'd started out. 'That is a blast from the past. I'm sure he hired some flash lawyer to smooth his case over for him and managed to get out on appeal. Import and export, he claimed. Only it was a cover for moving around illegal goods.'

'He's got a temper on him though,' Lucy interjected. 'And he didn't seem like a happy-chappy today, Sarge. Seems to us like he was gunning for his son-in-law. We could feel the hate radiating off him in waves.'

'Right, well, Holder, I want you to run the checks on the E-fit,' DS Morgan instructed Holder before turning to Lucy. 'I've arranged a press conference for an hour's time. And I'd like you to lead it. We need to gain the public's support and compassion on this one, and I think that having a female officer lead the appeal will aid that.'

'Of course, Sarge. No worries,' Lucy said, aware that Holder was looking at her now, sensing a concerned undercurrent to DS Morgan's tone and trying to read her expression.

'Okay, well, how about you step into my office and we can go over a few things first?'

'Happy to help, Sarge,' she said with conviction that she didn't feel, not wanting to show her apprehension about being bombarded with questions from most of London's hungry journalists.

Because she knew before she even entered the press conference, that the police had a world of pressure on their shoulders now. There was a sadistic attacker out there on the streets of London. His target: pregnant women. Shelby Cooke had been one of the lucky ones; she'd managed to escape. But if Lucy and her team didn't move fast, the next victim might not be so fortunate.

CHAPTER SIXTEEN

'Is everything really okay, Lucy?' DS Morgan said, offering Lucy a chair before making sure the door to his office was closed.

He wanted to talk to Lucy about the press conference, but he'd also wanted to make sure that she was really all right. Because he had a feeling that she wasn't.

'Not exactly, Sarge, no,' Lucy said honestly. 'Look, I wasn't going to do this now. What with everything we have going on. But I have been going through some stuff.' Lucy shifted in her chair, uncomfortable with how vulnerable she felt when she opened up about how she was really feeling. But if there was one person she trusted completely in her life, that was DS Morgan.

'I'm not really sleeping, and I've lost my appetite. I think that's why I fainted this morning. I've just been really overwhelmed.'

'I thought as much.' DS Morgan nodded. 'And it's this case that's set you off? Because my offer still stands. I can still pull you from this?' He guessed that he'd been right all along and that this case was too close to home for Lucy. Which was completely understandable, given what she'd been through in her past.

'No, Sarge.' Lucy shook her head. 'I want to do this. It's not about the case. Well, not exactly, though I expect that's playing some small part in all of this. Something happened…' Lucy said, unsure how to explain the next bit without sounding like a crazy person.

She took a deep breath.

'I think I can remember what my mother's killer looks like.'

She stared at her boss, searching his face for signs of a reaction, but ever the professional, there was none. DS Morgan didn't react. He was listening without judgement.

'I mean, I know I can. I've seen his face,' Lucy continued, explaining herself. 'I have the same nightmares over and over again. I have done for years. And each time, they're the same sequence of events, replayed in my head of that terrible night. Only, a little while ago, it all changed. And instead of seeing the shadowy black figure that murdered my mother, I finally saw him. I mean, properly. His face, his eyes, his features. And I've seen him every time since. Shit! I know it sounds crazy…'

DS Morgan hesitated, taking in this new information for a few seconds before he spoke. Because he knew how sensitive this was to Lucy and he wanted to get it right.

'Okay then. What would you like to do?'

'Do?' Lucy said, shaking her head, as if not understanding the question.

'Going forward. If you are certain that you remember what your mother's murderer looks like, then I can organise a meeting with a specialist cognitive witness interviewer for you, and we could compile an E-fit. If this new information leads to a new suspect, it may open the lines of enquiry enough for us to prompt a cold case review.'

'You'd really reopen the case? After all this time? It's still possible?' Lucy said, surprised that after all this time it would still be an option.

DS Morgan nodded.

'Of course. Though identification evidence alone is never enough for a conviction, as I'm sure you're aware; but we would do everything in our power to look for this man. And if we did find him, we could revisit forensics. It's a start, at least.'

It was Lucy's turn to fall silent then.

She hadn't thought any further than talking to her sergeant. She hadn't even considered that the case would be reviewed and that there was a chance to reinvestigate. Suddenly she felt filled with fear once more at the thought of having to go through it all again.

'I'm not sure I can put myself through it all again, Sarge. It's just such a lot…' Lucy said, recalling the countless therapy sessions she'd endured over the years. The way that revisiting her mother's murder always seemed to leave her anxious and emotionally drained. She'd end up having to take time off from work. And it wasn't just herself she had to think about. 'And what about my nan, Sarge? I don't think she's able for it either. She's been through so much. She still is going through stuff, right in the midst of it all. And she's not really coping all that well. Some days she's so confused she barely even recognises me. What if this pushes her over the edge? Because the press will be all over it, won't they? One of the lead detective constables on this case, investigating a pregnant woman being murdered, another being attacked. They'd have a field day if they found out that my own pregnant mother had been murdered too, and the killer had never been caught.' Lucy stared out into the main CID room and seeing Holder working away at his desk. His head down as he pored over some files. The rest of her colleagues busying themselves on the case. 'And everyone would know…'

This was part of the reason she'd kept her past a secret from them all. Because the second she told people about her ordeal, they'd treat her differently. Even if they didn't intend to, that's just what people did. They couldn't help themselves. And part of her would always be tiptoed around. Part of her would always be Lucy Murphy – the victim.

'Baby steps, Lucy,' DS Morgan said, pursing his mouth, unable to say anything different or offer any reassurance that that wouldn't be the case, because he'd been thinking the same himself. This case was high-profile and so far, they had very little to go on.

Lucy was right; once the media found out about her past, she would be publicly scrutinised. They all would, and he knew how much Lucy wouldn't want that. Morgan sat back in his chair. There was no one in the world, other than Lucy, who wanted Jennifer Murphy's murderer caught more than him. But this was Lucy's call. All he could do was advise and guide her.

'If you start overthinking it and worrying about every aspect of this case, you'll drive yourself crazy.'

'Even more crazy than I already feel?' Lucy laughed, secretly hoping that DS Morgan didn't think of her that way.

DS Morgan smiled.

'You're not crazy, Lucy. You're still grieving and no doubt, in some ways, you always will be. What you decide to do from here on in is down to you. Like I said, it's one baby step at a time. Zack's still here. Maybe you could talk this through with him? As a forensic profiler, and a bloody good one at that, he might be able to give you his insight on the attacker. Then you can weigh up your options. No pressure, no expectations. Just see how you feel. And once it's done, you can decide from there where you want to go next. If anywhere. We can keep it between us.'

'Maybe you're right. Maybe I should do that at least,' Lucy conceded. 'Because I feel as if I need to get this image out of my head. Maybe then the nightmares will stop.'

'Well, we have the specialist cognitive interviewer and Facial Imaging Officer still here at the station too. If you wanted to have a chat with them, now would be the perfect time to do so, without drawing any suspicion from the rest of the team. They'd all assume that you were talking about Shelby Cooke's case. And I can get Zack on the phone now, and see if he's free too?' DS Morgan shrugged. 'We've got the press conference lined up shortly, but maybe you could speak to him afterwards? Unless, you think it's too much, doing it all today, I understand. I'm sure we could work something out for another day.'

DS Morgan could see that Lucy was considering her options.

'And I know you're worried about how this would all affect your nan too. I've met Winnie. I know how strong she can be. But if this is all affecting you, there's no doubt it's affecting her too. Maybe you'll both finally get some form of closure. Maybe you won't. It's always a risk, you just have to weigh up what would be best for you both.'

Lucy nodded slowly. DS Morgan was right. She was scared, of course she was, but maybe she had to do this, regardless of whether she wanted to or not. Because there would be no end otherwise. She and her nan would forever live in limbo. Dancing around the subject of her mother's murder, both pretending to be okay, when inside they were both slowly drowning in pain. But if she was going to do this, then she would have to speak to her nan.

'I might as well go all in, Sarge. And see them all while they're still here at the station. Before I lose my bottle. Hopefully, like you say, no one will get suspicious. And maybe having the press conference in between will keep my mind focused on something else for a while.'

'I'll get them to see you right away.' DS Morgan picked up the phone and made the call. His hand covering the mouthpiece as the dial tone sounded.

'Whatever happens, Lucy, you have my full support. Whatever resources are needed, whatever it takes. It won't be easy, but I want you to know that you are not alone.'

'I really appreciate that, Sarge,' Lucy said, feeling the tears swell in her eyes at her boss's sincere words.

She knew that he wanted this as much as she did. To finally catch her mother's killer and see justice served. And after all of these years, bring some kind of peace to her and her nan.

CHAPTER SEVENTEEN

Finishing her second pack of biscuits and discarding the packet onto the floor, Imelda George took one last swig of tea, recoiled at how cold it was now and let out a huge belch. Standing up, she placed her hand on her protruding ball of a stomach and smiled to herself as she cradled the round mound in her hands.

She'd always been fat; she was well aware of that. Having endured a lifetime of bullying and looks of disgust from strangers wherever she went, making no secret of their contempt at the sheer size of her, she'd have to have been deluded not to know otherwise. But they couldn't call her fat now, could they? The rotten bastards.

Massaging her bump, Imelda no longer cared about any of that now that she had a good reason to eat until her heart's content and not be made to feel guilty about it. She waddled when she walked these days and now instead of disdain, people would smile at her encouragingly. As if offering their support. They'd see her obvious rounded bump and actually get up out of their seats on the bus and let her sit down.

And Imelda liked it. Basking in the sudden attention that she got for being pregnant made her feel like royalty. People actually went out of their way now to engage in conversation with her. They wanted to talk to her. Her pregnancy meant that she was suddenly no longer invisible. She was a somebody now. A mum to be. And people asked her all kinds of questions.

Is it a boy or a girl? Have you had a good pregnancy? Have you had any weird cravings?

And, stranger still, they genuinely wanted to know details that almost nobody else would have found interesting in the slightest. They wanted to know it all. Every last mundane detail and tedious bit of minutiae. It was such a revelation to her, people engaging in conversation with her.

When are you due?

That was the one awful, burning question that Imelda had spent most of her lifetime dreading, for the fear of having to admit that she was simply just fat. Recalling how her face had burned a deep red with humiliation every single time she'd had to correct someone. Often, in the end, she'd just gone along with it to save embarrassment and pretend that she was pregnant after all. But she didn't need to pretend any more. Not only did she relish these words now, she welcomed them wholeheartedly.

Making her way to the small bedroom at the front of the flat, Imelda sat down in the rocking chair in the corner of the room, looking around with glee. The rest of the flat was run-down and tired-looking, as expected in such an old, decrepit building, but Imelda had worked tirelessly making this room just perfect. And it was perfect.

She'd lost several hours each day just sitting here, breathing in lungsful of the faint smell of the freshly painted white walls and the lingering scent of the new soft, grey carpet at her feet. She absently rocked back and forth in her nursing chair, staring at the beautifully dressed cot and thinking about all the exciting times she had ahead of herself as a new mum.

It wasn't as fancy and posh as some of the nurseries in the mother and baby magazines that she spent her days poring over. But she'd tried her very best, filling it with bargains that she'd bought from sellers on Facebook, and upcycled second-hand furniture she'd managed to source from charity shops. Only the best for her baby.

And once the baby was here and she knew what she was having, she would finish the room accordingly. A splash of pink or blue. And secretly she hoped it would be a girl. A little daughter would be the dream. She'd have her best friend for life then. Someone to talk to and laugh with.

Because most days all she had was the television set for the company. Still, the TV was better than nothing to help her whittle away the boredom. Making her way back into the lounge, she slumped back down onto the sofa and turned the TV on, pushing the piles of new mother and baby magazines and her jumbled mass of abandoned knitting projects onto the floor. It turned out she didn't really have the patience for knitting.

She caressed her bump absently as she flicked through the channels, until the E-fit image of a man's face filling the screen on the local news bulletin almost her made drop the remote control.

'What the hell?'

Frantically, Imelda pressed the volume button so she could hear what the young female police officer now on screen was saying.

'A young pregnant woman, local to the Wandsworth area, was attacked late last night. The attacker is thought to be in his mid- to late-thirties, roughly five foot eight, slim frame and was wearing a black tracksuit with a navy jacket over the top. The hood has a bright pink or neon orange lining.'

Imelda could feel her pulse quickening as she read the police officer's name at the bottom of the screen.

'Detective Constable Lucy Murphy, Wandsworth CID.'

She watched in horror as she saw the cameraman zoom in on the common just outside her flat. The crime they were talking about happened right here, practically on her doorstep.

'I would urge anyone who thinks that they might recognise the man in the E-fit to contact us as a matter of urgency. As you can imagine, this was a very traumatic ordeal for the victim and we are determined to find the person responsible and bring them to justice.'

'Is it true that you've linked this attack to the murder of Liza Fitzgerald, also pregnant, who was killed over at Richmond Park last week? Do you think you're looking for a serial killer?' One of the journalists at the front of the room called out.

Imelda's chest was tight now. The walls were closing in. She held her breath as the camera zoomed in to the female officer's face, as Imelda and the room awaited the police officer's answer.

'As yet, that's not something that we can confirm. We are carrying out a full investigation and right now our priority is finding the person in the E-fit image.'

'Is it true that this victim on Wandsworth Common lost her baby?' another journalist asked.

Imelda felt her heart thump erratically inside her chest, her stomach consumed with a sinking feeling of dread.

'The shock of the attack did bring on early labour, but the victim has given birth to a healthy baby boy. I can confirm that mother and baby are doing well under the circumstances.'

As the press conference ended and the news presenter moved on to the next subject, Imelda got up and started pacing the floor, one protective hand still on her bump, filled with a bubbling anxiety as she eyed the phone. In two minds if she should make the call.

Because she'd seen him. The man from the E-fit photo. She was certain of it. And the chances were he'd seen her too.

CHAPTER EIGHTEEN

'We've got a fucking problem,' Sam Boland said, the second his brother Russ walked back into the flat, having gone to pick up some money they were owed from one of their regular borrowers.

'I had Ashley Cooke on the phone earlier. He's saying that his missus was attacked last night. It looks as if Jay-Jay got too heavy-handed with her. The stupid fucker had a knife on him too, apparently! That wasn't what we agreed, Russ.' Having stewed on the conversation waiting for his brother's return home, Sam was seething now. 'What the fuck is he playing at?'

'What? Jay-Jay? Are you sure? Our guy on the inside vouched for him, didn't he?' Recognising his brother's rage slowly building, Russ recalled the exact words of the prison guard that they had on their payroll. 'Made out that he was a hard bastard. That he could handle himself when he needed to. But he said that he mainly kept his head down. He wasn't any trouble, that he kept himself to himself.'

'Well, he left out the bit about the man being a fucking knife-wielding lunatic then, didn't he?!' Sam spat. Furious now at what Ashley had told him. Because if Ashley was already holding them accountable, it wouldn't be long until the police would too. And this wasn't how Sam liked to work. In his game, discretion was everything.

'He said that the police think Jay-Jay murdered another woman too? Last week. I looked it up. Some pregnant bird over in Richmond park was stabbed. We can't be involved with all this. We're going to have to deal with him.'

'What do you want to do?' Russ said, taking a deep breath as he accepted there wasn't going to be any reasoning with Sam on this. And if what Ashley had said was true, and Jay-Jay did attack Shelby Cooke, then there was nothing that Russ could say or do to help him. The man had fucked this up on his own.

'We can't have any of this come back on us.'

About to nod his head in agreement, Russ stared ahead at the TV, his eyes widening in shock as he took in the image of Jay-Jay Andrews's face as it filled the screen.

'Fucking hell! What are the chances?' Russ said, lurching across the sofa and grabbing the remote control. Cranking up the volume on the TV, the two brothers stood in silence, staring at the 52-inch E-fit of Jay-Jay Andrews gawping back at them through their television screen. They listened intently as the camera zoomed in on a female police officer – DC Lucy Murphy according to the name printed at the bottom of the screen – and managed to catch the tail end of the statement as she addressed a room full of press.

'As you can imagine, this was a very traumatic ordeal for the victim and we are determined to find the person responsible and bring them to justice.'

'Is it true that you've linked this attack to the murder of Liza Fitzgerald, also pregnant, who was killed over at Richmond Park last week? Do you think you're looking for a serial killer?'

'A serial killer? Oh, you have got to be fucking joking!' Sam said, staring at the TV in disbelief at the kind of lunatic they'd got themselves involved with. 'Trust us to throw a bone at someone who's on a fucking killing spree of pregnant birds, Russ! For fuck's sake man! One job and already his mugshot's all over the bloody news. This was not what we need to be dealing with,' Sam spat. 'It can't be him though, can it? When did he get out of the nick?'

'Ten days ago,' Russ said, a sinking feeling in his stomach as he realised that the timeline fitted. That Jay-Jay would have been out when the woman in Richmond Park was murdered.

'Fuck! We need to make sure that he keeps his gob shut about working for us. Because the police will catch up with him for this, and when they do, he ain't dragging us down in the shit with him. This is on him and him alone. We need to make sure that he understands that.' Sam nodded to the safe over in the corner of the room, which held their guns, so that his brother was under no illusion just how serious this was, and just how much Sam wanted to make sure the trail didn't lead back to them.

'Come on, Sam. Jesus! We don't need to fucking take him out. And especially not if the police are hot on his tail. They'll come looking for us for answers if we take him out. We'll have to play it safer than that. I'll speak to him; I'll make him see sense,' Russ said, knowing that if he had to wipe Jay-Jay out of the picture for good, he would do it. Of course, he would. He had no qualms about that. Like Sam always said, this was business and they did what they had to in order to survive.

Russ had only spoken to Jay-Jay for all of five minutes, but he'd thought the guy was sound. He'd certainly never have suspected he was capable of such sick and twisted acts. And if he was being totally honest, part of Russ felt a little impressed. It just went to show that there were some real sick fucks walking amongst them.

'Are you having a laugh, Russ. A word? All it will take is "a word", just one from him when the police catch up with him. And they'll fit this shit on us in a heartbeat, and you know they will. This is their golden opportunity. And you think he won't try and pin it on us, if it means there's a chance he won't go back inside? If they offer him a deal. He's desperate, Russ. And desperate men are a fucking liability.'

'He won't talk!' Russ said with certainty. 'That's a fact, because I'll make sure of it.'

'That's just it though, Russ. We don't know that for a fact, because we clearly don't know him,' Sam said, jabbing his finger on his temple to show that Jay-Jay wasn't all there in the head. The man was mental.

'But like you said, Sam, even if it's true and he did do this, we didn't tell him to do this. This has jack shit to do with us.'

'And you reckon the police will give two shits about that tiny detail? Come on, Russ! All he has to say is that he's working for us and they'll make it fit. They'd love that, wouldn't they? The golden opportunity to finally send us down. No, he needs to be sorted.'

'Okay, Okay. I'll do whatever needs to be done,' Russ said, getting up and sending a text to Jay-Jay's phone.

A few minutes later the reply came in, just as he knew it would, and he turned to Sam. 'I told him that I'm going to come and pay him the money for last night's job. He's told me to meet him at some dive of a pub in town.'

Grabbing his keys from the side, Russ turned to his brother and said: 'Leave it with me, yeah! I'll make sure he knows the score. I'll drum it into him personally if I have to. And if he tries anything stupid, then we'll do it your way. Yeah? Either way, I'll sort it.'

CHAPTER NINETEEN

'That lot can't help themselves, can they? They feed like vultures. They're bloody ruthless,' Holder said, referring to the press. He switched off the TV that he'd been watching the press conference on as Lucy walked back into CID. 'You did good though! I thought you handled it really well!'

'Well, I did what I could, but as you no doubt heard, they've already done their homework and linked it to the murder enquiry over in Richmond, so that lot will be having a field day. The pressure is well and truly on now!'

'Hey, kiddo! That's how we roll. We should be used to that by now,' Holder said with a smile, trying to make light of the situation as he recognised the ashen look on Lucy's face. 'You look as shattered as I feel.'

'It's been a long day!'

'Hasn't it just. And I see your mate's back…' DC Holder said with a chuckle. They both watched as DS Morgan stepped into his office to where Zack Lownrey was waiting. 'He's been sitting in there waiting patiently for the press conference to finish. Doubt he has anything more to add to the case yet though? Anyway, I'm starving, and you must be hungry too? Do you fancy going to grab a quick bite to eat, seeing as they're clearly busy?'

'I can't.'

'Course you can. I mean, all right, it's almost three o'clock so, it's not technically lunch, but we do have to eat at some point. And you look like you could do with a break.'

'I've already made arrangements.' Lucy shifted awkwardly on her feet, diverting her gaze from Holder's, before covertly glancing over to where DS Morgan and Zack Lownrey were standing in the office, both men looking over in her direction now. Lucy waved in acknowledgement, letting Zack know that she would be with him shortly. Turning and following Lucy's gaze, Holder laughed as he realised the score.

'He's waiting for you?' Holder said, shaking his head, unable to feign his surprise as Lucy's cheeks flushed red in answer. 'Man, that bloke works fast!'

'It's not like that,' Lucy said, trying to explain, only she knew exactly how it looked. Which was purposely why she hadn't mentioned her meeting with Zack to Holder in the first place. Especially as Holder had done nothing but wind her up, by saying that he thought Zack had the hots for her. 'It's strictly work. I just wanted to talk to him about the case. Get more of a handle on the attacker's profile,' Lucy lied, trying to play down the meeting, because the last thing she needed right now was to confess to Holder what this was really about. Though she could see by Holder's expression that he wasn't buying it. And after the day that she'd had, she really didn't have the energy to go into it all with her friend. Because she knew that it wouldn't be an easy conversation to have. It was bad enough that she was going to have to speak to Zack Lownrey about it, but Lucy knew that she didn't have much choice now.

DS Morgan would be filling him in on the situation right at this very moment. And Lucy had already come this far. She'd spoken to the specialist cognitive interviewer and done an E-fit with the Facial Imaging Officer. Now she just wanted to speak with Zack and find out his thoughts on her mother's attacker and get this over and done with.

'Look, you don't need to play it down to me. I mean, if you and Zack are starting a thing or whatever. Well, it's none of my business… Clearly!'

'Oh, don't be like that, Holder,' Lucy said, picking up on the man's annoyance that she was keeping things from him.

'It's cool. We can grab something to eat another time. I hope you have a nice time. Don't let him be a cheapskate though, yeah? Make sure he foots the bill,' Holder said, winking at Lucy before grabbing his keys and making for the door, to show Lucy that there were no hard feelings.

Though Lucy could tell that Holder was upset with her now. And she felt bad then, keeping things from him. Because as unlikely as it had seemed when they'd first met, she and Holder had become a close-knit team while working together the past few months. And Lucy had actually grown to really like the man. Despite his blunt, sarcastic ways, Lucy classed him as a good friend. A friend she could trust. Only right now, it wasn't a case of not trusting him. It was more a case of having to work out what she wanted to do next. Because right now Lucy didn't have a clue where to start with any of it.

CHAPTER TWENTY

'Well, this is a little bit fancy just for a bit of lunch, isn't it?' Lucy said, feeling a little out of place and very much underdressed in her workwear as the waiter guided them over to the table of the fancy brasserie on the corner of King's Road, which Zack had suggested they go to for their late lunch meeting.

'I just figured it would be quiet here at this time of day. And trust me, the food here is the best. Do you like French food?' Zack asked, pulling the chair out for Lucy and trying to make her feel comfortable now that they were away from the station and away from prying eyes or ears.

'I guess…' Lucy said, scanning the fancy à la carte menu for something vaguely familiar, unable to make heads nor tails of the dishes that were listed there.

But Zack was right about one thing, the place was quiet and for that she was grateful. Eyeing the only two other occupied tables in the restaurant, Lucy guessed that the place would normally be heaving if it was lunch or dinner service. They were here in between both main services and almost had the place to themselves.

'It's very pretty in here,' Lucy said, hoping the distraction would be her best attempt at not looking so ungrateful. She took in the sight of the rich decor, the vibrant purple fabrics that stood out boldly against walls which were awash with an elegant emerald green. Her gaze was drawn then to sparkling gold edging that lined the dark polished timbers of the feature bar which stood prominently in the middle of the restaurant. A large crystal chandelier twinkled above a cluster of staff as they milled around, trying to look busy beneath it.

Only she just couldn't relax no matter how quiet and lovely it was. She felt out of sorts here and uncomfortable. But that was partly because of the conversation they were about to have, no doubt.

'This place must cost a fortune,' she said, thinking out loud as she scanned the menu once more. A bottle of their fanciest Champagne would probably set her back the best part of her week's wages. Which instantly made her think of Holder's earlier comment about making sure that Zack footed the bill. Lucy bit her lip to stop herself from smiling.

'How's the case going?' Zack said, sensing how uncomfortable Lucy seemed, and hoping to break the ice and put her at ease.

'So far, we don't have much to go on other than the E-fit. The press conference should help…' Lucy shrugged. 'And we're currently making our way through all the CCTV in the local area, as well as doing a door-to-door for any witness statements. It's still early days,' Lucy said, though she was genuinely hopeful that the attacker would be caught. 'Shelby managed to get a really good look at him. The E-fit is really clear and she's certain it's an accurate likeness. So, I think we will get him,' she said with certainty, hoping she would be proved right.

Zack nodded, noting how Lucy twiddled her napkin awkwardly.

Something else clearly playing on her mind.

'Which was what I wanted to speak to you about. I take it DS Morgan filled you in?' Lucy said, her voice quieter then, as if she was almost too scared to broach the subject.

'He did. And I'm so very sorry to hear about your mother. It must have been extremely traumatic to witness what you did.

Especially at such a young age,' Zack said, knowing that Lucy probably just wanted to get this conversation over and done with; already it was lingering in the room between them.

'Thank you. Yes. It's been tough,' Lucy said, not playing it down, grateful for the waiter who approached them and began pouring water in their glasses. Giving her a few seconds to gather herself, before she managed to find her voice as it lodged somewhere deep inside her throat.

'But other than the E-fit, I don't really know where to start with it all, or even if I want to full stop. It's been twenty years. What are the chances that we'd even find him now after all this time?' Lucy said with a shrug. 'DS Morgan suggested doing the E-fit, and he said that it might be a good idea to speak with you. But that's as far as I've got with everything. I don't know, I guess I just wanted to know all the facts before I make my decision on what I should do next. Because it would mean dragging everything back up again. Bringing it to forefront of my life again. And not just mine. My nan's too. Only her health is deteriorating and I'm not sure that she'd be able to cope with any of it.'

'It's a tough decision to make. I don't envy you.'

'I just wonder if seeing his face, what if it isn't enough…' Lucy paused.

'But what if it is?' Zack said, finishing Lucy's sentence for her.

Lucy nodded.

'Well, as you can imagine, reopening the case after all these years will prove a challenge. But it's certainly not impossible,' Zack said. 'If we can identify the suspect, and you never know, it could happen, then it will be a case of trying to work out if there's any way of placing the suspect at the scene of the crime. We'd need to rule out any alibis. And we would, of course, need to revisit forensics, which wouldn't be a bad thing. We've come a long way in the last twenty years, so you just never know what might pop up now…' Zack said, narrowing his eyes. 'But I'm guessing that you know all this already. DS Morgan seems like he's on the ball on this one. He was one of the original investigating officers on the case, wasn't he? And from what I understand, he would pursue whatever avenues that he thought possible, if it meant he could finally bring your mother's killer to justice,' Zack said finally. 'So, is there something else?' he asked as the waiter approached the table once more to serve them both some warm bread rolls.

Lucy waited patiently until he had left.

'I wanted to ask you if you would profile the killer for me,' Lucy said then, matching Zack's bluntness.

'Well, gladly. I mean if the case is reopened and yourself and DS Morgan request that I…' Zack said, watching closely as Lucy shook her head, shifting uncomfortably in her chair.

The expression on her face telling him that this wasn't what she had been getting at.

Zack frowned.

'What if we don't reopen the case?' Lucy said, not wanting to divulge any further details to Zack just yet. 'Could you still profile him?'

Zack nodded now in understanding. Lucy wanted answers, but she was wondering how much she could access unofficially. Off the record, to see if it was worth her while going public with everything. Or if this was a gamble that didn't have any chance of paying off. Zack could understand that. Once Lucy opened this can of worms, there'd be no going back.

'It's not something that's possible without all the information. I'd need to see the cold case file,' Zack said, pursing his mouth. 'My job is to compile and compare data from similar crimes, and in order to do that I'd need to know exactly what I'm dealing with. I'd need to have access to every bit of crime scene evidence that was collected and the witness reports. It's a lot more complex than just giving my opinion; there's a lot of data to analyse.'

'But if DS Morgan gave you that access… off the record…?' Lucy said hopefully, knowing what a big ask it was for Zack to do this for her. To go over a historic murder case with a fine-tooth comb and try and profile a murderer who had, so far, managed to slip beneath the police force's radar for the best part of two decades.

'I'm happy to have a look at the files,' Zack said finally, the look on his face showing Lucy that this wasn't a spur-of-the-moment decision. He'd seen this coming, suspecting that this might be the reason that Lucy wished to speak with him since having the conversation with DS Morgan, and he'd clearly given it some thought.

'Even if I decide not to go ahead with it all and reopen the case? It's a lot of work.'

'Even if you decide not to proceed. I know what you went through must have been horrific, Lucy. Really, I can't even imagine,' Zack said then, selecting his words carefully. Not wanting to show Lucy how sorry he felt for her. He could see that she didn't need his sympathy. What she needed was his help. 'I'll be happy to do whatever I can to help. Whatever you decide.'

'Thank you, I appreciate it.' Lucy smiled then. Relaxing now that the hard part of the conversation was over as she saw the waiter lingering once more near their table, with his notepad in his hand ready to take their order.

'Now, maybe your first port of call is going to be helping to translate the menu for me.' Lucy grinned. 'What would you recommend?'

CHAPTER TWENTY-ONE

'Right!' said Vivian, scrutinising the Scrabble board before eyeing her letter options for the umpteenth time. They were almost at the end of their game, but there was still everything to play for. 'I'm only in the lead by a few points.'

'Well then, everything counts on this last go,' Winnie said. The confident gleam in her eyes told Vivian that the woman had been dealt a good hand of letters this time. Unless Winnie was doing her usual and pulling the ultimate poker face on her. Either way, Vivian was in a dilemma.

'I've got a word, but I don't think it's appropriate,' Vivian said, pursing her mouth and wondering if she should just play the damn letters. 'It's a swear word. I don't think swear words count?'

'Course they do. Though, personally, I find them vulgar and offensive… but if it's all you've got,' Winnie said pointedly with a shrug. Her eyes challenging the younger woman to play her word and defy her. Which only made Vivian chuckle.

This was the Winnie she had grown to love. And tonight, the woman was on top form. Completely in the zone, forgetting entirely that this was just two friends playing a friendly game of Scrabble to pass the time. Winnie was acting like she was a contender in the British Scrabble championship.

'Okay then. Well, I'm going to play it. Sorry if it offends you, Winnie. It is all that I've got. "Shit." That's seven points.'

'Shit?' Winnie said, turning her nose up in disgust.

'I take it you can do better, Winnie?'

'Better than your "shit" attempt.' Winnie smirked. She arranged her own letters on the board quickly and looked at Vivian with triumph in her eyes.

'Fuckers?' Vivian squealed indignantly. 'You said swear words offend you? I almost didn't play mine!'

'The term is calling your bluff.' Winnie shrugged, grinning now from ear to ear. 'And I don't like some swear words, but fuckers, now that's a proper swear word. How many points is that?'

'Sixteen,' Vivian said, shaking her head. 'So, your final total is a hundred and twelve.'

'Ooh, which makes me the champion! Not bad, eh? Considering I've never played the game before,' Winnie said, with no memory of the countless other games she'd played with Vivian and Lucy over the years. 'So, that means that I get the last Jaffa Cake!' She shoved it into her mouth triumphantly before Vivian could protest. Or remind Winnie that she'd eaten the majority of them already, anyway.

'Well done, Winnie,' Vivian said, showing the lady that she was not a sore loser and she would take her defeat on the chin. 'Christ, if anyone could see the intellect that goes on in our games, Winnie. You're a bad influence, did I tell you that already?' Vivian laughed and started packing the game away as Nurse Hamilton came into the room.

'All done, Winnie?'

'I won!'

'Oh, well I didn't expect you not to.' Nurse Hamilton smiled.

'Same time tomorrow, Winnie?' Vivian said.

'If you can face the humiliation of losing to me again,' Winnie said, her tone deadpan. Winning the game had completely gone to her head.

Vivian played along.

'Oh, I don't know. I'll give it my best shot. Night night, darling!' She got up and gave Winnie a kiss on the cheek before turning to leave and smiling at Nurse Hamilton. 'Night.'

'Lucy didn't make it again?' Nurse Hamilton said, knowing how time-consuming Lucy's job could be. She'd been due to visit tonight.

Vivian shook her head.

'She sent me a text to say she'd been held up. She'll be kicking herself. But fingers crossed she'll see her tomorrow.'

'Indeed,' Nurse Hamilton said, leading Winnie away as Vivian let herself out the main doors and made her way across the car park.

She stopped abruptly as Lucy's car drove through the entrance and pulled up next to her. Lucy wound down the window.

'I've missed her again, haven't I?'

'She's just gone off to bed, but don't worry, she kept me busy this evening,' Vivian said, giving in to another of her raucous laughs. 'It never fails to surprise me how that woman is still as sharp as a knife when it comes to her Scrabble games. Sometimes, it's as if she's not sick at all. Though tonight she thought she had beginner's luck. She had no recollection of all the games she's made me play before now, bless her. Oh, she's as crafty as they can get when she's on top form.' Then seeing the crestfallen look on Lucy's face, Vivian added: 'Hey, there's always tomorrow, Lucy. Don't be hard on yourself. You're working and, let's face it, you don't have an easy job.'

Lucy nodded. Grateful that Vivian was here tonight when she couldn't be. That helped ease her guilt.

'Do you fancy a lift? It's the very least I can do,' Lucy said, leaning over and opening the passenger side door before Vivian could refuse.

Vivian smiled and got in.

'Thank you, darling. It beats catching the bus. How was your day?' Vivian sensed that Lucy was exhausted.

'Tough. We're in the middle of a murder enquiry. There was an attack on another potential victim. Luckily she managed to get away.' Lucy shrugged her shoulders. Her eyes fixed on the road. As if there something more she wanted to say.

But Vivian knew not to pry.

Lucy's job was confidential, and even the very little that Lucy told her was forbidden.

'Can I ask you something, Vivian?' she said finally.

'Of course, anything.'

'Do you think that it would make my nan worse if my mother's case was reopened?'

'Your mother's case is being reopened? Has something happened? Do you have a suspect?' Vivian said.

Lucy had filled Vivian in on everything about her mother's death previously, because she knew that working in such close proximity to her nan for the amount of time she did, would throw a lot of things into light, and she wanted the woman to be prepared to deal with anything that might cause her nan to be upset.

And that obviously included her mother's murder. It had affected Winnie badly at the time, but her illness seemed to bring it all up again, almost daily. Winnie was always so confused. Sometimes she forgot her daughter was even dead at all. Other times she remembered the pain of finding out over and over, as if she was reliving it all once again.

'We don't have anything concrete, no. But I remember something. His face. I remember his face. And I don't know what to do. Because the last thing I want to do is cause my nan any more distress by dragging it all up again.'

'Oh, my! Lucy!' Vivian said, seeing the dilemma the girl was in. 'That's an awful lot for you to shoulder, honey. Have you spoken to anyone else?'

Lucy nodded.

'I spoke to DS Morgan earlier today. And he advised me to talk to a forensic psychologist. But other than that no. Only you.'

'Well, that's good. I'm sure that DS Morgan will support you in any way that he can. He cares about you, and your mother's case. He cares about your nan too,' Vivian said, knowing how close Lucy was with DS Morgan. How she trusted him implicitly, and how he cared for Lucy enough to ensure that she did the right thing, for her.

'Regarding your nan, I couldn't really say. You know that I live by the term that honesty is not always the best policy when it comes to caring for someone with dementia. Those little white lies we feed our patients aren't to make our job easier, they are to spare them from any unnecessary upset and distress.'

'So, you think it would be too much for her to be questioned about it all? That it wouldn't be a good idea for me to talk to her about it?'

Vivian pursed her mouth.

'Their brains are often experiencing a completely different version of reality from us and anything like this, well, I don't think she'd entirely understand it. I think it would be too much for her to process.'

Lucy nodded. That was what she'd thought. That she'd be dragging all of this up again, and for what? To upset her nan and cause her more heartache. Because it had been twenty years now. They hadn't caught her mother's killer back then, and there was no guarantee that they'd be able to catch him now. Especially when all she had to go on was a vague recollection of a face in her dreams.

'But you need to do what's right for you, too, Lucy,' Vivian said as they pulled up outside her house a few minutes later. 'You've got too much going on to suffer alone with this one. I'm always here for you, if you need to talk. You know that, don't you?'

'I do. Thank you.'

Satisfied with that, Vivian leaned over and kissed Lucy on the cheek.

'I'll hopefully see you tomorrow evening?' Vivian said as she got out of the car, leaning down and giving Lucy a small smile. 'Because I'm not sure I can take one more arse-whooping from that grandmother of yours. She takes Scrabble far too seriously.'

Lucy couldn't help but laugh at that. Watching as Vivian made her way into her house, the windows all lit up, the movement of people inside, she felt a slight tinge of jealousy then as she pictured Vivian's family. The loud, raucous laughter around the dinner table. The arguments. The love. She pulled away and made her way back to her nan's empty house.

CHAPTER TWENTY-TWO

'Fuck me, you're really pushing the boat out, Jay-Jay. All the pubs in London and you pick this dive?' Russ Boland said, standing over the man and eyeing him with disgust as he shoved half a cheeseburger in his mouth and a trail of ketchup ran down his chin.

It was no surprise to Russ that he, Jay-Jay and the barman were the only three people in here.

'Nothing a lick of paint and a new carpet wouldn't sort out.' Jay-Jay shrugged. He wasn't fussed about the place's decor. The food was warm and the beer cold. Compared to the squat he was currently staying in it was a palace.

'A lick of paint?' Russ laughed at the man's optimism. 'The only thing that would improve this place is a fucking inferno! And is he fucking deaf or what?' Russ nodded over towards the barman, who was standing directly under the huge flatscreen TV that hung over the bar, noise blasting from its speakers. 'Cos if he ain't already, he soon will be with that thing blaring. Still, at least the telly's drowning out the noise of you shovelling that food into your face. No one's gunna steal it on you, mate!' Russ smirked.

He and Sam had it on good account from a mutual acquaintance in Wandsworth nick that Jay-Jay Andrews could more than handle himself, which is why they had offered the bloke a job when he'd got out in the first place. The man fought like an animal when he needed to, they'd been told. Though looking at him now, Russ could see that he ate like one too. 'You look as if you haven't eaten all week.'

'And?!' Jay-Jay said, confirming that Russ had hit the nail on the head as he greedily swallowed down the mouthful of his food. Glaring at Russ now.

He just wanted Russ to pay him and fuck off so that he could finish his meal in peace. He'd spent the past ten days fending for himself and scouring in the bins behind the local parade of shops for anything remotely edible. And he'd found a few decent morsels. One man's rubbish is another man's treasure and all that. But this was the first real bit of decent grub he'd had since he'd got out of prison. He wanted to savour it.

'You sorted it then?' Russ asked, referring to the first job that they'd sent Jay-Jay on.

Jay-Jay opened his mouth, ready to fill Russ in on the shitshow that had been last night.

The victim sprawled out on the ground. The knife dropped on the floor. Only he knew that once he told Russ about last night's colossal fuck-up, and how quickly everything had seemed to escalate completely out of control, he could kiss goodbye to the money they'd promise him, and he'd have no work with them in the future.

'What?' Russ said. Narrowing his eyes then, and feigning ignorance. Knowing full well that something was up. 'Please tell me you didn't fuck it up. Because between us, mate, I heard things got a bit heavy-handed.'

'Heavy-handed?' Jay-Jay said feigning ignorance, deciding to keep his mouth shut and not incriminate himself. He wondered what exactly it was Russ claimed to know.

Jay-Jay was depending on this money so that he could eat properly over the next few days. He wanted to buy some decent bedding too. He was fed up with sleeping on some old piss-stained

sleeping bag on the freezing cold floor of the derelict house he was squatting in. This was the price he paid for wanting to stay off the grid. For not taking the handouts offered to him when he'd got out. For not opting for assisted housing and benefits. He'd declined the proposal of being put up in a hostel, knowing that if he did, he'd be beholden to the system. Depending on state benefits and handouts while having some do-gooder case worker keeping tabs on him. But Jay-Jay didn't want to be in debt to anyone. He wanted to earn his own way and be his own man. This gig with the Boland brothers might just be the making of him. He couldn't fuck it up.

'All you need to know is that it's done. I sorted it,' Jay-Jay said, just wanting to get paid his money and get the fuck out of here.

Only he could see that Russ still didn't look convinced, scrutinising Jay-Jay intently as he'd picked up on a trickle of doubt in his body language. The man clearly wasn't as stupid as he looked. Jay-Jay needed to make this look good. Or at least believable.

'Look, let's just say, I made sure she got the message,' Jay-Jay said with finality. He wiped the ketchup from his chin with the back of his hand, before shovelling a handful of chips into his mouth and trying to appear complacent. As if Russ's suspicious stare wasn't affecting him one bit.

'You know what, fuck it, while I'm here I may as well join you. It ain't as if you can catch salmonella from a pint, is it? Mind you, this place might be the exception,' Russ added, not waiting for an invite as he slid in to the tatty, worn pub booth before shouting over at the barman.

'Oi, mate. I'll have a pint if it ain't too much trouble. Wouldn't want you to miss whatever shite you're watching on the box!'

'I ain't staying. I've got places to be,' Jay-Jay lied, trying and failing to hide his irritation that Russ had decided to join him and was dithering over giving him his money.

The last thing Jay-Jay wanted to do right now was sit and have a drink with the man, because he'd encountered men like Russ and Sam many times in his life. They were always the ones out to prove a point. Acting the big-I-am. Trying to make trouble just for the thrill of it. And he could tell that Russ was in the mood for trouble today. He had that air about him.

'You'll have to let me know if you've got any more work lined up for me,' Jay-Jay said, testing the waters and trying to gauge Russ's reaction. 'Proper work this time though, yeah? I'm drawing the line at threatening women,' he added bitterly.

Annoyed now at how last night had played out. He hadn't signed up for that shit.

'Threatening women? Is that what you call it?' Russ laughed. 'You know, that bird you paid a visit to last night is Pete Baker's daughter. You heard of him?'

Jay-Jay shook his head. Not fussed whose daughter the woman was.

'The man's an old face. And I mean that literally too. Personally, I think he's well past it. But give him his due, he was a proper fella in his day. And he still has a lot of contacts and a lot of clout.' Russ shook his head, his brother's words still ringing in his ears after he himself had endured the lecture.

'According to Sam, he ain't someone that we want to start a war with.' Russ shrugged. 'And between us, I don't think he'd be too fussed about the beating we dished out to Ashley. We've heard he ain't much of a fan. Ashley's that kind of bloke. He's got more enemies than acquaintances. Besides, even if he did cop the hump, it's tough shit. Pete Baker knows only too well how this game works. We just want back what we're owed. This is business. It ain't personal. But last night, well, it got personal, didn't it?'

'What the fuck...?' Jay-Jay murmured, no longer listening to Russ. Instead, he was staring at the TV screen.

'A young pregnant woman, local to the Griffin Estate, was attacked in the early hours of the morning while making her way towards Wandsworth Common…'

'Oi! Earth to Jay-Jay!' Russ raised his voice, not used to being ignored.

Though as he turned to see what had caught the man's attention, Russ shook his head in resignation. Taking in the sight of the giant mugshot of Jay-Jay's face staring back at him from the TV. The camera cut to a news reporter standing in front of the two tower blocks of the Griffin Estate.

'The attacker is thought to be in his mid- to late-thirties. Roughly five foot eight, slim frame and was wearing a black tracksuit with a navy jacket over the top, the hood has a bright pink or neon orange lining. I would urge anyone who thinks that they might recognise the man in the E-fit to contact us as a matter of urgency. He is believed to be extremely dangerous. And we are advising members of the public not to approach him.'

Shifting awkwardly in his seat, Jay-Jay was aware that the clothes that had just been described were what he was still wearing now. That they were the only clothes he really had.

Russ glanced over at the barman and satisfied himself that he wasn't paying the bulletin any attention, his back to the screen as he busied himself pouring Russ's pint.

The two men focused their attention back on the news bulletin and listened in to what was being said, as the cameras changed to the footage of a female officer speaking at a press conference.

'Is it true that you've linked this attack to the murder of Liza Fitzgerald, also pregnant, who was killed over at Richmond Park last week? Do you think you're looking for a serial killer?' A journalist's voice cut in.

'As yet, that's not something that we can confirm. We are carrying out a full investigation and right now our priority is finding the person in the E-fit image.'

'Shit! SHIT!' Jay-Jay said, visibly paling at the news as he screwed his fists up, not knowing what to say or do.

'See, here's the thing,' Russ said with a loud whistle, turning and facing Jay-Jay, a twinkle of malice in his eyes. The lack of reaction to this sudden revelation told Jay-Jay all he needed to know. It might be the first time Jay-Jay had seen that he was a wanted man, but Russ and Sam already knew. Which meant they knew that he'd royally fucked the job up. He could forget about getting paid.

'I thought I could be a sick fuck when the mood took me, but this?' Russ laughed then and held his hands up, seeing the horrified look on Jay-Jay's face. 'Hey, mate. We all need to get our rocks off somehow. There's no judgement from me.'

'That isn't it. Fuck! You don't understand…' Jay-Jay said, unable to hide the panic in his voice now as he pulled his hood up around his face. He fell silent as the barman approached them and placed Russ's beer down on the table in front of him. God knows how many people had seen that E-fit by now. Shelby Cooke had got a better look at him than he'd realised. He was royally fucked now.

'She's okay though? The copper said.' Jay-Jay said when they were alone again. His skin had paled to almost translucent. He looked as if he was going to be sick too. 'The baby is okay?'

'No thanks to you,' Russ said with a nonchalant shrug of the shoulders. 'And see, here's where we come to the end of the line, Jay-Jay. Because fuck me, mate, I wouldn't want to be in your shoes when that old bastard Pete Baker catches up with you. This will be on you now, you know that, don't you? His daughter is the apple of his eye. If he gets wind that this was your doing, he'll bury you alive. So, I'm warning you to keep a low profile. Leave London, get as far away as you can from here. And if anyone, and I mean anyone, starts asking questions, you leave me and my brother out of it. Do you understand?'

Russ took a large gulp of beer, revelling in the fact that he was clearly putting the shits up the man opposite him.

'Because this has fuck all to do with me and my brother. We didn't tell you to go around carving pregnant women up. Even we ain't that sick and depraved. So, if I get wind of the police getting any ideas about us from you, I'll deliver you to Pete Baker personally.'

Russ glared at Jay-Jay.

'Like I said. For us it was strictly business. But you, Jay-Jay, son, have just made this personal. We can't be associated with any of this. Or with you. You're on your own, mate, and there's no going back from here.'

CHAPTER TWENTY-THREE

'You've got a visitor, Winnie, my love.' Nurse Hamilton smiled as she guided Winnie across the dayroom to see her awaiting guest. Walking patiently as Winnie took her time.

The woman's face lit up at the sight of her visitor.

'Jennifer, darling!' Winnie exclaimed, mistaking her grand-daughter for her late daughter and throwing her arms around her. 'I knew you'd come and see your old mum.'

'It's me, Nan. Lucy,' Lucy said firmly, trying her hardest not to react or take it personally that her nan didn't recognise her.

The past couple of days had been some of the longest, hardest days that Lucy had endured in a long time. Having to do the press conference to help find Shelby Cooke's attacker yesterday, as well as sitting with the Facial Imaging Officer to describe her own mother's attacker for an E-fit, and having a frank discussion with Zack Lownrey about her predicament had left her emotionally drained. And today, making numerous door-to-door enquires had taken it out of her physically too. To say she was completely exhausted now would be an understatement.

All she wanted to do was get home and get a good night's sleep, but she knew she couldn't hold off coming to see her nan any longer than she already had. It wasn't fair on the woman. Winnie was confused enough as it was, and now that Lucy was here, she could see with her own eyes how quickly her nan could deteriorate. She knew how debilitating her nan's illness could be, but it didn't get any easier.

'You look lovely, Nan.' Lucy smiled, eyeing her nan's usual eclectic style of bold and bright outfits. Today's ensemble consisted of a pair of soft cotton leopard print pyjamas, layered with a huge knitted red-and-white striped cardigan. A slick of bright orange lipstick, and her usually bouffant, curled hair flattened to her head with what looked like gel finished the look. 'Your hair looks different, Nan! Have you been styling it?'

From afar, her nan looked radiant, if eclectic. To a stranger, you probably wouldn't even realise that the woman was losing herself to dementia. But Lucy knew. She could see it in her nan's face, how her expressions were contorted. Mirroring how disorientated and confused she was. The lights of her eyes dimmed by a heaviness that lurked behind them.

'Oh, yes, I saw a picture in a magazine. Thought I'd try something new. What do you think? All the models wear their hair like this you know.'

'She used up half the pot of butter,' Nurse Hamilton interrupted. 'Almost started a war at breakfast when the other residents were trying to butter their toast. Then you refused to have a shower, didn't you, Winnie?' Nurse Hamilton shrugged. 'Pick your battles and all that. She's not having the best day, so we figured we'd leave her be, and just wash it out before bedtime. There's no real harm and it's better than causing more upset.'

'Oh dear!' Lucy muttered, sensing that her nan had been difficult today, and grateful that Nurse Hamilton and the other staff here at Treetops always seemed to be so patient with her.

'I'm sorry I haven't been in the past couple of days, Nan. We've had a lot going on at work. It's been so busy,' Lucy said, playing down that they were in the middle of a murder investigation. The fact that it was pregnant victims and the last attack had happened on the Griffin Estate had only given Lucy another reason to stay away the past few days.

It was all too raw. Dealing with all of that, and then coming here and seeing her nan like this again – catapulted back to a place and time where she believed the memories that were locked inside her head were real. That she was living in a time before all the hurt and devastation had so turbulently entered their lives, uninvited, unwelcome guests. Burdening them with their presence ever since.

'I brought you your favourite magazine, and some of those sweets we had last week. The lemon bon-bons. You ate the whole bag last time.' Lucy smiled, gently planting the seeds of her nan's real memories back inside her head as she helped Winnie into the chair opposite her.

'You look tired, Jennifer,' Winnie said, scrutinising the weary look on Lucy's face.

'I am, Nan. I haven't been sleeping much lately.' Lucy persevered, keeping the conversation as normal as possible, knowing that at any minute her nan could change and be back with her, here, in the present moment. But already, she could see that her nan had lost her focus and was looking around Lucy and scanning the room as if she was looking for someone.

'Are you okay, Nan? Who are you looking for?' Lucy asked, following Winnie's gaze, unsure why she was looking so flustered.

'Hmm. I can't see her. Where is she?' Winnie bristled, screwing her face up, angry now.

'Who are you looking for, Nan?' Lucy asked again, a wave of sadness engulfing her then as she braced herself for Winnie to say that she was looking for her daughter. For Lucy's mother. It was what she always did when she finally remembered who Lucy was. Still confused, she'd wait for Jennifer to turn up then too.

It pained Lucy that they'd never really get past this. No matter how many times they went over it. Which was often. Her nan would always forget that Lucy's mother was dead. And some days it took all of Lucy's strength to have to play along and pretend that this was all completely normal. To not let it show that her grandmother's dementia wasn't affecting her too. Only Winnie's next words surprised even Lucy.

'Who do you think? That bloody woman. My stalker!' she exclaimed, looking at Lucy with a deadpan expression, as if it was Lucy who was losing her mind. 'She turns up everywhere I go.'

'Your stalker?' Lucy almost laughed. But she could see from her nan's pained expression that she was genuinely on edge. She believed what she was saying. And she seemed distressed.

'Maybe it's just another resident here. The same as you, Nan…'

'No. She's not. She's a stalker. She follows me around like a bad bleeding smell. I can't get away from her.'

Lucy exchanged a look with Nurse Hamilton, who smiled back and nodded, confirming to Lucy this was exactly what she'd hinted at when she'd indicated that Winnie was having one of her more challenging days.

'It's just Lucy here now, Winnie.' Nurse Hamilton cut in, taking this new development entirely in her stride. 'Your nan's already had her dinner, Lucy. So, I'm sure she'd love to have some of those lemon bon-bons you mentioned. Shall I get you both some tea? I expect you could do with a nice strong cuppa?'

'Please.' Lucy nodded, not wanting to admit that once again she couldn't stay long this evening. She felt guilty enough as it was that she hadn't been around much the past few days. A quick cup of tea wouldn't hurt. Besides, she'd missed her nan and, by the looks of it, Winnie was really struggling.

'We like a nice cup of tea, don't we, Nan?'

Only her nan didn't answer; instead her eyes continued to sweep the room. 'I bet she's hiding because she knows you're here,' Winnie said finally. Shaking her head as if almost disappointed.

As if she'd built herself up to say something to the woman, only now she couldn't find her.

Winnie brought her gaze back to Lucy then. Fixated on her, she smiled. But Lucy could see she was still back in her own make-believe realm.

'How's the baby?'

For a second, Lucy faltered. The conversation seemed almost normal as she thought of Shelby and her newborn son, Riley. Only as her nan's eyes moved to Lucy's stomach, it was clear that she wasn't asking about Shelby's baby. Of course she wasn't; why would she?

'Stop, Nan,' Lucy said, raising her voice louder than she'd intended. 'I'm not her. I'm not Jennifer. I'm Lucy. You remember that, don't you? Mum is dead. She's not here. It's just me, Nan. Lucy.'

As soon as her angry words left her mouth, Lucy instantly regretted them when she saw the sharp jolt of pain flash across her nan's face at the sting of her outburst. That fleeting look of doubt as she questioned what she thought to be real. It was like watching the woman physically deflate before her very eyes. Sinking down into her chair, looking so small and frail.

'I'm sorry, Nan. I didn't mean that. I'm tired. I've been having bad dreams again.' Lucy thought about the file that was still in her bag from yesterday. The image of the man who haunted her dreams. She'd been so busy that she'd barely had a chance to look over it again.

She felt sad then, thinking about how once she would have gone to her nan for advice without a second thought; only now her nan could barely even function for herself. Let alone help Lucy.

'What did you have for dinner, Nan?' Lucy said, changing the subject and hoping to focus her nan's attention back onto something else.

The last thing she wanted to think about right now was her mum and the baby.

'Dinner? Have I already had it?' Winnie's voice wobbled. A flash of fear in her voice as she bit down on her lip. A habit of hers when she was feeling anxious.

Lucy felt terrible then for losing her temper. She hadn't meant to upset her nan more than she already was. This wasn't her fault. None of this was either of their faults.

'There you go, ladies. Tea and biscuits,' Nurse Hamilton said, appearing and placing a tray down between the two women, sensing the tension between them both.

'My nan can't remember what she had for dinner,' Lucy said, trying to keep her tone light.

'Oh, well now, let's see,' Nurse Hamilton said, recalling what Winnie had eaten tonight. 'You had chicken and mushroom pie with green beans and mash potato.'

'Yes. That's it,' Winnie said, victoriously almost, at the snippet of memory that flashed in her mind.

'Three cups? Are you joining us?' Lucy smiled, hoping that Nurse Hamilton would. That another person in the mix would help to ease her nan's fractious mood.

'Oh, as much as I'd love to, I've got too much to do this evening. That extra one's for Vivian. She was outside, just hanging her coat up… Oh there she is!'

Lucy turned towards the doorway just as Vivian entered the room and waved dramatically in their direction. 'Just in time for a brew, am I?' Vivian beamed as she approached them. Frowning then as she looked at Winnie's vacant chair.

Lucy followed her gaze, narrowing her eyes as she realised that her nan's chair sat empty where Winnie had quickly bolted from it, and was now crouching down on the floor behind it.

'Nan?' Lucy asked, wondering what she was doing now.

'Oh, is Winnie not about this evening? That's a shame. I was hoping to have a cup of tea with her. I've got a pack of her favourite biscuits with me.' Vivian winked at Lucy, oblivious to Winnie's mood, and thinking that she was playing along. That Winnie was having some kind of a joke with her. Only Lucy shook her head, warning Vivian that Winnie wasn't playing. Something was wrong.

'I told you she'd be lurking about… That's her…' Winnie whispered to Lucy. Scowling now. Visibly distressed at the sight of Vivian standing amongst them. 'Always talking. Always pestering me…'

'Nan. This is Vivian. She's a very good friend. She used to care for you too.' Lucy closed her eyes, mortified at her nan's sudden outburst and the rude reception that she'd just given Vivian, after Vivian had no doubt trekked halfway across London on public transport just so she could visit the woman. As she did most days.

'That's what she'll have you believe…' Winnie shook her head, unconvinced. Her steely gaze fixed on Vivian.

'She doesn't mean it.'

'Of course she doesn't,' Vivian said with a small smile, noting Winnie's adverse reaction to her, but not giving her one back. 'Lucy, the last person you need to explain anything to is me, trust me, darling. I've got skin thicker than a rhino, me.'

'Get her away,' Winnie said, her voice quiet and almost inaudible. Only her words weren't working. They weren't listening to her. 'GET HER AWAY. GET HER AWAY!' She shouted now, standing up from the chair and gripping it tightly with both hands before throwing it towards the small coffee table.

Vivian, Lucy and Nurse Hamilton all stepped back just in time as the tray of tea was knocked to the floor, along with Lucy's handbag, the contents spilling out across the floor.

'I'll wait outside,' Vivian mouthed to Lucy, not wanting to antagonise the woman any further. Nurse Hamilton rushed to

Winnie's side, wrapping her arms around her as she stood now, rigid with fear, her fists clenched at her sides. Only after the nurse had whispered soothing words in the older woman's ears did Lucy see her nan begin to physically relax.

'I'm going to take Winnie back to her room for a lie-down. I think today has been too much for her,' Nurse Hamilton said.

'What's that?' Winnie said, staring at the mess on the floor, as if she had no idea how it all got there.

'That's the tray of tea, Winnie. You knocked it over. Never mind, eh. Accidents happen. Don't worry, I'll clean it up,' the nurse said, hoping to reassure the woman. Only Winnie refused to budge.

'No,' Winnie said, irritated then as she stared down at the contents of Lucy's bag, which had tipped over and spilled out across the floor. 'That.'

Her eyes fixed on the paper. Following her nan's gaze, Lucy saw the E-fit. Her colleagues had let her keep a copy, and she'd hurriedly shoved it into her bag before going into the press conference yesterday. *Shit.* Now her nan was going to start asking questions about who the man was, and Lucy would have to tell her that she'd seen him. The man who murdered her mother. That she'd finally remembered his face. But before she had time to think of a cover story about who the man was, Winnie bent down and picked up the piece of paper.

'Well, now. That's a face that I haven't seen in a while,' Winnie said, eyeing the image with horror. Her face twisted then as if she was in some kind of pain.

'You know him, Nan?' Lucy said, shocked that her nan would recognise the man in the image.

Her heart started thumping wildly inside her chest and her blood whooshed loudly inside her ears. As her nan looked up at her and nodded, she felt almost for a second as if the world had stopped. As if time had frozen, and all they had was this. This one moment.

'Why are you asking me such a stupid question, Jennifer?' Winnie said, exasperated. 'Of course, I know him. You do too. It's Lucy's father.'

CHAPTER TWENTY-FOUR

Having managed to avoid the small cluster of journalists who stood around in the car park below, Ashley couldn't help feeling a bit smug as he made his way up the back stairwell that led to his flat. The investigating officers who had taken Shelby's statement yesterday afternoon, had warned the family that the press would no doubt hound them for their story over the next few days.

As it was, news of the attack was already splashed all over every newspaper and news channel available. The press was hovering around like hungry vultures now, waiting to pounce on their prey and pick apart the local tenants for any information they could get on Shelby and the attack.

Ashley didn't have time for any of that. All he wanted to do was get his head down for the night before going back up to the hospital first thing in the morning.

Only as he reached his floor and stepped out on to the balcony that led to his flat, Ashley faltered, thinking that one of the journalists had worked out which flat they lived in, when he caught sight of the woman loitering right outside his front door.

Ready to give the journalist a piece of his mind and tell her to get lost, Ashley relaxed as he recognised the short, dumpy woman to be one of the tenants from a few doors down.

Imelda? Or something like that. He couldn't remember exactly, but he knew that Shelby had spoken to the woman on a few occasions. Though, he certainly wouldn't have classed the two women as friends. An oddball, but completely harmless. That was how Shelby had described her when talking to Ashley about the brief, awkward encounters. They'd both joked that the woman had the hots for him, because apparently she always asked after him, despite the fact that Ashley barely gave the woman the time of day if he saw her. Still, he couldn't blame her for having good taste. And he guessed that she was probably lonely too. An expectant single mother, due to give birth any day now going by the sheer size of her.

The woman had latched on to Shelby because they both happened to be pregnant at the same time, but Ashley knew that was really the only thing that Shelby would have had in common with the woman. There's no way that Shelby would have even entertained a friendship with the woman otherwise. They were polar opposites.

Though just because she thought she was a friend of Shelby's, didn't mean that she was going to get special treatment and that Ashley was just going to feed her with gossip and give her the lowdown on his wife's ordeal, just so that she could tell every other nosey bastard on the estate all the gory details. If that's what she was here for, she could think again.

Nodding in her direction was the most attention he was willing to give her as he got his key out and turned his back to her.

'Was it Shelby?' Imelda said, not taking the hint as Ashley stepped around her and made a beeline for his front door.

'They didn't name her on the news, they just said a local woman. But I knocked and there's no one home… Well, I mean you're here now…' Imelda said, giggling nervously, so acutely aware of her cheeks glowing pink that she could barely bring herself to look Ashley in the eye. 'Only I haven't seen her. So, I just thought that… maybe it might be her… It was, wasn't it? I have had a bad feeling in my stomach since I heard. I can sense these things…'

About to step into his flat and close the door behind him, Ashley hesitated, hearing the genuine concern behind Imelda's question. The way that the woman hopped awkwardly from one foot to the other as she spoke, as if full of anxiety. Her hand protectively cupping her own bump as she spoke.

Shelby might not class Imelda as a good friend, but it was clear that Imelda did her.

'It was her, wasn't it? Someone attacked her. Oh my god, how awful. Part of me didn't want to believe it,' Imelda said now, practically pleading with the man to be straight with her.

'It's Imelda, isn't it?' Ashley asked, waiting for the woman to nod before he continued. 'Can you keep this to yourself?' he said, looking along the balcony before breaking the news to his neighbour. 'Yeah. It was Shelby. The press are down in the car park grilling everyone for information, and well, I'd like to get her back home without the awaiting circus if I can. So please, I need your word that this won't go any further, yeah?' Ashley said, feeling guilty then at judging the woman so harshly.

The Griffin Estate was rife with crime. The place was known for the endless stabbings, muggings and vicious domestic attacks. But the attack on Shelby had sent shockwaves through the entire estate. And Imelda being pregnant and a friend of Shelby's would no doubt only heighten the woman's own safety concerns. The very least Ashley could do was try and put the woman's mind at ease.

'The police have got a good description of the attacker though. They think they'll get an arrest quite quickly,' he said, repeating what DC Murphy had said to them when she'd come to take Shelby's statement.

'So, Shelby saw the attacker? Is she okay? And the police seem confident that they'll catch them?'

Noting the strain in Imelda's voice, Ashley softened some more, recalling how Shelby had told him that she and Imelda were close in due dates. Imelda was probably thinking that the attack could have easily been on her. It was no wonder the woman seemed so visibly shaken.

'They seem very confident,' Ashley said.

As police officers went, Ashley quite liked Lucy Murphy. Because despite the way that the rest of Shelby's family treated him as if he was a spare part in all of this, despite how Pete and Janey had almost taken over, Lucy had been sensitive to the fact that he was Shelby's husband and the father of their baby. And she'd made a point to include him in every part of the process when discussing his wife's ordeal and how they were going to carry out the investigation. In fact, she'd been the only person so far to actually ask him how he was, and genuinely seemed to want to know the answer.

'Yeah. She's doing great, considering. I mean, the shock of it all set off her labour. I expect you heard on the news, she's had the baby. We've called him Riley. You should see him, a real little smasher he is. He's a little on the small side, so they're keeping them in, just to keep an eye on his feeding. But other than that, he's doing amazing.' Ashley beamed proudly, glad to give the woman the positive news and hoping it helped her to not dwell on the bad so much.

'Riley? That's perfect,' Imelda said, so overcome with emotion then that she started to cry.

'Here, it's okay!' Ashley said, wrapping his arms around the woman awkwardly as she sobbed briefly, before pulling away from him, embarrassed.

'I'm sorry. It's my hormones,' Imelda said, blushing now at Ashley's show of affection towards her. 'Thank God he's all right. That they're both all right.'

'Oh, you know Shelby. She's not one to mope about. Told me when I go back up to the hospital first thing in the morning that I need to bring some of her things. She gave me a list longer than her legs.' Ashley rolled his eyes then playfully. 'Said the hospital dressing gown looks like a rag on her; she wants her own one. And of course, all her make-up too. Won't let me put any photos of her and the little one on Facebook until she's sorted her face out. Apparently, the whole world's going to be wanting to have a look at them, according to Shelby. And going by that lot downstairs, she could be right. Though, I think Shelby thinks she's going to end up on the front of *OK* magazine or something, going by the amount of outfit changes she wants me to pack.'

Realising that he was rambling, Ashley nodded down at Imelda's swollen stomach, before adding: 'Guess you won't be long now either? I'm sure Shelby told me that you were due around the same time. A little playmate for Riley, eh?!'

'Any day now,' Imelda said, her hand cupping her stomach.

'It doesn't seem real,' Ashley said with a laugh. Only going by the confused look on Imelda's face, he'd clearly said the wrong thing. 'I mean, of course you know… it's real. You're the ones going through it all,' Ashley explained, seeing Imelda's expression change to one of wariness now. 'You women just make it look so easy, I suppose. It's probably just me, being a man and all that. Experiencing pregnancy from the outside looking in. But the entire time Shelby was carrying Riley, it just didn't feel real to me. I mean, sure, I'd feel the odd little movement or kick, but sometimes I'd sit and think, Christ, there's a real live human in there. But now he's here and I can actually see him, I just can't get my head around the fact that he lived inside her. That there's a real live baby in there too.'

Reaching out without thinking, Ashley touched Imelda's bump, then instantly regretted his movement as the woman jumped back. As was expected. Clearly shaken from the news of the attack and the fact she barely knew Ashley. Yet here he was, reaching out to touch her baby.

'Shit, sorry,' he said. 'I didn't mean to startle you. I wasn't think-ing.' He rubbed his forehead then, exasperated. Women! Maybe it wasn't just Shelby that overreacted at the slightest little comments and gestures while she'd been pregnant. Maybe all women were the same. Sometimes Ashley couldn't do right, for doing wrong. 'I haven't slept, and I'm knackered.' Ashley hoped that his feeble excuse would be enough to excuse his thoughtless actions.

Only Imelda still looked alarmed. Her body language suddenly off, as if she couldn't wait to get away. Ashley could see that Shelby's attack had affected her badly. He made a mental note to mention it to Shelby when he went back to the hospital. Maybe Shelby could call Imelda and put her mind to rest that she really was okay.

'Kate?' Ashley said then, his cheeks suddenly burning red as he looked past Imelda and stared at the beautiful woman who sashayed through the stairwell door and down the balcony towards them. 'You didn't have to come here. I could have come to yours.'

His first thought was that Kate would have had to walk past all the press. That it was a huge risk her coming here, because even though it was near on impossible, part of him couldn't help but worry that someone might recognise Kate. That they might link her to him and work out that Ashley had been up to no good.

Shelby might find out about them.

Meanwhile, Imelda felt her hackles rise as she picked up on the sudden high pitch to Ashley's tone. Panic? A look of guilt flashed across his face. Imelda looked Kate up and down as if she was something she'd just stepped in. All dolled-up with a face full of heavy make-up and a dress that left very little to the imagination.

She could see why Ashley seemed completely distracted now. Kate was attractive, Imelda couldn't dispute that. And men were fickle. Even Ashley.

'You want something?' Kate said tartly, as Imelda stood there gormlessly, her stare fixed on her for a few seconds too long.

Though Kate didn't appear fazed – she'd spent a lifetime batting off the jealous disapproval glances towards her from other women. If anything, Imelda's reaction just irritated her more than anything.

'I was just going,' Imelda said, feeling her own cheeks flush then at the woman's curt comment and taking the hint that she was no longer wanted here as Ashley ignored her, preoccupied now as he immediately ushered Kate inside his flat.

Imelda started to walk away, then turned back as a flash of rage shot through her. 'But please tell Shelby when you see her that I'm glad she's okay. And that the baby's okay, Ashley.'

She couldn't help herself but throw in a comment about Shelby and the baby. To remind Ashley of who he should be focusing his attention on right now. Not some other stuck-up tart.

Her mind instantly went into overdrive about who this Kate was, and what she was doing alone in the flat with Ashley, while Shelby was in hospital.

'Will do!' Ashley called out, sensing the sudden shift in Imelda's mood and the blatant disapproval towards Kate's untimely visit.

Part of him wondered if Imelda would keep her mouth shut about seeing Kate here today. If he should maybe ask her not to mention it when she saw Shelby. Or would that only make his guilt more obvious and only add fuel to an already smouldering fire? Maybe he'd just keep his own mouth shut and hope for the best? But Imelda was already gone.

He watched as Imelda turned her back on him once more and waddled towards her own flat, before rolling his eyes then. *Women!* Ashley thought as he closed the door to his flat. Still, right now, he had more pressing matters to tend to. Like Kate. And how he was going to get the Boland brothers their money back.

*

'Well, she seemed really lovely!' Kate said, her tone loaded with sarcasm now that they were alone inside Ashley's flat. 'A friend of yours, is she?'

'She's a mate of Shelby's. She's just worried about her, that's all,' Ashley said.

'And how is Shelby doing?' Kate asked, perching on the edge of Ashley's sofa and hoping that Ashley would at least offer her a drink. She was still in shock at what she'd heard had happened to Ashley's wife. She didn't necessarily care for the girl, but she wasn't completely heartless either.

And Ashley, standing awkwardly, lingering by the lounge doorway, looked as if he could use some support.

He didn't seem like himself. He seemed on edge, distracted. Still, she guessed that was as much to be expected after what he'd been through.

'She's doing okay. She's tough,' Ashley said, feeling uneasy at the fact that they were both sitting in his and Shelby's flat. Talking about his wife who had just given birth to his child. After what they'd both done a couple of nights ago.

Remorse wasn't a feeling that Ashley had ever been consumed with before, until now.

'So, you're officially a daddy now. What did you call him?' Kate asked, aware how stilted the conversation seemed between them, how off with her Ashley suddenly seemed.

'Riley.' Ashley felt disloyal even discussing his newborn son with her.

Kate took the hint and changed the subject.

'This place is nice,' she said, her eyes lingering on a photo frame with Ashley and his wife staring out from it, back at her. Smiling.

Shelby was pretty, though she had a hardness about her that made it look as if she was trying too hard. They looked happy though. She hadn't expected that. Their home looked nice too. Cosy. Taking in the soft matching cushions and the scented candles she guessed that these weren't Ashley's attempts at adding some feminine touches. 'It's very homely.'

'Did you get it?' Ashley said, cutting to the chase and deciding that he just wanted Kate gone. It didn't feel right having her here, in his and Shelby's home while Shelby was at the hospital. He just wanted what he'd asked her for.

'I did, indeed!' Kate nodded. Rummaging around in her handbag, before pulling out the CD in a clear Perspex case, that contained the club's security footage from last night before waving it triumphantly in Ashley's face.

Glad to see him visibly relax then that she'd come through for him and managed to steal the copy from the club. Though unfortunately for Ashley the relief was going to be short lived.

'The police have already seen it!' she said bluntly, figuring there was no easier way of breaking it to him. 'They dropped by yesterday afternoon apparently. Just before you called me.'

'Shit!' Ashley said, running his hands through his hair then as he paced the room. He should have known that the two detectives at the hospital would have wasted no time in checking out his alibi from the other night. They probably went straight there.

Which meant that they knew he was lying about being attacked by a gang of kids.

'They weren't the only ones either, Ashley,' Kate said carefully, as she broke the really bad news to Ashley. 'Mia, she works doing promotions and events, said that she'd had someone come by just after they'd left. This guy. And he offered her money to see the footage. A lot of money. And, well, she's a single mum. She didn't see any harm in it, seeing as the police had already been and gone.'

'Who?' Ashley said, holding his breath. Already anticipating Kate's answer.

'He told Mia his name was Carl Rangers,' Kate raised her eyes knowingly, 'and I checked him out on the security footage when he entered the club. He's the guy that turned up at my flat at the crack of dawn yesterday morning, with your father-in-law.'

The two men that had frogmarched Ashley from her flat, straight up to the hospital.

'No, no, no!' Ashley said. Shaking his head now, as if the words he'd just heard would physically fall from his ears.

This couldn't be happening. Because if Carl Rangers was snooping about, it would only be on Pete Baker's orders. Which meant that they were on to him too, as well as the police. And Pete was already suspicious about Ashley's involvement with Shelby's attack the other night. Ashley could tell by the way the man kept glaring at him. And the fact that he'd caught him red handed with Kate hadn't helped matters in the slightest.

Ashley was on thin ice as it was, it wouldn't take much digging around for Pete to find out the two men dishing out the kicking to Ashley were the Boland brothers. And then he'd find out about the twenty thousand pounds that Ashley had stupidly borrowed and lost. He'd know that Shelby had been attacked because of him and his greed and stupidity. Pete would kill him.

He glanced at the clock. He only had a few more hours to work out how to get the money back to the Bolands. There was no way that he could ask Pete for help, not now. Things couldn't get much worse.

'Ashley, what's going on?' Kate asked, worried now. Because Ashley had lied to her too. He'd told her that he'd been attacked by kids, which after seeing the footage herself, she knew now was a lie.

'Nothing. Trust me, you're better off not getting involved. The less you know, the better.'

Ashley seemed stressed out and on edge, and she knew a good remedy for that. 'Well, I'm a big girl, Ashley. Maybe I can help?'

Walking over to him she pressed herself up against his body – but the last thing she expected was for Ashley to physically shrug her off.

'No. You should go,' Ashley said, just wanting Kate to leave now. 'I've got a kid now, Kate. I have to think about Shelby and Riley now. I've been a complete shit, I need to stop all this. I need to start putting them first.'

He wanted to be alone with his thoughts. He needed to work a way out of this mess.

'But Riley doesn't have to change anything, Ashley? We can still work this out. We can still be "us".'

'Us?' Ashley said, narrowing his eyes, not sure what Kate was talking about.

Though he could see by the look in her eyes that she thought their relationship meant something to him.

'Yes, us, Ashley. We can still be together. And if you and Shelby call it quits, I could help you with Riley. I've always fancied being a mum, I'm good with kids. A natural.'

Ashley shook his head, astounded that he always managed to get it so wrong in these kinds of situations with women. He never seemed to realise how clingy and needy they were until it was too late. Why did women always do that? As soon as they started sleeping with him, it was as if suddenly they had the right to start making claims on him. He'd thought Kate was different. He thought she wanted the same as him. No strings. Just a bit of fun.

'Kate, we fancied each other. We shagged. That was it,' Ashley said, aware he was taking his temper out on the woman, only he no longer cared. Kate wasn't taking the hint and he just wanted her gone. Out of his flat, and out of his life. This had all been one big mistake. He should never have gone back with her that night.

'There is no you and me. There is no us. Now, I think you should leave.'

Glaring at Ashley then as if seeing him for the first time, Kate was only too happy to oblige.

'You know what, Ashley, get fucked. You can't just go around treating women like this. You can't just use us to get what you want and then treat us like we're nothing,' Kate said, storming past the man. 'Because you've done it to the wrong woman this time – I'll teach you a lesson that you won't forget anytime soon.'

CHAPTER TWENTY-FIVE

'That's my father?' Lucy said, convinced that her nan was fabricating another story. That she must have got it wrong.

That it couldn't be her father in the E-fit, could it? Winnie seemed so convinced. But that was what dementia did, wasn't it? It brought on confabulations. Fabricated distorted versions of memories. Her nan wasn't being malicious. She believed what she was saying. And Lucy was used to not taking these misinterpreted memories to heart. But there was something about the way her nan seemed so certain, so sure that she knew the man in the photo, that made Lucy believe that perhaps she actually did.

'You must be mistaken, Nan. He can't be…'

'Why are you asking me such stupid questions, Jennifer?' Winnie said, her face blazing with anger now as the paper was snatched from her grasp. 'You know who he is. What's wrong with you? Why is she asking me these things?' Winnie said, turning her attention to Nurse Hamilton now.

'Nan, this is important. Who is he?'

'I've already told you,' Winnie said, visibly distressed as she picked up on Lucy's sudden frustration as she continued to quiz her. Mistaking Lucy's urgent need for answers for anger.

'What have I done wrong? Why is Jennifer shouting at me?' Winnie asked the nurse. Because something had upset Jennifer and Winnie couldn't understand what it was.

Had she done or said something? She couldn't remember. Her head was hurting. She was tired.

'Is she sick? Is there something wrong with her? Is that why she's shouting?' Throwing a look to Nurse Hamilton, Winnie wondered if the nurse standing next to them was here for Jennifer. 'I think you should sit down, Jennifer. I don't know why you are so angry. I told you he was trouble. I told you to stay away from him. But you wouldn't listen.'

Lucy bit her lip, knowing that battling against her nan wouldn't get her anywhere. She was just prolonging the agony of not knowing how to make sense of this revelation. She changed tactics, hoping that playing along with her nan's make-believe world would be more effective.

'Sorry. Of course, I know who he is,' Lucy said, throwing a coded look to Nurse Hamilton that she was now playing along and pretending to be her own mother. It wasn't ideal, but she had to do this. She had to know the truth. Sitting back down on the chair, Lucy slipped into her role, hoping to defuse the heated tension between them. It worked. Winnie faltered then. Her guarded body language visibly relaxing as she mirrored Lucy. Sitting down opposite her granddaughter.

Lucy finally spoke.

'We didn't tell Lucy about him?' Lucy said, hoping that this tactic would work. That her nan would tell her what was going on. Because something wasn't right. She had the feeling that her nan had been keeping something from her.

'Of course not. We agreed. We said she must never know the truth. It was for her own protection, remember? We made a pact,' Winnie said sadly as she looked down at the floor, sombre then. 'Oh, Jennifer, why didn't you listen to me? Why didn't you stay away from him? I should have made you listen to me. I should have made you stop,' Winnie said eventually. Her voice wracked with what sounded like guilt.

'I'm sorry, I should have listened. You were right…' Lucy said, not daring to disagree, in case she broke the spell.

'You knew how dangerous it was, Jennifer. You knew that but you chose to ignore it. You knew that every time you did your "job", if you can call it a job!'

Lucy held her breath. The realisation of what her nan was implying shaking her to her core.

'My job?'

'Yeah, well. That's being polite. I wouldn't call sleeping with men for money a vocation. But you insisted that you had no other choice. Insisted that it was the only way you'd ever get off that goddamn estate and make a proper life for yourself…'

'No.' Lucy gasped, wincing as her nan confirmed the worst. She shook her head. Refusing to believe what her nan was saying.

That her mother had been a sex worker? That wasn't possible. And even worse than that, she had known her killer all along? And her nan knew too. Lucy knew her mother, inside and out. She'd idolised her. Knew everything she could know about her. She and her nan had talked about her constantly, always making a point to keep her memory alive.

The woman who danced and giggled around the flat with her on rainy afternoons. The woman who snuggled up with her on the sofa, watching movies and reading fairy tales together while eating ice cream.

Lucy didn't have many memories from that early age, but the few she did have of her mother she cherished. And now her nan was tainting her mother's good name. Confused and fabricating fragments of someone else's stories that flitted into her head and churning them out as her own. Because her mother wasn't like that. She didn't do that.

Still Lucy continued, hoping that her nan might be able to explain the E-fit image at least. Because she seemed so certain that she knew him, and Lucy just needed a name. She could check the information out herself after that.

'And what about him?' Lucy said, nodding down to the bit of paper on the table. 'Who is he? What's his name?' she asked, almost not wanting to hear the answer now. Unsure how much more she could take.

'You know who he is. He's trouble, that's what. Kevin, though he always went by the name of Bodge. Stupid bloody name that was, mind.' Winnie almost spat the man's name from her mouth. She held Lucy's gaze. 'You should have stayed well away from him. But you wouldn't listen, would you? And look what happened. Look how you ended up. And I had to live with it,' Winnie said, clenching her fists tightly in her lap, angry now. 'I knew that it was him that did it. I always knew it was him. Of course, I did. But what could I do? I couldn't tell a single soul, because if I did, if I ever even thought about going to the police, he would have killed Lucy too. Or worse still, he would have taken her eventually too. Staked his claim on her as her biological father. I wouldn't have been able to fight that. To fight him. Then look where she would have ended up. In that life. Doing those things. He would have forced her to, because that's all he cared about. He didn't care about you and he certainly had no interest in Lucy. But you wouldn't listen to me, Jennifer. You always thought you knew better.'

Her watery eyes were boring into her with a stubborn anger that Lucy had never felt directed at her before. Only it wasn't aimed at her this time either. Not really.

'He used you. For the money. That's all you ever were to him. A form of income. Oh, you may have foolishly loved him, but he didn't care about you. Not one bit. And Lucy coming along was a hinderance to him. It meant you couldn't work as much. That she was your focus instead of earning money for him.' Winnie shook her head sadly. 'And when he found out about the baby… Oh, well, he couldn't force you to get rid of it, could he? Though Christ knows he tried. And I guess he didn't have to in the end. Because he did the job himself, didn't he? Killing you both.'

'He was her pimp? This Kevin or Bodge or whatever he called himself?' The words coming from Lucy's mouth in a mere whisper as she tried to make sense of what her nan was saying.

Could it really be true?

She'd spent her life not knowing who her real father was, and her nan was always vague and edgy if Lucy ever broached the subject. Was this why? Because all this time she was keeping the truth away from Lucy. Shielding her from it.

She felt sick then. Only when Winnie didn't answer her question, Lucy grew frustrated. She wanted answers. She demanded answers.

'Nan? Was he her pimp?'

Why was she only just learning all of this now? That her mother had secrets. That her nan had always known the truth, or at least had her suspicions.

'Nan! I need you to tell me what you remember, please? I need to know the truth.'

'Lucy?' Winnie said, shaking her head slowly, as if realising for the first time today that this woman sitting in front of her was her granddaughter, and not Jennifer at all. As though all of her jumbled memories of the past merged in union with the present day. She stared around the room now, as if she'd just been transported there without her knowledge. As if she had no idea how she'd got there.

'Oh, Lucy. What's happening to me?'

Her hands shook, her voice trembled. The pain of her daughter's death hit her with its full force once again, as she realised that Jennifer wasn't really here and mixed with the fear of being so out of control. Of not being able to know or trust her own mind.

'Poor, poor Jennifer. She didn't deserve what happened to her.' Winnie started to cry.

'It's okay, Nan,' Lucy said, crying then too, reaching over and placing her hand on top of her nan's to offer the woman some comfort. Knowing that she had pushed her too far.

'I think that's enough for today,' Nurse Hamilton said softly, seeing her patient so visibly distressed. Knowing how, like all of the residents here at Treetops, Winnie's emotions could cycle the highest of highs and the lowest of lows so quickly that it would leave her physically exhausted. 'I'm going to take Winnie back to her room, so she can get some rest.'

Lucy nodded.

'Come on, Winnie. Let's get you showered and tucked up in bed. I'll bring you a fresh cup of tea. Would you like that?'

'Oh, yes.' Winnie smiled, stepping around the teapot that was still lying on the carpet from where she'd thrown her chair at the table. 'Did some eejit drop the last one?'

'Something like that, Winnie.' Nurse Hamilton laughed as she led the woman from the room. 'Something like that!'

CHAPTER TWENTY-SIX

Pacing up and down the cold, wet floors of the derelict house that he was currently staying in, Jay-Jay's head was pounding. He should have been out spending the money from the job the Boland brothers had sent him to do; instead, he was having to cower away here. In this run-down cesspit that, for now, was home.

The only good thing about the place was that there was no electric, and the handful of down-and-outs that he shared the place with weren't the type of people with access to the TV or internet anyway. So, there'd be no way of them finding out that he was a wanted man.

They were all like him. The forgotten dregs of society that, somehow, along the way had managed to slip through the cracks and end up here. Jay-Jay hadn't even bothered to enquire what their names were. Because he had no interest in getting to know any of them. A couple of heavy drug users, and an alcoholic. Wasters. The type of people who would sell Jay-Jay out for a packet of fags and a cheap bottle of cider, if they realised that he was worth anything right now. Which of course, he was. There was a manhunt on, and Jay-Jay was top of the wanted list. Fuck!

He sank down on to the piss-stained mattress that he'd been using as a bed. The pain behind his eyes from the stress of his predicament was building intently. He didn't know what to do. How to get out of this mess. Because if the police caught up with him, they'd send him back to prison, and Jay-Jay wasn't sure he could take another stint inside.

He wasn't cut out for being held captive in a tiny cell, caged like an animal. There was something so degrading and demoralising about being locked up, away from the rest of society. And if they sent him down for murder, what would he get? Fifteen, twenty years? Life? Maybe he'd never get back out. The thought of that terrified him.

Placing the palms of his hands over his eye sockets, Jay-Jay hung his head to put pressure on them. Moving his hands in circular motions to try and iron out the pain. Only nothing was working. He couldn't seem to shake it. He thought about the E-fit that he'd seen flash across the huge television set back at the pub.

How the fuck had Shelby Cooke managed to get such a good look at his face the other night?

He remembered it all, only he couldn't pinpoint that precise moment when she'd properly seen him. Because he'd been careful, hadn't he? He'd leant over the balcony and spotted her walking across the communal garden of the Griffin Estate, dragging a small suitcase behind her. And he'd taken his cue. Running down the stairwell in a bid to catch up with her. Determined to do the job he'd been sent to do, so that he could finally get his hands on some decent money. Only she'd been on to him, aware that he was lurking behind her; she'd turned at one point, and he thought she'd seen him. But he'd comforted himself with the fact that it had been so dark, and Jay-Jay had pulled his hood up over his head in a bid to conceal his face before pressing himself up against a wall, out of sight. Hiding amongst the shadows. Or so he'd thought.

But Shelby Cooke had described him to a T. The girl must have X-ray vision. It wouldn't take a genius to ID him now. Anyone who saw the E-fit image and knew him would know that had been his ugly mug blaring out from the TV. So, he knew that it was only a matter of time until someone recognised him.

Cracking open one of the cans of Stella that he'd nicked from an off-licence, Jay-Jay gulped one back greedily. He needed something to take the edge off his fractious mood. Something to numb the anxiety that raged inside of him as he recalled the look of amusement in Russ Boland's eyes when he'd told him that he was on his own now. That this had nothing to do with them. How they refused to be associated with someone with so much heat on them. Someone wanted by the police for murdering a pregnant woman and attacking another. And what could Jay-Jay say in his defence? Nothing.

He was a convicted criminal with a long record of violence. There was no talking his way out of this. No one would believe a word that came out of his mouth, no matter what excuse he gave them. And now he was here, back at this shithole dive he was staying at, and right back at square one. Sleeping rough for God knows how much longer and scouring the local bins for food, in order to survive. Maybe he'd be better off if he went back to prison.

Taking another big glug from the can, Jay-Jay leaned back against the wall and stared around the place in disgust. The dirt and grime seemed suddenly magnified as he realised that this was all he was destined for now. Because this wasn't freedom. Holed up here and hoping the police didn't catch up with him.

Finishing the first can, Jay-Jay opened another, welcoming the feeling of numbness that was starting to set in as he drank that one quickly down too. His head was still throbbing, but suddenly he felt lighter as an idea came to his mind.

He replayed the conversation he'd had with Russ Boland. The chat about Shelby Cooke's dad, Pete Baker. What had he said? That the man would be on the warpath now too, because his daughter and no doubt his grandson were his most treasured possessions.

That the man had once been a face. That he was still a big player in the London underworld. Or at least, still well-respected.

Jay-Jay wondered how much of that was true. Because if it was, then that meant that Pete Baker wouldn't be short of a few quid. And like Russ said, Shelby and her baby were the old man's most prized possessions. Maybe there was another way out of this, another option for him. Maybe he didn't have to resign to this shit way of life after all?

He'd lost his opportunity of working for the Boland brothers, but there were other ways he could earn some serious money. He smiled then, wiping his mouth with the back of his hand as he set his plan in motion in his head. Rich men thought that money could buy them everything. And rich, desperate men always paid out.

CHAPTER TWENTY-SEVEN

Stepping out of the lift as the doors opened on the postnatal ward, Imelda eyed the empty corridor, surprised at how quiet the place was.

She'd expected a scene from one of the birthing shows she'd been watching religiously on television in preparation for having her baby: wailing women and beeping monitors and nurses rushing about in a panic.

Placing one hand protectively over her bump, she made her way through the main doors that led to the unattended nurses' station. Wondering, were all the shows staged then? Edited to show giving birth to be more dramatic than it was, to hold the viewers' attention?

Part of her couldn't believe that she was actually here. In this place. Because she'd thought about it often. Especially as her due date loomed. After spending months trying to imagine how it would feel. To be in the full blows of labour. Wondering if she'd be here on a ward like this, or if they would put her in a private room. She'd want a room, if given the choice. She wouldn't want to share such a private, precious moment as giving birth with a room full of nosey strangers.

And she wouldn't want any pain relief either, unlike some of the mothers she'd watched on the birthing programs, who played on every tiny bit of pain, so melodramatic and exaggerated, demanding every bit of pain relief that was going.

That made Imelda's blood boil. Because giving birth was a privilege. It was an exceptional experience and she wanted to feel it all. Every wave of agony, every rip of pain. Magnified. She was feeling clammy now. Angsty. Annoyed that so many women didn't make the most of the gift that had been bestowed upon them.

Staring up at the board behind the nurses' desk, she eyed the names and times of admissions, scanning the names of the babies born recently, the dates and times of birth scrawled underneath the names of the mothers, as she searched for Shelby's name.

'Can I help you?' a voice called from behind her, breaking Imelda's train of thought and making her jump with fright. As if she'd been caught out doing something wrong.

'Sorry. I was miles away,' Imelda said, making excuses as she desperately tried to compose herself.

'Are you all right?' the midwife said, looking Imelda up and down, noting her huge, swollen bump and guessing that Imelda might be in the wrong place.

'I was going to call, but I live nearby. So, I thought I'd just come in,' Imelda started. Wondering if she should just come clean and admit that she was a friend of Shelby's.

If she could confess that she hadn't been able to sleep. She'd been so worried thinking about what had happened to Shelby and Riley. Part of her had just wanted to see for herself that they were all right.

She was dying to see little Riley. Imaging his jet-black hair and dark brown eyes like his father. Or perhaps he'd be blonde like Shelby.

And she couldn't stop thinking about Ashley leading that woman into his flat. How he'd been acting so shifty, as if he was up to no good.

Because Shelby deserved to know, didn't she? After everything she'd been through. That Ashley wasn't the man she thought he was. He wasn't the man that Imelda had thought he was. Shelby deserved to know what he was doing behind her back.

But now she was here, Imelda wasn't sure that it was the right thing to do at all.

Shelby might find it weird that she'd come here, seeing as they'd only spoken a few times. And she might not even believe her.

She might think that Imelda was making it all up. And chances were the fact that she wasn't family would mean that the nurse would say it wasn't possible to see her anyway.

Imelda panicked.

'I've been having twinges. I thought maybe I was in labour, but they've stopped now. Sorry to waste your time.'

'Oh, well now. This is the postnatal ward, for women who have already had their babies. And it's still very early, so most of them are still fast sleep,' the midwife said, making a point to keep her voice low. 'If you were in labour, you should be down on the maternity ward.' She was used to new mothers being paranoid and neurotic and thinking that every twinge and ache in the later stages of their pregnancy meant that they were about to give birth.

Only this woman seemed so poised and composed, almost robotic-like when she spoke. As if she was making a point not to show how anxious she was. The fact that she'd come to the hospital this early in the morning, on her own, showed that she must be very worried, even if she was playing her concern down now that she was here.

'How long ago was the last "twinge"?'

'Oh, I'm not sure. Maybe about fifteen minutes ago? Maybe longer,' Imelda said, backtracking now and deciding to leave as she stared at the doors behind the nurse. She shouldn't have come here. She realised that now. 'It's probably nothing, knowing me, it's probably just wind.'

'How far along are you?' The midwife eyed Imelda's stomach.

'Thirty-seven weeks. I mean, thirty-eight; I've still got two weeks to go…' Imelda said. The midwife's intense stare was making her fumble her words. It felt as if the nurse could see straight through her and her lies and knew why Imelda was really here. Pretending that she was going into labour, this midwife wasn't stupid. She'd been naive to think that she could just stroll in here, and that somehow, she'd be able just to walk in and say hello to Shelby. Or if they were sleeping, she could just stand and look.

'Honestly, it's probably nothing. In fact, I feel silly now for bothering you… I'm sure you have better things to do with your time. I'll go.'

'Look, seeing as you're here anyway, why don't we just get you checked over first? I can do that here for you. It's no bother,' the midwife insisted, convinced that something about the woman didn't seem right. Her eyes were darting up and down the corridor anxiously. Her body language was all wrong. And as much as she seemed adamant she would be wasting the midwife's time, a quick check-up might just put the woman at ease.

'Honestly, I'm sure you've got more important things to be doing,' Imelda said, though she stopped protesting as the midwife gently took her arm and guided her over towards the private room opposite them.

'It's no trouble. I'm Katie Farmer, the midwife on duty this morning. What's your name?'

'Lizzie,' Imelda said, the word slipping from her mouth before she'd even had time to process it. Unsure where that manufactured name had come from. She didn't even know a Lizzie.

'And is this your first baby, Lizzie?' Sensing the woman's unease, she nodded towards the bed, indicating that Imelda sit down, before closing the door behind them.

'Yes. My first.' Imelda nodded.

'I know it can be daunting. But you're in safe hands. I'll give you an examination and take your blood pressure. You've probably had a bout of Braxton Hicks. Have you heard of that? It's when the womb repeatedly contracts and relaxes, but it's like a false labour. It's very common in the third trimester, but it's usually just a false alarm.' Placing a hospital gown on the bed, the nurse paused and took a deep breath.

'You wouldn't think it was April, would you? They've got the heating on full whack; it's almost tropical. Are you hot too?'

Imelda shrugged, not really feeling the temperature either way.

'Mind you, I have been running around like a headless chicken. Lots of new babies earlier; we've been run off our feet. Right, you pop yourself into this gown. I'm just going to slip my cardi off,' the midwife said, turning her back to Imelda and slipping off her cardigan, before placing it on the back of the door. 'Have you had a show, yet?'

'A show?'

'Oh, you'd know if you'd had it. It's when a plug of mucus from the cervix comes away.' The midwife frowned then. 'Did they not tell you about it in your NTC classes? They should be teaching you all of this, so you know what signs to look for.' The midwife was about to continue the lecture on the classes not focusing on all the important things when it came to labour, only to stop mid-sentence as an alarm screeched loudly from a room further down the corridor.

'I'm going to have to check that. It's one of my ladies and we're a bit short-staffed,' the midwife said apologetically. 'You get yourself comfortable and I'll be back in a few minutes.'

Imelda nodded obediently, waiting until the nurse had left the room before she finally relaxed back on the bed. Relieved that the alarm had gone off and that the midwife had left her. Before she slipped back off the bed and pushed her feet back into her shoes and took her opportunity to leave.

CHAPTER TWENTY-EIGHT

Waking up from a deep sleep, Shelby Cooke stared over at the crib that sat just beneath the window of the hospital suite, unable to help herself as she smiled. Riley hadn't arrived under the best of circumstances given the horrific attack she'd endured. They were the talk of London now, their story was all over the news, and the fact that her attacker had yet to be caught made her feel physically sick. Especially knowing what she did now: that the man who'd attacked her had more than likely killed someone before her. And her baby. She had been lucky, and thankfully, her son seemed none the wiser to the ordeal they'd both suffered. It certainly wasn't the best start in life for him, but he was here and safe and that was all that mattered to her now. And a part of Shelby still couldn't believe that he was finally here.

Reaching for her phone on the bedside table, she flinched at the time, surprised that it was almost five o'clock and Riley had not woken her with the sound of his hungry cries. She'd last fed him at midnight and she finally felt as if she was getting somewhere. Riley was starting to have an appetite and was feeding so much better. She reassured herself that the fact that he was still blissfully sleeping meant he was clearly just as content as she was. Like mother like son. It also meant that they'd both hopefully be allowed home today, and she couldn't wait.

She'd spent months decorating Riley's nursery and shopping for only the best nursery furniture and bedding. It looked beautiful, and Shelby couldn't wait to get him home to see it. Though part of her dreaded going back to that estate, at least while her attacker was still on the loose. Still, she'd have Ashley to look after her. Because Shelby had every faith now that things would change for good. Now that Riley was here, their son would be the one to ensure that they were a proper family. Ashley wouldn't need to go out so much. He could stay at home, with them. At least, Shelby thought, she could live in hope.

Tapping her feet impatiently beneath the covers, she resisted the urge to jump from her bed and scoop Riley up from his crib. She'd only been awake a few minutes and already she was longing to feel his soft skin against hers and smell that familiar soothing new-baby scent of his. Riley was like a drug to her. Only she knew that she should let him sleep for as long as possible. She'd have all day to spoil him with love and cuddles. For now, she was just going to enjoy a few moments of peace and quiet before Ashley and her parents turned up later and started fussing around her and the baby.

Switching the small overhead reading light on, Shelby sat up in the bed, grinning once more as the midwife from yesterday spotted the light while passing and popped her head through the gap in the door to check that Shelby was doing okay.

'You all right, Shelby, darling?' The midwife smiled. 'How did you sleep?'

'I was out for the count.' Shelby smiled, feeling surprisingly refreshed after just a few hours' sleep. She'd been dreading having to spend the night here alone, because she hated hospitals. Confined to this small room, it felt almost claustrophobic. And not only that, but she hated being away from Ashley even more. She thought of him then, at home, snoring loudly as he slept. Completely undisturbed by this new little being that had entered their lives. Men always had it easier than women.

'I'm not surprised. You're probably exhausted. You've been through a lot. Get your rest while you can,' the midwife said sympathetically, knowing the ordeal that Shelby had gone through that had brought on her labour. The woman was doing remarkably well considering.

'How did Riley do during the night?'

'He was an angel,' Shelby said proudly. 'I last fed him at around midnight and he latched on properly this time and managed to have a decent feed. He must have been nice and full up as he's still sound asleep.'

Shelby had expected the worst last night. After the past two days of struggling to get Riley to breastfeed, she'd been left close to tears with exhaustion, and worried that the midwives would have to intervene and put him on formula milk. It didn't help her angst that her mum kept offering her well-intended but not needed advice every five minutes either.

But Shelby was convinced that she'd mastered it now. She'd taken to motherhood more easily than even she'd expected.

She knew what her family thought of her. Ashley, her mum and her dad. That she wouldn't be able to cope on her own. That she'd need them all rallying around to help her constantly. That she'd need their support. Only she didn't. At least she didn't yet. So far, so good. Riley seemed like an easy, contented little baby. And Shelby was determined to do right by him.

'The breakfast trolley doesn't do the rounds until around seven. Would you like me to see if I can get you a cup of tea?'

Shelby nodded, picking up her phone again and flicking through her social media and reading all the messages of outrage and sympathy about what had happened to her, now that the press had got hold of the story and it had gone viral, as well as scrolling through the long list of congratulation messages too. She bet everyone was dying to see a photo of Riley.

And no doubt the press would manage to get hold of that, which is why she'd insisted to Ashley that he bring up a selection of her favourite outfits and her make-up bag when he came today. She'd ask one of the midwives to take a decent photo of the three of them and then she'd upload it as her profile picture. Let that go viral. Not only to show her attacker that he didn't get to her, but to show any of the stupid bimbos who had their eyes on her Ashley that he was a taken man now. Once and for all.

Because she wasn't stupid. As much as he liked to make out that she was paranoid and crazy, she knew what he'd been up to behind her back the last few times he hadn't come home. Still, that would all change now that Riley was here. Shelby felt excited to show her new family off to the entire world. Because she hated the thought of anyone thinking of her as a victim. She was anything but that.

Clicking on her private messages then, she smiled at the kind words of her friends until she came across a message that had been sent a few hours ago, from someone she didn't know, a woman named Kate.

The message had gone into a separate folder and Shelby had almost missed it.

Clicking the button, she stared at the words as her hands started shaking.

Let's hope your baby doesn't turn out to be anything like his cheating scumbag of a father.

'There you go. Two sugars and a splash of milk,' the midwife said, reciting how Shelby had taken her tea yesterday as she set the cup down on the bedside cabinet beside her. 'Who'd have thought having a baby would be such hard work, huh?'

Putting down her phone, Shelby tried to shake off the message.

It was probably nothing. Just some horrible ex of Ashley's trying to stir things up, jealous of their happiness.

And she didn't want anything to ruin today.

'This will have to be our little secret. If Ashley asks, I've been rushed off my feet. You can't let him know that I've been lying in bed, being served tea like Lady Muck,' Shelby said, putting the hurtful words out of her mind.

'Oh, don't you worry. I won't say a word. Discretion is my middle name,' the midwife said, before making her way to the end of Shelby's bed and checking information on Shelby's chart, to see what time she was due some painkillers now she was awake.

'I'll grab you some pain meds when you get your breakfast tray,' she said, satisfied that Shelby could start taking something once she managed to get some food inside her.

Then, making her way towards the crib to check on Riley, the nurse faltered.

'Oh, is Ashley already here then?' she said, turning to face Shelby, her brow raised expectantly. 'Only I didn't see him come in. I know you've been through a lot, love. But unfortunately, we have to be strict about visiting hours. He can't really be here until gone nine a.m. It's not fair on all the other mothers to change the rules for one…'

'Ashley's not here,' Shelby said, puzzled, as she tried to work out why the midwife's tone had changed so suddenly. 'He'll probably be making the most of his lie-in. It's the last one he'll be getting in a while,' Shelby said with a grin, trying to make light of the midwife's sudden abrupt tone.

Only the midwife didn't smile back – instead, a flash of panic spread across her face. Something was wrong.

'Why, what's the matter? I don't understand…'

'Who's been in here? One of the other midwives? A doctor?'

'No. No one. Only me.' Shelby shook her head, a trickle of fear spreading through her as she picked up on the building hysteria in the midwife's voice. 'I don't understand. What's the matter?'

Her eyes went to the cot. The blue woollen blankets her mum had knitted for Riley were draped over the clear Perspex sides, blocking her vision of her son. Her mum had insisted that he would sleep better if he was cocooned in, and she'd been right. Hadn't she? Riley had slept soundly; he hadn't made a peep. Though now, Shelby could feel a deep trepidation creeping over her as she realised how unlikely that really was.

'Where's Riley?'

'What do you mean?' Shelby laughed, the unnatural sound strained and twisted as it hit the air, as she hoped that the midwife was making some sick kind of joke. But the midwife wasn't laughing, and her expression was deadly serious.

'He's there in his crib,' she said, looking at the midwife as if she'd suddenly gone mad.

What was wrong with the woman? Why was she acting so strange and saying such stupid things?

Only as Shelby moved off the bed, panicked now too, she recoiled in horror when the midwife lifted the blanket to reveal nothing but the thin little cot mattress and sheet. It was empty.

Rushing to the wall, the midwife pressed the alarm. The noise filled the room, only to be drowned out by Shelby Cooke's hysterical screams.

CHAPTER TWENTY-NINE

Dragging herself from the warmth of her bed at the sound of loud banging at her front door, Lucy wrapped her dressing gown around herself before grabbing up her mobile phone from the bedside cabinet.

She frowned as she noted it was only five thirty and registered a flash of relief, realising that she hadn't overslept. So why was there a long list of missed calls from Holder on her phone? He'd rung her six times in the past ten minutes. *Shit!* She'd drunk so much last night, she must have slept through them. The strain of yesterday's revelation had finally got to her.

'I'm coming!' she shouted as the banging continued and she made her way down the stairs, guessing by the calls that it was Holder at the door. The urgency in his knocking, and the fact that he was here at the crack of dawn, meant that something had obviously happened. There must have been a development on the case.

Which made her instantly regret the copious amounts of vodka she'd knocked back the previous night, now she rationally thought about the volume of work they still had to do, if they were going to catch Shelby Cooke's attacker.

'Jesus, Lucy,' Holder said, noting the state of the woman as she pulled open the door. A trail of black mascara smudged down both of her cheeks from where she'd clearly been crying at some point during the night. Her hair a matted mess. 'No offence, but you look like a bag of shite,' he said playfully, not waiting for his invite as he stepped into the hallway and made his way into the lounge.

'None taken. Please, do come in,' Lucy muttered sarcastically, staring at her dishevelled reflection in the mirror and noting how Holder had a point. She looked awful.

'Bloody hell, do you want me to get scene of crime officers out here? You been burgled or something?' Holder called out.

Shit! Too late, Lucy remembered the mess she'd left the room in before she drank so much that she'd passed out. She quickly followed Holder through, doing her best to try and ignore her thumping head and the overwhelming urge to be sick now that she was upright.

'I was just sorting through some of my nan's stuff,' she said, following Holder's gaze as he stared around the chaos of the room, his eyes going to the piles of open photo albums that she'd left spread out all across the living room floor, before finally resting on the E-fit photo on the table. A bottle of vodka, almost empty, stood beside it.

'I had a few drinks last night,' Lucy said, nodding at the vodka bottle, hoping to take his attention away from the E-fit. She cursed herself for leaving it out on the table. She'd been so drunk last night that she hadn't realised just how much mess she'd made. She wished that she'd cleared up before she'd passed out in bed; though in fairness, the last thing she'd been expecting when she opened her eyes this morning was an uninvited visitor at this ungodly hour.

But Holder was right. The house was a tip. Lucy had pulled out every photo album that her nan possessed and had pored over each and every one, twice. Not really sure what she'd been searching for. Part of her thought that she might find the man in the E-fit staring back at her from one of the photos. This Kevin or Bodge, or whoever he really was. If only it could have been as simply solved as that.

'It turned into a bit of a late one,' she said, recalling the sense of panic that had filled her last night. Because as much as her nan got confused these days and came out with all her funny little stories, Lucy had seen the recognition in her nan's eyes when she'd looked at the E-fit photo and recognised the man staring back at her as Lucy's father.

And there had been something in the way that her nan had acted that made Lucy believe that this wasn't just her nan being confused. She really did think that it was him. And that there was more to her mother than she'd been told growing up. And that thought terrified her.

So much so that she'd craved the numbness from the vodka. She'd wanted everything that she felt to stop. How scared she was. How angry she felt. How alone she was.

She remembered downing the first drink, how it had burned her throat and the welcome warmth had spread through her. Immediately she'd poured herself another. And another. After that everything had become a blur. The only good thing from last night was that the vodka had managed to do the trick and knock her out. She'd slept through the entire night without a single nightmare. Small mercies and all that.

'You been working on the case?' Holder said, picking up the E-fit image and examining it closely. He guessed that the case must have really got to her; only on closer inspection, he noticed that although the date printed in the corner was from two days ago, this wasn't the E-fit belonging to Shelby Cooke's attacker. This was someone else completely.

'Who's this?'

'Oh, no one. It's nothing. I must have accidentally picked up some paperwork from the sarge's desk by mistake when I grabbed a folder or something,' Lucy said unconvincingly. She took the paper from Holder and shoved it back inside her bag before he could quiz her further. All the while not daring to look at him, because she knew that Holder would see right through her.

'Anyway. I'm sure you're not here to offer to do the cleaning. So, what's up?' Lucy said, glad to change the subject and take the attention away from herself. 'My alarm hasn't even gone off yet. I take it something has happened?'

'It has,' Holder said, leaning back against the doorway and trying to read Lucy. She played her cards close to her chest. He got that. She liked her privacy, but she was acting as if she was on edge about something. But Holder knew well enough by now not to push her. If Lucy wanted to talk about whatever was going on, she would eventually.

'You might want to go and get dressed, because we're needed back up at the hospital.'

'Shelby Cooke? Is she all right? Has something happened?'

'You could say that. She woke up a little while ago to find that someone had taken her baby.'

'Someone has abducted Riley? Shit!' Lucy said, shocked at what her colleague was telling her. 'Do we think that it's related. To the attack?'

Holder shrugged. 'It's too early to say. But DS Morgan wants everyone down there ASAP. This is big, Lucy. The press is already all over it. Someone leaked the story. Suffice to say, he is not a happy man.'

'Oh my god, poor Shelby,' Lucy said, running back upstairs and dragging some clothes on, all the while thinking of how distraught Shelby Cooke must be right now. And again, wishing that she hadn't let loose last night and drank so much.

The case they were working on had just taken a dreadful turn for the worst, and from what they were already concluding about the attacker, Lucy prayed that he didn't have Riley. Because his motives could only be sinister.

CHAPTER THIRTY

Jay-Jay stared out from behind a small cluster of trees just across from the hospital entrance.

He'd done his research well, spending the first part of the night in the internet café on Wandsworth High Street, making sure that he'd done all his homework properly when it came to Pete Baker and his family. He hadn't wanted to go back to the squat after that. He had been too fired up thinking about what he needed to do. So he'd decided not to wait, that he would put his plan into immediate action. Coming here to the hospital early, way before visiting hours, way before anyone else was around. And as it turned out, it was genius.

Because he knew in his gut, that by coming here today he would change things forever, but until just a few minutes ago, he'd had no idea on how big a scale that would turn out to be. Now he was just going to wait it out and see if the cavalry arrived. Which he was in no doubt that it would.

And to be fair, Shelby Cooke had made his research easy for him.

The woman put her entire life out there on social media for all and sundry to see. Jay-Jay couldn't understand that. Why would you want to tell hundreds of nosey strangers your every move? What you had for breakfast, where you'd spent your day. Just feeding people information about you. So that they could sit back and silently judge you. And Jay-Jay had judged the family.

Shelby Cooke was a spoiled little daddy's girl from what he'd seen. Pretentious and fake, her entire account was her posing in some obscenely overpriced designer outfit or a skimpy barely there bikini. Each post fishing for compliments. Or the other posts where she was having a rant. Publicly moaning about something meaningless and pathetic, as if she was entitled to take centre stage. As if it was only her opinions and thoughts that mattered.

And Jay-Jay was under no illusions now, that was exactly what Shelby Cooke was. He'd scrolled through the hundreds of photos and posts, memorising each family members' face. Ashley Cooke looked like a wide boy. Just the kind of man that he'd imagined would owe money to the likes of Sam and Russ Boland. He had trouble written all over him. Pete and Janey Baker looked like your average middle-aged couple.

Jay-Jay hadn't been expecting that. He'd expected someone a bit more flash looking. Although, from what he'd seen of the house they lived in, it was worlds apart from the squalor of the Griffin Estate. Expensive cars, nice holidays. All the evidence pointing to the fact that Pete Baker had done well in his life and was now reaping the benefits. The only photo Jay-Jay hadn't been able to see had been one of the baby. Which had surprised Jay-Jay, seeing as Madam Shelby liked to share even what she ate for bloody breakfast with the rest of the world. Though he guessed that she was probably playing the long game, aware that the media would be jumping on the first photo that she posted of her newborn, especially now that the police had linked her attack to the murder in Richmond Park. She might look like your typical bimbo, but in that sense, Jay-Jay guessed that she wasn't completely stupid. He glanced at his watch. Wondering how long he'd have to wait around until he saw a face he recognised. He didn't have to wait much longer.

A Range Rover Evoque screeched into the car park, skidding across the front parking bays right outside the hospital's main doors. Jay-Jay watched in fascination as the two men and a woman got out of the vehicle and ran inside, recognising them all as Pete and Janey Baker and Ashley Cooke.

He pursed his mouth, his eyes fixed on the main door as the security guards approached them, and all four took the stairs.

Seconds later he heard the blast of sirens, quickly followed by the sky lighting up with flashing blue lights as a fleet of squad cars sped into the car park now too. The officers abandoning their cars in a similar manner as Pete Baker had, before rushing inside the hospital.

Staring down at the large green holdall at his feet, Jay-Jay knew that he had to get the fuck out of there. Fast.

CHAPTER THIRTY-ONE

'The whole place has been put on lockdown, Sarge. No one is coming in or going out,' Lucy Murphy informed DS Morgan as he arrived at the postnatal ward, just minutes after Holder and Lucy had got there.

'All officers are currently giving the entire building a thorough search, Sarge. I've got a team sent down to cover the lift shafts and the car park too. A few of our CID are currently replaying all of the security footage from last night too,' Holder said as he followed DS Morgan and Lucy along the corridor towards Shelby's room.

'Good, because every second counts right now. Time is critical. How's Shelby doing?' DS Morgan asked.

'As expected, Sarge. Not good,' Lucy said as she opened the door of Shelby's private hospital room and the three officers stepped inside, immediately seeing the pained look on the woman's face. Her eyes were puffy from crying. She sat on the bed and stared at the three officers expectantly, desperate for news that they'd found Riley.

Only seeing the sombre looks on the officers' faces, she instantly lost her last glimmer of hope as she sank back in her bed.

'Where is he, Mum? Who would have taken him from me?' she sobbed.

'It's going to be okay, Shelby. They'll find him,' Janey said, fussing around her distraught daughter and pulling the blanket up around her to keep her warm, before stroking a long strand of hair out of Shelby's face.

'How can you still not know anything?' Pete Baker said, challenging the officers. Irate, watching his daughter crumble before his eyes. 'I mean, how the fuck can someone just walk into a hospital room and snatch a baby? How is that even possible? Don't these people have measures in place to stop this kind of thing from happening?' Pete continued his tirade of criticism aimed at the doctors and the midwives that were supposed to be looking after Shelby and Riley.

'It's not anyone's fault…' Janey started, though even she couldn't find the conviction for her argument. Because her husband was right: this shouldn't have happened. No one should have been able to simply walk in here and take their grandson.

'Of course it bloody well is. If the staff here weren't so incompetent this would never have happened. Why didn't anyone see anything? What about the security staff? What the fuck are they being paid to do, if not spot someone walking out of here with a newborn baby?'

Staring over at his beautiful daughter who was sitting silently, just staring into space, Pete could see how broken she was. How fragile she looked. She'd been through more than enough the past few days.

'And what if it's linked?' Pete lowered his voice now, so as not to alarm Shelby, directing his question at the officers. 'First she was attacked. Now Riley's been taken. It's too much of a coincidence, isn't it?'

Lucy and Holder looked down at the floor then, not wanting to answer the man's comment. Because they were all thinking the same thought. It was too much of a coincidence.

'Mr Baker,' DS Morgan said, taking the lead and knowing that this gentleman wasn't going to be easy to appease. 'I understand that you are out of your mind with worry, but I don't believe shouting and blaming everyone is going to help anyone right now.'

'Well, it will make me feel a bit fucking better,' Pete said, annoyed now, because part of him knew that the officer was right. But Pete always acted out in anger. What else was he supposed to do? Just sit here and take this? Knowing that someone out there had the nerve to snatch his grandson? 'Because if this is the same fucker that killed that woman over at Richmond Park – the same animal that attacked my Shelby – then I want to know what the fuck he wants with my grandson.'

'I have every available officer on this. We have locked down the hospital. If Riley is still here, we will find him.'

'And what if he's not? What if some fucking psychopath has taken him?' Pete asked.

Pete glared in Ashley's direction, then, as he sat on the chair in the corner of the room.

Not a peep out of him.

Which was a strange reaction to have when your child had just been abducted.

'If I find out that you are involved in this, in any way… I'll kill you, Ashley!' Pete said, raising his voice now and not caring if the police were there to witness the threat. He meant it. Clenching his fists tightly at his sides, it was taking every inch of will power that Pete possessed not to march over to Ashley and pin the fucker up against the wall. He was seething now, recalling the telephone conversation that he'd overheard shortly after Riley was born. His suspicions that Ashley might know more than he was letting on were growing by the minute.

'Dad! Why would Ashley be involved in our baby going missing?' Shelby cried, wishing that her dad would just give Ashley a break.

'For God's sake! Do you really think that Ashley's not suffering too? Just because he's not vocal about it like you. Riley is our little boy. So, please stop!'

Sensing the tension growing in the room, DS Morgan intervened, hoping to calm the situation down and to let Pete know that he understood and that he sympathised truly. He wouldn't wish this situation on his worst enemy.

'Pete, you have my word. We are going to do everything in our power to find Riley and bring him back to you all. What we need right now is for you to try and stay calm. We need to keep Shelby calm.' DS Morgan glanced over to Shelby as she stared ahead of her in a trancelike state, hoping that the man's soft spot for his daughter might just do the trick.

It did. As he cast one more look over to Shelby, his daughter looked so forlorn and broken that Pete wanted to break down and cry for her.

'You lot need to pull your finger out,' he said with finality, before stomping off towards the window and staring out into the car park.

'Are you okay, Ashley?' Lucy said, feeling sorry for him.

Though she too had noticed his lack of reaction.

Behaving the same way he had a couple of days previously: a completely cool, calm exterior, showing almost no reaction to the drama that was unfolding around him.

'As well as I can be.' Ashley shrugged.

Lucy wondered for a few seconds if that was just his coping mechanism. If maybe everyone was being too hard on him, just because he didn't scream and shout and react the way everyone else did. Maybe this was the way he dealt with things, by going into himself and not making any fuss. Only there was something in the way that he tapped his foot frantically against the floor, an anxiety to the way that he tightly clasped his hands together on his lap and fiddled with his thumbs repeatedly that made Lucy think that maybe Pete was right.

Maybe there was more to this than Ashley was letting on.

'Do you fancy grabbing a cuppa? I'm sure Shelby could do with a hot drink too. Wanna give me a hand?' Lucy said, glad when Ashley nodded and followed her out of the room and towards the vending machines.

'Go on then, how are you really?' she said, sensing the man felt like a spare part.

Pete Baker could be an intimidating presence, and between him and Janey it looked as if Ashley wasn't getting a word in when it came to looking after his wife.

'I'm okay.' Ashley shrugged as if he hadn't given how he felt a second thought up until now. 'I just can't believe that this has happened. I feel like I'm in shock. It's like my worst nightmare has come true. I've barely spent any time with the little fella and now someone's taken him.' He could feel the tremor in his words as he spoke. The raw emotion catching the back of his throat. 'Shit, I'm sorry,' he said, feeling embarrassed then at being so frank with the officer. 'It's just no one else, apart from you, has given a shit about me. I know it's Shelby that's gone through everything, but I'm Riley's dad. I feel this too.'

'I know, Ashley. That's what I thought when I saw you sitting on your own. This must be hard on you too. I thought that maybe you could do with a breather for a few minutes. Clear your head.'

'Why would someone take him? What would they want with him?' Ashley said, his eyes boring into Lucy's, as if she somehow held all the answers. Only Lucy simply shook her head.

'Ashley, I know this isn't the time. But I wanted to have a chat with you about the assault.'

'I told you, I wasn't there! What else can I tell you?' Ashley said, almost defensively then.

'No, not Shelby's assault,' Lucy replied. 'The assault that took place outside Smokes nightclub… on you.' She paused, watching for a reaction, and immediately she got one. 'I've seen the footage. I know it wasn't kids that did that to you,' she said, pointing at Ashley's bruised face, as he visibly flinched at being caught out. 'I saw that you got into a taxi afterwards too.' She didn't mention the attractive brunette, who worked in the club, who had climbed in the car beside him. Lucy guessed that was another reason why Ashley didn't want Shelby and Pete to find out all the details about his whereabouts that night.

He'd been cheating on Shelby while she was being attacked. No wonder he looked wracked with guilt.

'Look, I'm not here to judge you. Your private business is exactly that,' Lucy said, hoping that Ashley would trust her enough to open up to her. 'But I need you to tell me who those men are and what your involvement is with them.'

Knowing that there was no point in continuing the lie, Ashley knew it was time to come clean. He wouldn't win this one.

'I'm sorry. Please don't say anything to Shelby or Pete.' Part of him was glad to finally get this off his chest. 'You're right, it wasn't kids.'

Lucy nodded again. Waiting for Ashley to elaborate some more.

'I've got myself into some trouble. I owe some money, a lot of money. To the Boland brothers,' Ashley said, seeing the recognition in Lucy's eyes at the familiar names.

'Samuel and Russell Boland?'

Ashley nodded.

The footage Lucy had seen wasn't clear enough for her to recognise the two brother's faces, but the men had seemed vaguely familiar.

The Boland brothers were notorious in London. They liked to call themselves businessmen, but what they really were was a couple of thugs. Suspected of running protection rackets and dishing out loans with extortionate interest added on top. The brothers were well and truly on the police's radar. And from what Lucy did know about them, they were not the type of men that you messed with, and if they were the ones who had set upon Ashley that night, then Lucy figured that they were definitely more than capable of being behind Shelby's attack too.

'But they wouldn't have done this…'

Ashley bit his lip, shuffling his feet. He knew what Lucy was getting at, because he'd been thinking the same too. Since the minute he'd arrived at the hospital on hearing his son was missing, Ashley had thought about nothing else.

'He's just an innocent baby. They wouldn't take him, would they?'

Ashley's skin paled, turning a translucent white. Until now, in his head, it almost hadn't seemed possible. That Sam and Russ Boland would stoop to this new low. That they would take his baby as payment. Or to punish him. Now though, now that Lucy had said it out loud, the fact that the police even considered it a possibility made it painfully real.

Forty-eight hours they had said. And Ashley's time was up. 'Christ,' he said again, almost crying now as he cupped his hands around his head. Frantic that once again this was all on him. This was all his fault. 'They wouldn't do that. Surely?'

'I think that it's a line of enquiry that we're going to need to follow up,' Lucy said, giving Ashley fair warning that this was all going to come out, and seeing the look of dread spread across his face as he nodded in understanding.

'Look, get yourself a cup of coffee and maybe bring something back for Shelby. She looks like she could do with something sweet to take the edge off. It will be good for the shock. I'm going to go and speak with my sergeant and then I'm going to pop downstairs and see how my colleagues are getting on with the security footage that covers the main entrance.'

Ashley nodded, about to walk away, when Lucy stopped him, placing her hand on his arm.

'And maybe you should talk to Shelby? Tell her the truth, Ashley,' Lucy said, full of seriousness now. 'She's not going to like what she hears, but it's probably going to be better if she hears it from you. Don't you think? Because she will find out eventually. And probably very soon. It's just a matter of time now.'

'You don't really think it's possible, do you? That they're the ones that have taken Riley?' Ashley said then, praying that Lucy would tell him that she highly doubted it. That he was just being paranoid. That there was no way that the Boland brothers could be involved. Only Lucy didn't answer. Instead she squeezed Ashley's arm, her silence and the grave look on her face, speaking louder than her words ever would.

CHAPTER THIRTY-TWO

'We've gone through the tapes with your colleagues here and unfortunately the camera covering the main door of the ward wasn't in operation. It hasn't been working all week.' The security guard couldn't hide his embarrassment as DC Holder stared at him incredulously, in complete disbelief at what he was hearing. 'Maintenance were sorting it, but they were waiting for a new part to come in.' He shrugged apologetically, knowing there was still worse to come.

'And there's nothing covering Shelby Cooke's door either. It's just out of shot. The suites are right by the nurses' station, so it would have been covered by the same camera.'

'The main camera for the ward is out? You have got to be kidding me!' Holder said, though in all honesty, he wasn't entirely surprised. In his bitter experience on the job, things like this happened way too often, making their job so much harder than it needed to be.

'All we've got on here is a pretty standard night shift. Everything checks out. I've had the senior members of staff vouch for everyone on here. A couple of cleaners on the ward. All the midwives on shift last night. It all looks pretty much routine,' the security guard said, letting the tape run to the end, to the time when Shelby must have noticed that the baby was gone. Because the screen showed the nurses frantically running up and down the corridor then, setting off the alarms, before checking every room in a bid to find baby Riley.

'Where else isn't covered up here?' Holder said, closing his eyes in despair, wanting to make sure that he got as much information as possible, so he knew what they were up against. 'Is there any other way that a person could get in or out of the ward without being seen? Apart from, of course, the main door,' Holder said sarcastically.

'The fire exit stairwell. It's at the end of the corridor. Near Shelby Cooke's room.'

'Where does it lead to?'

'Down the side of the hospital, straight out to the car park.'

'Fucking marvellous!' Holder said, closing his eyes briefly in utter despair. 'So we've got fuck all then? Nothing on camera and two exits that are completely uncovered. And nobody saw anything dodgy?'

'Your lot are still questioning all the staff,' the guard said, defensive now. 'A couple of midwives went home after finishing their shifts. Think your boss mentioned that he was sending officers out to their homes to interview them too. I don't know, maybe we've picked up on something on the cameras that cover the hospital's main entrance?'

He was relieved when the detective constable got up to go and find out.

'Let's hope so,' Holder said, heading out the door after Lucy before he said something he regretted. He was willing to bet his monthly salary that the security guard and the rest of their team were nigh on useless when it came to keeping things in order around here on the night shift. Guessing that they were just as lapsed and lazy, that they wouldn't be very much help to him.

The security tapes were all they had to go on so far. They held the key to finding who had taken Riley. Because so far, they had no other clues. No sightings of anyone taking the child. It was as if the kid had just vanished into thin air.

Making his way to the security room by the main entrance, Holder hoped Lucy was having better luck.

'Have you got something?' He guessed, by the animated look on her face, as she stood with the phone to her ear, that she'd had more success than he'd had.

'Er, you could say that,' Lucy said, placing her hand over the receiver to fill him in as she waited for the person at the other end to pick up.

'Take a look at that. See anyone familiar?' Lucy nodded towards the screen that had been paused, the image zoomed in. 'We managed to get this from the camera covering the back of the car park. It's a bit blurry, but we think that is the time that Riley was taken. It's too much of a coincidence, isn't it?'

'You're fucking kidding me!' Holder stepped closer, inspecting the grainy image on the screen.

'Sarge. It's Lucy. You need to get down here now. We've got something,' Lucy said. She turned her attention back to the phone as DS Morgan's voice poured out from the other end.

'We've got an image of the man that fits the description of Shelby Cooke's attacker. An almost identical image to the E-fit. The camera has picked him up lurking in the car park around the time that Riley Cooke went missing.' She tapped at the screen, to draw attention to what sat at the man's feet for Holder's benefit.

'Shit!' Holder said. Going silent then as Lucy broke the news.

'He's got a large holdall with him, Sarge. Big enough and discreet enough to hold a stolen baby. And there's something else. We've had some calls come in from the press appeal, Sarge. The same name has been given to us three times. One caller seems like a reliable source too, claims that they are a prison officer over at Wandsworth Prison. We're following it up right now, but he says that the E-fit matches the exact description of an inmate who was recently released from there, get this, three days before the first victim was murdered in Richmond Park. Sarge, I believe the man we're looking for is a Jay-Jay Andrews.'

CHAPTER THIRTY-THREE

Little Riley Cooke won't stop crying. His voice fills the room with loud, rampant, angry sobs. And he won't stop. Lying on top of the duvet, he kicks out his arms and legs in his wild fury. Stronger and far more furious than a newborn baby should be.

It's as if his survival instincts have kicked in. As if he's battling for a feed. Hungry, perhaps, only he refuses to drink the bottle that is offered to him. His mouth pursing tightly shut, as if purposely protesting to keep the teat out. The milk might be too warm? Or maybe it's too cold? He screams some more. His nappy has just been changed, so it can't be that. He's tired. And so he should be with all the bawling he's done. Exhausted himself. Yet he's fighting sleep, and there's no sign of him giving in to it anytime soon.

Still he screams. Louder now, the noise echoing around the room. Nothing seems to stop it, not even for a few seconds. Nothing is good enough. Nothing is working.

It's like he knows, like he is picking up on the sinister vibe around him. Unsettled and pining for his mother. He doesn't feel safe. He's not happy. Only nothing seems to help, nothing will make him stop. And the noise is deafening now, the sound of his dull, constant whimpering turns into a high-pitched hysterical scream that fills the room.

Wrapped in extra blankets in case he's too cold. Taking them off again, in case he's too hot. Picking him up and praying that the rocking motion will help soothe him.

Only it doesn't. He's screaming louder now. A stream of tears running down his puce-red cheeks.

Placing him back down on the blanket.

The slam of a door. The noise quieter, muffled.

Nothing will make him stop.

CHAPTER THIRTY-FOUR

'So, it was all a lie?' Shelby said, open-mouthed as Ashley confessed to her the trouble that he was in with the Boland brothers – how they'd beaten him up outside the club the other night. 'It wasn't just kids? You knew these men?'

Ashley nodded, looking down at the floor now. He hadn't even told Shelby the worst of it, and already she looked ready to implode. But he knew he had to tell her. Taking his chance while they were finally alone. Like Lucy said, it would be better coming from him. Because this was going to all come out either way, and Ashley had to salvage whatever he could.

'I owe them money, Shelby. A lot of money. It was for us. I did all of it for us, you have to believe me.' Ashley was trying his hardest to make Shelby understand why he'd got in the situation in the first place. 'It was stupid, I know that now. But I was given some information about a bet. It was a dead cert. I was going to give it back straight afterwards.' Ashley knew that of all the things he'd asked Shelby to forgive him for in their relationship, this was going to be the ultimate. 'I just wanted to prove to you that I could get us out of that dump of a flat and that I could support you. I'm sick of your mum and dad looking down their noses at me, as if I'm a nothing. As if I'm just a waster. The money was going to be a big chunk of the deposit.' Ashley wiped the stray tear from his cheek. 'Only I lost the bet. I lost fucking everything. And the Boland brothers wanted their money back. I didn't think they'd carry out their threat when they said they'd pay you a visit too,' Ashley said, regretting saying so much as Shelby's head whipped around to face him then.

'Pay me a visit?' Narrowing her eyes. Ashley's words were going into her ears, but her brain couldn't make sense of them. What he was telling her couldn't be true. 'The attack? Someone threatened me with a knife. I could have been stabbed, murdered. Our son could have died. And all this time, you've known who it was? And you sat there like a gormless bloody idiot and kept your mouth shut?'

'I didn't know for sure, I still don't,' Ashley said, starting to cry properly now, because when Shelby said it like that, so bluntly, it sounded bad. Really bad. 'I thought they were just saying it. You know. And the police, they mentioned about your attack being linked to another attack over in Richmond Park. So, I figured it couldn't have been them.'

'A murder, Ashley. It wasn't just an attack; the woman was fucking murdered,' Shelby spat. Thinking how close she'd come to being a victim too. 'Anything you knew or even suspected should have been said.' For a split second she wondered why he was confessing all of this to her now. What did he have to gain by coming clean, or more importantly, what did he stand to lose?

'Oh my god. They've got Riley,' she said, then, as it suddenly dawned on her. 'That's why you are telling me all of this, isn't it? You think they have Riley?'

Ashley looked down at the floor, feeling heartfelt regret for ever getting himself tied up in such a mess.

'DC Murphy said that it was a line of enquiry that they would be looking in to, yes.'

Shelby was off the bed then. Launching herself at her husband. Beating him repeatedly over the head with clenched fists. Screeching every obscenity she could think of at the man as she directed all her anger, venom and hate towards him.

And Ashley just stood there and took it. Because he knew he deserved it and so much more. He knew that even after the Bolands had warned him they would target Shelby, he'd self-ishly still spent the night with Kate. That he'd put himself first throughout all of this. He'd put his own child's life at risk.

'Hit me!' he shouted. 'Go on, I deserve it. I know I do.'

'You fucking bastard! You lying piece of shit,' Shelby screamed, so deep in her rage that she didn't hear the door of the suite open or the officers all come running in.

DC Lucy Murphy wrapped her arms around her, pulling her away from Ashley.

'It's okay, Shelby. It's going to be okay!' the officer said, trying to calm her down. Shelby's whole body was trembling. Violently shaking, filled with fury and rage and something far more powerful than that. Real fear.

'How can it be okay? Someone has taken my child. My beautiful baby boy. I can't remember his smell,' she said then, the realisation coming in a panicked screech. 'He's only been gone a few hours. But already I can't remember his smell. What if he forgets mine? What if he forgets I'm his mum? What if someone hurts him? What if we never get him back?'

Shelby broke into hysterical sobs. As she collapsed into Lucy's arms, all Lucy could do was hold her, and allow her to let everything out. Until finally Shelby had exhausted herself and pulled away from the officer.

Pete and Janey came back into the room, thankfully having missed most of the outburst.

'I understand how difficult this is for you both and how distressed you must both feel, but we've got a press conference set up to start in fifteen minutes. I need you both to try and stay as calm and composed as possible,' Lucy said, hoping to finally defuse the situation. 'We need to do this for Riley. So that we can get him back. Do you think that you can both do that?'

Ashley nodded, holding out his hand to Shelby, asking for a truce. Shelby slapped it away.

'And I think you should both know that we've had a development,' Lucy said, the grave look on her face getting everyone's attention. 'I'm sorry to say that it looks as though the man who attacked you the other night, Shelby, was here at the hospital. We've got images of him outside in the car park in the early hours of this morning. We've got a name too. Jay-Jay Andrews,' Lucy said, in the vain hope that someone might recognise it.

Only nobody reacted.

'He was here? Around the time that Riley went missing?' Shelby said. An involuntary wail left her mouth before she could even properly register what she was being told. 'Please God no. Did you see Riley? Did he have Riley with him?'

'It's hard to say,' Lucy said honestly. 'He had a large bag with him, but we still don't know anything for sure. I want you to know, because when we do the press appeal, we'll be focusing it on our search for him.'

Shelby nodded. Robotic, almost, as if she was no longer in control of her emotions or her body.

'But I need you both to put on a united front. We can't show him that he's got to us. We have to show that we have every confidence in getting Riley back. And soon. Very soon. Because we have,' Lucy said with a fierce determination. She stared at Shelby, willing the woman to see that she meant every word she spoke. 'We will get him back, Shelby.'

'We'll do it. But when it's done, I'm going home,' Shelby said defiantly. Dragging her hospital gown over her head, before pulling her tracksuit on and scooping her hair back in a bun. 'I can't sit here in this bloody hospital just waiting. The sound of all these crying babies is sending me over the edge. I need to go home.'

'Of course.' Lucy nodded in understanding. She knew how hard this must be for Shelby. Desperately pining for her newborn son.

'Yeah, we can wait for news there, back at the flat,' Ashley chimed in, thinking that it was at least a start. That they could get home and get Riley back. And then they could start fixing this mess that he'd landed them in.

Only Shelby shook her head.

'No. I'm not going back to the Griffin Estate. Not after what happened. And not with you. You caused all of this. It's all your fault. I'm going home. We're done, Ashley. I don't want anything to do with you, ever again.' Then, looking over at her parents, Shelby's lip quivered with emotion once more as she asked: 'Can I come home?'

Both her parents nodded without question, and as they hugged her tightly to them, Shelby started to cry silently again.

CHAPTER THIRTY-FIVE

Staring at the TV screen, unable to believe what she had just seen, Imelda listened intently as a reporter announced that a baby had been stolen from the hospital. The camera zoomed in on Shelby.

Only it couldn't be Shelby?

It didn't look anything like the vibrant, flashy, dolled-up Shelby that Imelda knew. In fact, if Imelda had seen her out on the street, she was certain that she wouldn't have even recognised her at all. She would have walked right past her. She was devoid of the usual heavy mask of make-up and dressed down, wearing a plain old tracksuit.

Imelda stepped closer to the TV, so she could see her properly. Stunned at the sight of the broken shell of a woman before her. Shelby's face was bruised, her eyes dark and sunken. She stared at the camera, but there was nothing going on behind her eyes. It was as if the lights had gone out. It was probably the worst that Imelda had ever seen her look. And now the whole world was seeing it too.

Imelda stared at Ashley then too and couldn't help but feel sorry for him. Shelby had pushed him out. They were sitting next to each other, and it would be hard for others to see it, but Imelda could. Shelby's body language was off. She tilted slightly away from him, as if she couldn't stand to be next to him. As if she couldn't stand to be anywhere near him. And when he reached for her hand, Imelda could see the way that she flinched. It was such a slight, almost seamless movement that you wouldn't notice unless you were really looking.

But Imelda was really looking. She was taking it all in. How Ashley's hand clamped around Shelby's, but Shelby's fingers hung loose. Their bodies next to each other, but their connection worlds apart.

She wondered if Shelby knew about the woman that went into their flat yesterday.

This 'Kate' that Ashley had seemed so pre-occupied with. Maybe he'd told her, or Shelby had somehow found out?

Listening as the female detective made the statement. Appealing for the general public to be vigilant and keep a look out for the missing baby. Imelda's eyes went to the photo again of Shelby's attacker. They'd named him now.

Jay-Jay Andrews.

Imelda stared at the image. Shivering as she recalled the same cold glare that had met hers the night she'd walked across the estate's communal gardens. Remembering how she'd told herself that she was imagining the pair of eyes that she could feel on her. Watching her from the shadows. Only she hadn't been imagining it at all. He'd been there. He'd seen her.

Going to the front door, Imelda reached for the top bolt and yanked it into its lock, before crouching down and bolting the other new locks that she'd taken the initiative to install. Because she didn't feel safe anymore. She didn't feel safe in her own home.

And she needed to keep him out.

Going to the window, she stared out from behind the net curtains. Her eyes searched up and down the balcony. Wondering if he'd come for her too.

CHAPTER THIRTY-SIX

'Well, this is worlds away from life over at the Griffin Estate, that's for sure!' Lucy said, unable to hide her surprise as she eyed the double-fronted period home in the middle of the private road, set just off the southern border of Wandsworth Common.

'Shelby Cooke must really love the bloke to downgrade from this,' Holder added in agreement as the two officers got out of their unmarked car and made their way through the wrought-iron gates towards the large front door. Lucy rang the bell and they waited. 'I mean, he's got a lot to live up to, hasn't he? Poor bloke. There's just no competing with this, is there?'

'DC Murphy, DC Holder. Is there any news?' Janey Baker said, opening the door and faltering at the sight of the two officers standing on her doorstep, trying to read the officers' expressions. 'Please God, say you've found him?' she said hopefully, praying that they were both here to tell them that they'd found Riley.

Holder shook his head. 'We're still fully investigating every avenue, Mrs Baker. Which is why we're here. Is Shelby around? We'd like to ask her a few questions, if possible.'

'Er, yes, of course. Sorry, we just weren't expecting you. Yes, of course. Come in.'

Following the woman through the house, Lucy made eyes at Holder. Janey seemed on edge. More jittery than normal.

'They've probably had a row or something? Pete Baker seems like he'd be a challenge for anyone to live with,' Holder whispered as Janey led them through to the lounge, where Shelby was sitting on the sofa. A blanket was draped over her and the log fire was lit.

'Shelby, love, DC Murphy and DC Holder are here. They wanted to speak to you.'

'Have you found him?' Shelby said, sitting up straight, her eyes wide, her voice hopeful.

Lucy shook her head. 'Not yet. No.' She could see the woman's disappointment as she sank back down in the chair.

'Can I get you both some tea? Or coffee?'

'Yes, that would be lovely,' Lucy said, more so that Janey would leave them for a few minutes to speak to Shelby alone.

'It's lovely and cosy in here,' Lucy said, smiling at Shelby once Janey was gone.

'I can't get warm,' Shelby said, as if she hadn't noticed the warmth of the room. 'I feel cold down to my bones. It's probably because I'm so tired. But I can't sleep.' She shrugged. 'I know I should, but every time I close my eyes, I can see him. Wrapped up in his cot. Sleeping soundly. And then I remember that he's not here. That he's gone. That someone else has got him, and it's like a flood of panic takes over me.' Shelby stared off into space again. Not really addressing her grief to anyone in particular. Just making sense of it herself, out loud. Shaking her head as if she realised this, she looked at Lucy.

'What did you want to talk to me about?'

'We have been going through the security footage, Shelby. And one of the midwives that went off shift this morning was seen with a patient who came in, around 4.30am,' Holder said, sitting down on the couch next to Shelby and opening up the Mac laptop. The video footage was already paused, ready for him to press play. Shelby stared at the screen as he continued, talking her through it.

'We don't have anything from the camera over the postnatal ward's main door, but we do have this footage.' Holder pointed to the image of a pregnant woman making her way into a treatment room with a midwife. Shelby pursed her mouth, not sure what she was looking at.

'This is probably nothing to do with the investigation. We just need to rule it out. This woman was on the ward around the same time that you were there. It looks as though it was just a routine examination. Only we can't get hold of the midwife in question, so we wanted to ask you if you recognised her?'

Shelby stared at the image on the screen as she saw the woman re-emerge from the room.

'Oh! Wow. Yeah. I do. That's Imelda George. She lives a few doors down from me. We were both due around the same time. Maybe she was in labour? Poor cow still has to go through all that. It's bloody horrendous. I was terrified.' Shelby shrugged.

'Why? You can't seriously think she's involved, do you? What, that she's teamed up with the man who attacked me, and they both stole my baby?' Shelby laughed then. 'She's harmless. Trust me. She wouldn't hurt a fly. And we're friends. Kind of,' Shelby said, realising that in some ways they actually were. They'd struck up a strange little friendship throughout their pregnancies.

Seeing the fleeting look that passed between the two officers, Shelby figured that they didn't share her optimism.

'It's just, if she was in labour, she'd have been down on the maternity ward…' Lucy said, sharing her doubts with Shelby.

'Look, she might have been trying to get in to see me while she was there. She was worried about me. That's not a crime, is it?' Shelby shrugged again, remembering how Ashley had mentioned that Imelda had waited outside their flat, and that she'd seemed really shaken by the news of Shelby's attack.

'Shelby? What's happened?' Pete's voice came bursting into the room before he did. Still dressed in his coat and shoes, he eyed the officers expectantly, having seen their car parked in front of the house. 'Well? Have you found him?'

'Sorry, no. Not yet,' Lucy offered, getting up from her chair. They didn't want to impose on the family for longer than they needed to. 'We've got everything we need for now. Thanks for your help, Shelby,' Lucy said as Janey came back into the room with a tray of cups and a teapot. She placed it down on the table and stared meaningfully at her husband.

Lucy could see anger in her eyes as she raised her brow, as if to encourage Pete to say something. Only Pete instantly rejected her suggestion with an abrupt shake of his head, cutting her dead.

'Right, well, I'll show you out,' he said, in an attempt to avoid the subject, eager to see the two police officers off.

Only Janey, furious now, took her moment. 'Tell them,' she said, her words trembling with anger as she stood in the middle of the lounge, her fists clenched to her sides.

'Not now, Janey,' Pete said, dismissing his wife with a wave of his hand. Pretending that what she had to say wasn't of any real importance.

'Tell them. Or I will.' Janey stood her ground.

'Mum?' Shelby asked, not used to seeing her mother speaking so firmly to her father.

They could all feel the growing tension in the room.

'He's my grandson too, Pete. And I will not just stand here silently playing the dutiful wife. Not when so much is at stake. Tell them. Tell them, for fuck's sake.'

'Dad? What's going on?' Shelby said, staring at her father questioningly. Her mother never swore.

'Nothing...' Pete said, looking uncomfortable now that the police officers were staring right at him.

'Just bloody well TELL THEM,' Janey bellowed.

Pete hung his head. 'I got a phone call about an hour ago. They didn't leave their name, but it was a male caller. His voice sounded muffled. Disguised. But it was definitely a male,' Pete said, coming clean. 'I was told that if we wanted Riley back, then there was a ransom to pay.'

Lucy and Holder looked at Pete incredulously.

'Please tell me you didn't pay it,' Lucy said, knowing full well that that was exactly what was coming next. High-profile cases like this one, with the amount of media attention on it, were prone to fraudsters chancing their luck on making money from vulnerable parties.

'How could I not? This is my grandchild. I had to,' Pete said, his voice breaking with emotion.

'Mr Baker, with all due respect, you should have told us about the call,' Holder said, thinking exactly the same as Lucy, and not wanting to voice his concerns that the caller could have been someone looking to make money out of the family, completely unconnected to the abduction.

'And what about the press? They are out there, just digging around for their next headline. What if you were followed? What if they saw you? What if they mess the exchange up? There's a lot of factors that can go wrong,' Lucy said then, picking up her radio and knowing that now they were racing against time.

'Where did you leave the money, Mr Baker, and what time is the exchange being made?'

'I don't know,' Pete said desperately. 'I was just told to leave the money in the bin, at the children's playground on Wandsworth Common. I wasn't told anything else.' Pete knew how pathetic he sounded. He'd just left a considerably large amount of money out in the open, for anyone to find, and had no real confirmation that he'd get Riley back once the abductor had been paid. He'd acted in haste. For the first time in his life, he felt as if he had no real control. As if everything around him was crumbling down, and there was nothing he could do to fix it. He had always protected his family no matter what. And that was all he wanted to do now too. Fix this. Make it right again. To get Riley back home and stop Shelby from hurting.

'I had no choice. I couldn't just sit around and do nothing. I had to at least try and get him back.'

'How much was the ransom?'

'Twenty thousand pounds. Cash. I took it from the safe in my office.'

Janey Baker closed her eyes and shook her head. 'I told you it was a stupid idea. I told you to call the police…'

'Well it's done now, isn't it?' Pete said, his whole body sagging with the realisation that, of course, as always, his wife was right. He'd played right into the caller's hands. Oh, how the mighty had fallen. How stupid he'd been. Because that was what these types of people did, wasn't it? They preyed on the desperate, the broken, the weak. And just when you were on the brink, they bought you down to your knees.

Pete should have known better. He'd dealt with some real scumbags in his time. Men who had the morals of an alley cat and zero integrity to go with it. He, of all people, should have known not to give in like this. And a small, terrified part of him couldn't help but realise that maybe he had really fucked up now. That by paying this money, he'd gained absolutely nothing. Not even the safe return of his missing grandson. All he could do now was hope and pray that the call had been genuine. That the money he'd left would bring Riley home to them all.

'There's no need to point the finger of blame.' Holder nodded in agreement, feeling sorry for the man. It was done. Now they had to move fast in the hope of rectifying it.

'Sarge, we need some undercover officers down at the children's play area on Wandsworth Common,' Lucy said, getting on her radio as the officers quickly left the house. 'We've got a possible ransom demand for the safe return of Riley Cooke. We need to get someone down there pronto.'

Because right now that money was the only real lead they had to finding the man who had taken Riley.

CHAPTER THIRTY-SEVEN

Sitting in the unmarked police car at Wandsworth Common's entrance, Lucy stared up at the gloomy backdrop of the two towers of the Griffin Estate, just off in the distance, while Holder kept his gaze focused on the bin inside the entrance to the children's park.

'What if the money's already been taken?' Holder said, his stare unwavering. Because they had everything riding on this. Whoever had demanded the money would lead them to Riley. They were almost certain of that. It wasn't even worth thinking of the outcome if this was all some kind of farce. If they'd been led on a wild goose chase by someone trying to cash in on the family's misfortune. 'I mean, Pete dropped it off personally, himself, and then walked back to the house. What if Jay-Jay Andrews has already picked it up, and we're just sitting here staring at an empty bin?'

'Do you want to risk it, and go and take a look?' Lucy said, knowing full well that they were just going to have to take their chances for now, and wait this one out. 'Because if I didn't want to get caught doing the pickup that's where I'd be waiting. Over there,' Lucy said, nodding in the direction of the line of dense trees that formed a row along the common's edge. 'Making sure that Pete was a man of his word and that I wasn't being stitched up. We're lucky we turned up at the Bakers' house when we did; the drop had only just been made. Chances are the money is still there. And he's out there somewhere too. Watching and waiting.'

Holder nodded in agreement, his eyes scanning the foliage; only, he couldn't see anything untoward.

'I see the cavalry's just arrived.' Holder grinned, eyeing the female jogger running down the pathway with her headphones in. Lucy followed his gaze, both officers immediately recognising their colleague from CID, who had slipped into her gym gear and made her way to the park in just minutes.

Another colleague, male this time, was walking the opposite perimeter. Taking his time. A casual afternoon stroll to anyone without a more watchful eye.

'It's starting to get dark,' Lucy said, her eyes not leaving the silhouettes of the towers. The grey, moody skies behind them made the place look even more sinister.

She shivered. Surprised at how that place could still affect her so deeply. How it caught her unawares sometimes. When she was least expecting.

'Maybe that's what he's waiting for. Maybe that's when he'll strike? We could be here for a while!' Holder said, before side-eyeing his colleague with a smirk and changing the subject.

'So, how was your late lunch date the other day with Zack Lownrey? The rumours around the station are rife by the way.'

'I bet they are. Well, for your information, like I told you yesterday, it wasn't a date. I wanted to talk to him. Strictly professional. I just wanted to talk through the case… And he suggested we grab something to eat…' Lucy said, blushing. Realising how it must have looked to the rest of the team, and that she'd probably been the talk of the station yesterday, if news of her conversation with Zack Lownrey had been passed around and made it back to Holder. 'Come on, we're in the middle of a murder enquiry, I'm not just going to go out on a date in the middle of it all, am I? So maybe next time you hear a "rumour" you could kindly put it to rest!'

'Oh, of course. My bad!' Holder laughed, shaking his head. 'It was a team meeting just for two, wasn't it? I'll be sure to let everyone know.' He raised his brow, teasing her now. Lucy was far too easy to wind up. 'I mean, you know he likes you, right? You can admit it if you have a crush on him. I just don't know what you see in the bloke. He's so smarmy.'

'Smarmy?' Lucy shrugged, knowing that Holder had taken an instant dislike to the man. Only she still couldn't work out why. 'I don't know what your issue with him is. He seems nice enough.'

'Nice enough?' Holder scoffed. 'Up his own arse, more like. A bit, I don't know, Pompous.'

'Whoa! You really don't like him?' Lucy said, raising her eyes, trying to work out what had pissed Holder off so much. 'I mean he can be a bit intense, I guess,' Lucy said, recalling how he'd kept staring at her throughout their meal. Holder was probably right; maybe he liked her. But Zack wasn't Lucy's type. She just didn't feel the same way. Still, she wasn't going to put Holder out of his misery anytime soon. 'Anyway, I just genuinely wanted to hear what he had to say about the case. The psychology behind the profiling is fascinating. Don't you think? Getting into the mind of a killer. Finding out what makes them do it,' Lucy said, not admitting to Holder that, in actual fact, she had talked to Zack Lownrey about her mother's case.

She decided that she would put Holder right eventually, because the last thing she wanted was all her colleagues speculating and gossiping about her.

'Not only that but if this abduction is linked to the murder and Shelby's attack, then it's good to have as much information on the perpetrator's profile as possible, don't you think? Zack is on our side. Seriously, I don't know why you don't like him.'

'It's not that I don't like him…' Holder started. His tone was earnest for once as he turned to face Lucy now. About to say something serious. 'It's just that… I like—'

'And bingo! What did I tell you…?' Lucy said, cutting Holder off and staring out across the park, nodding towards the thick growth of trees. 'He was hiding out over there. He probably saw the money being dropped off and was making sure that no one was going to come and stake the place out. More fool him, huh!' Lucy said, cocky now that her prediction had come true.

They hadn't deterred Jay-Jay Andrews from making the collection. The man had no clue that the park was currently surrounded. They watched as the dark silhouette of a figure made his way towards the children's playground. Getting nearer now. His head down. Opening the gate, he stepped inside and made a beeline for the bin, before glancing quickly around to make sure no one was watching, then leaning down and retrieving the bag of money.

'Holy shit!' Lucy said as she and Holder finally saw the man's face.

The two officers were rendered silent at the unexpected turn their operation had just taken.

'That's Ashley Cooke,' Holder said finally, just as bewildered as Lucy. 'What the fuck is he doing bribing Pete for money? Do you think he knows where Riley is?'

'Well, there's only one way we're going to find out,' Lucy said, thinking about their conversation earlier about the Boland brothers attacking Ashley.

Up until now they had no proof of the Boland brothers being involved in Riley's abduction. This would get them the evidence they needed to tie the men to the case, if they were indeed involved. Getting on her radio, Lucy told her fellow officers to stand down.

'If he's taking the money, then we have to see where he goes next. And pray to God that he leads us straight back to Riley!'

CHAPTER THIRTY-EIGHT

Pulling up his Range Rover at the back of Broomwood Road, Pete Baker slipped his black leather gloves on and got out of his car.

'They're all still inside?' Pete asked, nodding curtly at Carl Rangers, who stood on the edge of the pavement, patiently waiting for him, before marching to the boot. Because despite what the police and Janey clearly thought of him, Pete was far from fucking stupid.

And he was never going to simply just hand over a bag full of money to some chancer when his grandson's life was at stake.

The police were doing their best, but so far, their best hadn't got Riley home, had it? So Pete was doing things his way now.

He'd ordered Carl to follow the money and whoever collected it, and not let the bastard out of his sight.

And that's exactly what Carl had done. Only the last thing Pete had expected to hear was that his son-in-law had been the one to do the pickup, and that he'd then made his way here to the Bolands' place.

He should have known.

Ever the slippery little fucker, Ashley always seemed to get away unscathed. But not this time.

Carl had managed to check out the nightclub's security footage for clues about Ashley's attackers, and Pete's instincts about Ashley being involved with something dodgy had been spot on.

They'd since found out that the Boland brothers had been the ones who attacked Ashley, not kids as he'd tried to have everyone believe.

Only it had taken Shelby finally confiding in her parents today about the trouble Ashley was in with the Boland brothers, for Pete to know the reasons behind the attack.

According to Shelby, Ashley owed these two fuckers a lot of money.

The only good that had come out of it all was that Shelby had come home.

Shelby couldn't trust Ashley, only it had taken something like this to finally make his daughter see sense.

'Yeah, Ashley only went in five minutes ago,' Carl confirmed.

'And you're sure that this dump is their place?' Pete said, turning his nose up at the run-down-looking mid-terrace house. His eyes swept the state of the rickety-looking back fence and gate which were rotten and faded in places. He could see makeshift bits of material hanging at awkward angles in the upstairs windows. The windowpanes condensated and mouldy.

The place was worlds away from what he'd imagined two flash twats like the Boland brothers would be holed up in.

But then again, Pete knew how these things worked.

Having made it his business this afternoon to do his homework on the two men, Pete knew that the brothers were making a real name for themselves and were both on a serious earn.

Flaunting their wealth would only draw attention to them while they were on their way up the ranks.

This place was no doubt a front. That was how the game was played.

'Yep! This is their place.'

'What the fuck is Ashley playing at?' Pete asked, shaking his head sorrowfully. Still unable to believe that in the midst of his own child's abduction, Ashley was still thinking of himself, and trying to save his own arse.

There was nothing lower as far as Pete was concerned.

And he was under no illusion that Shelby might ever forgive him for what he was about to do.

Rummaging around inside the boot of his motor, Pete pulled out his shotgun, which had been carefully concealed in a hidden compartment under the boot liner. He cast his eye along the street to make sure that they weren't attracting any unwanted attention, before he placed the gun inside his jacket.

This was it; he wasn't fucking around anymore.

'What if you're wrong, Pete? What if this is Ashley's way of getting him back? Riley might be in there?' Carl reasoned, realising now just how angry Pete was.

That his temper had finally got the better of him and he was no longer thinking straight.

He'd been Pete's right-hand man for longer than he could remember, and they'd found themselves in all kinds of predicaments over the years. Yet, he'd never seen Pete so angry.

The man was fit to kill.

And as much as Carl despised Ashley, Carl only cared about Pete. He didn't want his friend to do something out of anger that he might later regret.

He had a family to think about.

Going down for attempted murder, or worse, could cost him dearly.

'What? You really believe that do you? That Ashley's suddenly the modern-day hero? Don't you think if this was legit, and he was really trying to get Riley back, he would have come to me for my help? Only instead, he took it upon himself to fleece me for £20k and do this sneakily behind everyone's backs. What does that tell you, Carl? That he is trying to get his son back? Or is this typical bloody Ashley again? Using the opportunity of his newborn son going missing to pay off a couple of fucking loan sharks. Once again, that imbecile is only thinking of himself and saving his own arse. Either way, this all leads back to Ashley,' Pete said, shaking his head.

Carl wasn't a stupid man; he knew as well as Pete did that this was exactly the sort of stunt that Ashley was capable of pulling.

'And there's only one way to find out!' Pete said, giving Carl the nod to take the lead as he followed him inside the back gate and up the pathway towards the back door.

'Because if my grandson is in there, God help them all. And if he isn't, then not even God will be able to help Ashley!'

CHAPTER THIRTY-NINE

'Well, fuck me. If it isn't the infamous Ashley Cooke. Your mug's been all over the telly today,' Russ Boland said, opening the front door and staring at Ashley Cooke as if he was a mirage or something. 'I've just been watching you do the appeal for your boy. I mean, it's a shame your face is all smashed up. Doesn't paint you in the best light, does it? But still… everyone gets their five minutes.'

'Five minutes? This ain't about fame. This is about my son,' Ashley said, seething at the flippant welcome Russ Boland was giving him.

'Who is it?' Sam Boland shouted, walking up behind his brother and taking a look for himself. 'Well, this is a nice surprise,' Sam said, eyeing the rucksack that Ashley was clutching so tightly, before raising his brow.

'Don't tell me you're finally paying up? How the fuck did you manage all this then? Get the father-in-law to help you out, did you?' Sam said, ushering Ashley inside the flat so he could make sure it was all there. He'd half expected Ashley to go on the missing list again, convinced that there was no way Ashley would be able to pay up.

He was late, but the fact that he was here at all was a miracle as far as Sam was concerned, so he'd let the stupid fucker off.

'Something like that. Yeah,' Ashley said, throwing the bag down on the table and staring around the flat expectantly. 'It's all there, every penny. Where's Riley?'

'Where's Riley? Who? Your kid?' Russ burst out laughing, unable to believe what he was hearing. 'You've got to be fucking kidding?' He was doubled over now, as if it was the funniest thing he'd ever heard. 'Oh, Ashley. You're a fucking card, mate. We ain't got your kid. Is that what you seriously thought? That we were behind all of this?'

By the confused look on Ashley's face, it seemed that was exactly what the man had thought. He was deadly serious.

'We may be a lot of things, but we don't fuck around with anyone's kids,' Russ said then, glaring at the man, the very real accusation of stealing kids giving him the hump.

'Woah!' Sam said, placing his arm in front of his brother as a warning for him to back off so that he could defuse the situation.

'We haven't got anything to do with your son going missing, Ashley. You have my word on that,' Sam said, seeing the look of confusion on Ashley's face, quickly replaced with a look of distress as he realised that coming here tonight and paying his debt off wasn't going to get him his son back, as he so clearly believed.

'But I thought…'

'We know nothing about Riley's disappearance. All we know is what we've been following on the telly. It's all anyone is talking about right now,' Sam said, letting the news sink in.

The world and his wife were talking about Riley. How could they not? The disappearance of a one-day-old baby boy from hospital had everyone's attention.

'I'm sorry that it's happened to you, Ashley. But trust me, like Russ said, kids ain't our style. We draw the line at that sick shit. It's not something we'd ever get mixed up in.' His tone was genuine, sympathetic even. 'But I'm glad you saw sense and finally paid up,' he added, opening the bag and eyeing the piles of money.

'The police are looking for a Jay-Jay Andrews. He works for you? He's the guy who attacked Shelby, isn't he? If you haven't got Riley, then he has,' Ashley said, unwittingly raising his voice a few notes, panic consuming him now that the trail might run cold. That he might never find Riley. He'd fleeced Pete for twenty grand in the hope that the payback would be bigger than the fallout. On the understanding that as soon as he brought Riley back his father-in-law would forget all about the money. He'd be forgiven. Shelby would forgive him too.

Only if Ashley didn't find his son, and the police got wind of the payout, it would only be a matter of time before they realised that he had demanded the ransom. That he'd once again dragged his entire family through a complete shitshow.

'He don't work for us. Like I said, we don't get caught up in any of that shit. That bloke's got fuck all to do with us,' Russ said, kissing his teeth, making sure Ashley heard the message loud and clear.

'Just tell me where to find him, please?' Ashley said.

'You what?' Russ raised his voice, riled up now. 'Didn't you hear what I said? He's got fuck all to do with us.'

Ashley had paid them their money. Now he needed to leave. Only he was still standing there gormlessly in their flat. Acting as if they owed him something.

'We don't have to tell you jack!'

Sam raised his hand again, silencing his brother. 'It's all right, Russ. It's only an address. Look at him, man. The lad's broken. It's the least we can do.'

He recited the address to Ashley as he scrawled it down on a bit of paper for the man, before he showed him out and closed the door behind him. Ashley Cooke was one of life's leeches. Sucking the blood out of anything and anyone that he came in contact with to get what he wanted from life.

How he'd managed to marry into Pete Baker's family, Sam Boland had no idea, and he was willing to bet all the money that Ashley had just given him that it had come from Pete Baker. Because there was no way that Ashley could come up with the cash on his own. It was unfortunate that a little kid had gone missing in the process. But that really wasn't any of his or Russ's concern.

'Why are we cutting Ashley favours? When all we've done for the past few days is chase the man for what he owes us?' Russ asked, confused as to why Sam had been so accommodating.

'Because it wouldn't surprise me if that fucking weirdo Jay-Jay has taken the kid.' Sam shrugged, seeing the way that Russ looked at him then. 'I mean who the fuck goes around threatening pregnant women with knives? And that woman over at Richmond Park, she had her stomach slit right open.' Sam grimaced as he spoke. That shit was too dark even for him. 'It ain't no skin off our noses if Ashley goes around there, is it? They can both give each other a pasting as far as I'm concerned. Two less beatings for us to dish out. I just wanted the bloke out of my hair and out of my house. Now, let's get this money dished out. It's payday!' Sam grinned, letting his brother know that he hadn't gone completely soft as he grabbed the bag of money and started dishing out the piles of cash, fairly, between them both.

CHAPTER FORTY

'Okay, Sarge, so Ashley is now leaving the address on Broomwood Road that is believed to be the residence of a Samuel Boland and his brother, Russell. He went in with the ransom money, and he's come out empty-handed.'

'And there's no sign of Riley?'

'No, Sarge.'

'Shit!' DS Morgan said. His team were still standing by – they'd gone with Lucy's suggestion of following the money, hoping it would lead them to the missing child. But so far, they'd drawn another dead end.

'Shall we bring him in, Sarge? Only, I spoke with him at the hospital and he admitted that he owed money to the Bolands, so I don't know if he's just paid off his debt to them or if he is trying to get Riley back,' Lucy said. 'But my hunch is still on Riley. He's dropped the money off, but he's not heading in the direction of home, or Shelby Cooke's place. Maybe he's paid the ransom, but Riley isn't being kept there. He might be on his way to pick him up.'

DS Morgan was silent at the other end of the phone, trying to work out which shot to call. They had units placed outside Pete Baker's house and back at the Griffin Estate.

'We've come this far, Sarge. I think we need to see where he's going next,' Lucy said, sounding more definite about her decision than she felt.

'Okay,' DS Morgan said, knowing that his younger colleague was right to want to stick with this.

So far, they had one suspect for who had attacked Shelby Cooke and had taken Riley; it was the same man: Jay-Jay Andrews. Recently released from prison, and no fixed address. Finding him was proving nigh on impossible because he lived off the grid. There was no record of him, no paper trail leading back to him. Lucy was right. This might be their one and only shot.

'Okay. Stay with him, Lucy,' DS Morgan instructed the officer. 'Take another officer with you; tell Holder to stay put and watch the Bolands' place. If anyone goes in or out, I want to be the first to know. And as soon as you find out where Ashley is heading, you let me know.'

'Will do, Sarge.' Lucy hung up then looked at Holder. 'Did you hear all that?'

'Yes, ma'am.' Holder nodded. 'You go. And I hope you're right and he's not just off to get a shag somewhere,' he said, recalling the footage they'd seen at Smokes nightclub.

Ashley was used to living a secret, double life it seemed. The man could be currently heading anywhere.

'Wouldn't that be amazing,' Lucy said, rolling her eyes and flashing Holder a grin. 'Catching the bloke with his pants down. Christ! Wish me luck.'

Getting out of the car, Lucy made her way down the road to where another unmarked vehicle sat. She'd follow in the car for as long as possible and then do the rest of the route on foot.

CHAPTER FORTY-ONE

Hearing the loud bang as the back door came crashing in and smashed against the kitchen wall, Russ and Sam Boland jumped to their feet.

Startled at the sudden forced entry, their immediate thoughts were that they were being raided by the police.

That Ashley had somehow set them both up.

'Pete?' Sam Boland said, recognising one of the two men now standing in his kitchen. Wielding a shotgun in their general direction, Pete Baker looked seriously pissed off. His fury magnified by one of his men who stood menacingly at his side.

'What the fuck?' Russ said, sensing the danger they were in and moving fast in the direction of their safe, to retrieve their own guns.

Only the unnerving calmness of Pete's voice when he gave out the next command stopped Russ in his tracks.

'Don't fucking move another inch, or I'll stick a bullet in the pair of you right where you're standing.'

Recognising the words for what they were: real. Not a veiled threat. Russ did as he was told.

The room fell silent, until Pete spoke once more.

'Where's Riley? Where's my grandson?' Pete asked, his eyes flashing with fury as he scanned the dingy kitchen for any signs that his grandson might be here. 'And where the fuck is Ashley?'

'For fuck's sake, not you as well?!' Russ said, visibly relaxing as he realised that this was all just a simple misunderstanding. Pete Baker hadn't come for the money. This was about the kid. And Russ and Sam had nothing do with any of that. 'We told Ashley, we don't know anything about any kid.'

'Any kid? This isn't just about "any kid!"' Pete bellowed. 'This is about my grandson, Riley. He's missing, and I want him back. Now stop playing fucking games with me!'

'Pete, mate! We don't have him,' Sam said, sensing the imminent danger. Pete Baker was a man on the edge. Wearing the deranged expression of someone who had completely lost it, Sam knew that Pete was capable of doing them both some serious damage. Or worse.

'Ashley's just left, Pete. We told him the same. I don't know what the fuck is going on, mate. But trust me, we ain't involved with taking your grandson. We don't know anything about it. Ashley owed us money and he's paid up. That's all we know,' Sam said as Pete's eyes went to the table.

He recognised the rucksack that he'd personally packed with the cash. The money from his safe had been poured out on the kitchen table and was in the process of being divided up into two piles.

'Where's Ashley gone now?' Pete stepped closer to Sam, keeping his gun aimed directly at him.

Right now, it looked as if Pete had been right about Ashley all along.

He hadn't come here for Riley; he'd come here for himself.

He'd ripped his own family off to save his own arse. While his own newborn son was missing.

The bloke was the lowest of the low. Nothing more than scum.

When Pete finally got his hands on him, he was going to wipe the man off the face of the planet.

'I said WHERE THE FUCK IS HE?'

'He's gone looking for Jay-Jay,' Russ intervened. Genuinely scared then this mad fucker before them would do something stupid and shoot his brother.

'Jay-Jay?' Pete narrowed his eyes, recognising the name of his daughter's attacker that the police were so desperately searching for. The man who had more than likely been involved in abducting his grandson.

'Jay-Jay Andrews?'

'Yeah, he thinks that he must have the kid. Your kid. Your g-grandson…' Russ said, stuttering as he corrected himself. Because not only was Pete glaring at him like a maniac, he could feel his brother's eyes on him too. As if he'd said too much.

'And what's Jay-Jay Andrews got to do with you two? How do you know him?' Pete said, sensing that there was more to this than these two fuckers were letting on. That maybe these two were involved in some part of his grandson's disappearance and Shelby's attack after all.

'We ain't involved with him, Pete,' Sam said, silently cursing his brother for even bringing Jay-Jay's name up. Because it wouldn't take a rocket scientist to work out the connection between the men.

Pete Baker pointed the gun back at Sam. The man was clearly out for blood and the manic look in his eyes told Sam that Pete was capable of getting it.

'Ashley thinks that Jay-Jay's got Riley. That's where he's gone now. To see if he can get him back.' Then sensing that Pete wouldn't take kindly to being fobbed off, Sam took a risk. 'Look, Pete, I'll lay everything out there for you, mate. We didn't know about the attack on your daughter, and we didn't know that the fucking lunatic was going around slashing pregnant women open… not until afterwards,' Sam started. Wanting Pete to know that they didn't condone Jay-Jay's behaviour.

'We sacked him off as soon as we knew. We told him that we couldn't be associated with him. That it wasn't what we were about. We don't work that way…' As soon as the words left Sam's mouth and he saw the thunderous expression flash across Pete's face, Sam Boland knew that he'd said the wrong thing.

'So, he was working for you?' Pete asked.

The room fell silent once more as Sam realised he'd called the wrong shot.

'You sent that fucking animal to collect your debt from Ashley, didn't you? And what? When he saw that my Shelby was fair game, he decided to rough her up instead. You stupid fucking bastards!'

Tucking the butt of the gun tightly into his shoulder, Pete's finger pressed against the trigger, just as an almighty bang sounded from the front of the house.

Thinking fast on his feet, Carl Rangers ran at Pete, forcing him to drop his gun on the floor between them all.

Just seconds before DC Holder's voice and a horde of police officers filled the room.

'POLICE! Put your hands in the air where I can see them.'

CHAPTER FORTY-TWO

Eyeing the broken fragments of glass hanging in front of the partially boarded up windows, Ashley figured that Sam must have been taking the piss. This house looked abandoned. The windows and doors all shuttered up, and the front garden full of weeds and bags of overflowing rubbish scattered everywhere.

'For fuck's sake!' Ashley muttered, guessing that he'd been purposely sent on a wild goose chase. The two brothers were probably both pissing themselves laughing at him right now, while they both counted their money. The two of them taking great delight in Ashley's misfortune, and neither of them giving two shits that his son had been kidnapped.

Narrowing his eyes, Ashley checked the piece of paper once more, in case he had made the mistake. Only Sam's scrawled writing matched the number printed on the plaque next to the front door: this was the place.

'Fuckers!'

Turning to leave, he stopped, hearing a noise coming from inside the house. A loud bang. Something falling? There was someone inside.

Making his way around the side of the building, Ashley held his breath as the sharp acrid stench of piss burned the back of his throat. Further down, he saw an opening. A large piece of jagged boarding had been prised open and pulled away, to reveal a half-open doorway. Getting his phone out as he peered inside through the pitch-black darkness, Ashley shone his torch. The light bounced off crumbling, graffitied walls. The concrete floors were bare of carpets, covered in rubbish instead.

He wondered if Jay-Jay Andrews was inside. Scanning the garden, he spotted an old broken chair lying on its side. Standing with his foot on the main body of the seat, he held on to the metal chair leg and twisted with all his strength, pulling backwards with everything he had until it finally snapped off.

He stepped inside, armed with only a metal bar and the element of surprise. His eyes cut through the darkness as he followed the torch's steady beam of light, peering into the far corners of each room that he passed for signs of life.

The only noise was his shallow breathing and the crunch of God knows what beneath his feet as he made his way along the damp, moulding hallway. Looking down, he grimaced at the trail of used needles and discarded food and rubbish strewn over every inch of the floor. He was still trying to hold his breath, breathing only through his mouth, because the smell was so much stronger in here. Like a stinking, overflowing bin. Pungent and rotten. Everything inside the building was encrusted with a thick film of dirt and grime.

Finally, he reached the last room. At the front of the house, where the large window was boarded up. He guessed this would have been the lounge once. As he shone his torch around, he saw the occupied mattress in the corner of the room.

A huddled figure was sleeping in the middle of the mattress, cocooned beneath what looked like a thick green blanket and a blue sleeping bag. Ashley shone the light briefly on the sleeping figure's face. It was him. Jay-Jay Andrews.

Ashley had only seen his E-fit, but Shelby had described him perfectly to the police. Shining the torch back around the room, Ashley searched for any signs that Riley had been here. A box used as a crib. A ball of blankets twisted into a makeshift bed. There was nothing. No sign of him. It was just Jay-Jay here, all alone.

Bang. A noise again, this time from upstairs. Jay-Jay wasn't alone after all. Though Ashley guessed that this place was full of people like Jay-Jay. Down-and-outs, druggies and addicts, all using the derelict squat as somewhere to stay.

Standing inside the doorway of the room, Ashley gripped the bar tightly with both hands. Creeping towards the sleeping bag, ready to batter Andrews; to cave the bastard's head in for what he'd done to Shelby. Only as much as he wanted to murder the man, he had to let him live because he had to find Riley. Ashley brought the bar down hard on the man's stomach instead.

The sudden fury of the impact abruptly woke the man, though the padding of his coat and bedding protected him from the worst. Within seconds, Jay-Jay Andrews was up on his feet. Towering above Ashley, his frame might have been slim and undernourished looking, but the evil look on his face made Ashley instantly regret thinking that he could take this man on. He was no match for him. But Ashley had made the first move; now he had no choice but to hit out again.

Swiping again, the bar clanged against Jay-Jay's skull, knocking the man backwards, unbalanced, off his feet as the pain erupted through him.

'Where's Riley?' Ashley said, holding the bar up and threatening to hit him again if he didn't speak. 'You attacked my wife and you took our son.' Ashley watched the recognition of who he was sink in on the man's face. His furious anger at being attacked replaced by something else. Shock? Confusion? He held his hands up, begging Ashley to stop.

But Ashley wasn't going to stop. Not until he told him where his son was. The bar came down again, splitting the man's scalp and sending a stream of blood trickling down his forehead.

Jay-Jay fought back. Scrabbling to his feet, he punched out, his fist locking with Ashley's jaw, sending the man flying across the room with the brute force of pent-up rage now, incensed at being so viciously attacked.

'I haven't got your kid. And I didn't attack your fucking wife.'

He grabbed the bar, smashing it down on Ashley's body; losing control, he hit Ashley over and over again, as the younger man cowered on the floor amongst all the dirt and debris.

Suddenly, light filled the room as the sound of a commotion came through the lounge door.

'Put the weapon down. NOW!' Lucy Murphy shouted, holding up her badge, two other officers behind her.

She took in the scene: the mess that was Ashley Cooke, lying on the floor battered. Jay-Jay Andrews looming over him.

Jay-Jay shook his head.

'And what are you lot? The fucking cavalry? Can't a man even get a few hours' kip in peace?' Jay-Jay smirked, dropping the bar and holding his hands in the air to show compliance. Part of him glad that it was now over.

CHAPTER FORTY-THREE

'Well, that was a turn up for the books!' Holder said now that they were back at the station and going through a quick briefing before they talked to Jay-Jay Andrews once again.

'The last person I was expecting to arrest today was Pete Baker. Looks like we got there just in time though, Sarge. Him and Carl Rangers are both insisting that they just "popped into the Bolands for a friendly chat", if you'd believe that. Only the Bolands aren't saying any different. Though I'm sure the fact that no one's talking isn't going to come as much of a surprise!'

'It's the law of the land, isn't it? Don't grass and don't incriminate anyone. Not even your enemies.' DS Morgan frowned, knowing that this would be the case. 'What about the shotgun?'

'Two handguns and a shotgun have been seized from the property and sent to Forensics. No one's staking a claim on them. I'd happily bet my life that the shotgun, at least, belongs to either Pete Baker or Carl Rangers, because there's no way that they turned up at the Bolands' place empty-handed. They were there for blood. Only without any evidence or allegations, we've got nothing on them. We'll have to let them go. And the Bolands will be the ones taking the rap for the firearms,' Holder said, glad that they had managed to have something concrete on the Boland brothers at least.

'Well, I'm getting nowhere with Jay-Jay Andrews,' Lucy said. 'He won't talk either. But it's pretty much a given now that he's linked to the Boland brothers, isn't it? Now that we've managed to link Ashley to both parties too.'

'And what about Ashley Cooke? How is he doing?' DS Morgan asked, knowing that the man had been taken to St George's in an ambulance. That Jay-Jay Andrews had left him in a bad way.

'It looked worse than it was, Sarge. He's got a broken wrist and a mild concussion, but luckily for him he'll live. At least until Pete Baker gets his hands on him, now that he knows that it was Ashley who fleeced him for the ransom money so that he could pay off the loan sharks he owed. Good intentions or not.'

'And still, we are no closer to finding out where Riley Cooke is.' DS Morgan rubbed his head, frustrated beyond belief. The first twenty-four hours of a child abduction investigation were the most critical and they were already twelve hours in, and still no nearer to finding who took the child. 'I want you in with Jay-Jay Andrews again. Something isn't right. Everything we have leads back to him. He must know something.'

'That's just it though, Sarge. Something doesn't feel right, does it? When I got to the house, he was bellowing at Ashley, saying he didn't have Riley and that he didn't attack Shelby,' Lucy said.

'And you believe him?'

Lucy nodded. 'He didn't know we were there at that point. Why would he say it if it wasn't true? And it doesn't fit. Why would Jay-Jay Andrews cut the babies from his victims' stomach? What's his motive?'

'Why do any of these sick fuckers do anything that they do?' Holder interjected, knowing that there wasn't always rhyme or reason to most crimes that were committed. 'Half the time, I don't think they know what motivates them. It's just an urge. Like some sick fetish…'

'But Jay-Jay doesn't fit the profile,' Lucy said, taking a sip of her coffee and drinking it down, despite the fact that it had now gone freezing cold. Currently twelve hours into her shift, with no sign of being able to finish for the day anytime soon, she figured she would need all the caffeine she could get.

'Zack Lownrey said something that stuck with me. Kidnappers' motives are usually money or power, so it would make sense if Jay-Jay had ordered a ransom for Riley's return, but he didn't. That was Ashley,' Lucy said, still trying to piece the puzzle together. Because they were trying to make Jay-Jay Andrews fit, but it didn't sit right with her.

'And if Jay-Jay did carry out the attacks on Liza Fitzgerald and Shelby, what was his motive? Because so far, none of this is adding up,' Lucy said as the penny finally dropped amongst her colleagues then, too, that she was right.

They were on the wrong track.

Then looking at her sergeant, Lucy added, 'I think I need to speak with Zack Lownrey again, Sarge. I think there's something we're missing here. And if I'm going to talk to Jay-Jay again, I need to have all my facts. Because whatever happens, he does know something. We just need to work out what.'

CHAPTER FORTY-FOUR

'So, you've got him then. Jay-Jay Andrews? You've brought him in?' Zack asked, guessing that there was a sense of urgency as he made his way into the incident room where Lucy was waiting for him.

DS Morgan had called him and asked if it was okay for Lucy to run a few things past him. And it wasn't until Zack had arrived at the station that he'd heard they finally had the suspect of Shelby Cooke's attack in custody.

'Yes, we've got him. Only he's saying he's not responsible, and strangely, I believe him. Something just isn't sitting right with me. I can't put my finger on it. I wanted to run something past you before I go back in and speak with him for a second time. Check I've got all my information correct,' Lucy said, waiting as Zack took the chair opposite her.

'Absolutely. Always happy to help.'

'In the first briefing that you did, you said that these kinds of attacks are very rare. That they aren't common here in the UK?'

'Yes, that's correct. Predominantly, the small number of these types of attacks that have been carried out have been in America. That's how the main study was recorded.'

'Do you know what percentage of men have been charged for attempting foetal abductions? How common is that?' Lucy said, knowing that if Jay-Jay Andrews was responsible for the murder and the attack on Shelby, as well as Riley Cooke's abduction, then Lucy and her team would need something stronger than just a hunch and an accusation in order to bring him to justice. Especially if the man wasn't willing to talk. Lucy needed all the facts.

'We don't have a figure. That's how rare the attacks are. Especially by men. I mean, it's not completely unheard of, but predominantly attacks of this type are carried out by women. Any men found to be involved have more than likely been working in conjunction with a female perpetrator. They were more likely emotionally connected to the main attacker. Be it as a boyfriend, husband or partner.'

'And again, that doesn't fit with Jay-Jay Andrews. He isn't in a relationship. At least, not that we know of.' Lucy pursed her mouth, deep in thought. 'And the main motive for such crimes if it were committed by a male? Violent, hate crimes against women? A sadistic fetish of harming pregnant women? Because at a push, that could fit him. Jay-Jay was in for a number of offences, including GBH. But still...'

Zack shook his head. 'These types of attacks don't appear to be random attacks. And I certainly wouldn't say that they were impulsive or that they're linked to being sadistic hate crimes as such. Though I wouldn't completely rule out an underlying mental health issue in the attacker. Crimes this horrific and callous would tend to indicate that the attacker could be experiencing an episode of psychosis, or that they may have a personality disorder. It's very hard to speculate. Every case is so individual. But the attacks themselves are rarely about the violent act itself. The attacks are often methodically planned and executed. We're talking months in the making. Shelby's attacker had a rope, a knife, not forgetting the surgical implements inside the rucksack. This wasn't just some spontaneous gruesome crime carried out on a whim. This was planned.'

'We had the DNA results back. Shelby's attacker is the same person who murdered Liza Fitzgerald in Richmond Park. It's a match,' Lucy said, sitting back in her chair now, her head spinning as she tried to make sense of the man's motive. Something was off about all of this. 'So, Jay-Jay would have had to have been planning the attacks on these women while he was still in prison? I don't see it. It just doesn't fit at all.'

'You don't think it's him?' Zack said with curiosity.

'Do you?'

'Well, I'd have to agree that he doesn't fit the profile. But the issue we have is the surviving witness. Shelby Cooke saw her attacker. She can confirm it was him. And like I say, the forensic profile is usually accurate, but it doesn't always fit the bill. Every crime, motive, and killer is unique. It's rarely a case of "one box to fit them all". I think the only way you'll crack this one is to work out what the motive was. Because the vast majority of abductors in these kinds of attacks, their motive is the prize. It's about the end game. The physical abduction of the baby. The child.'

'And that's exactly it. What motive would Jay-Jay possibly have to abduct a baby? He was living in squalor; he seems barely able to look after himself. And he certainly doesn't seem to be the paternal type. I just don't think that this was him.' Lucy sighed, almost certain then that they'd all wasted so much valuable time concentrating on Jay-Jay Andrews when he wasn't their man.

'I need to get back,' Lucy said, her head still spinning at the thought of having to speak to Jay-Jay Andrews again. She'd been hoping that talking to Zack would shed some light on the situation, that she might unveil a vital piece of information that might hold more clues.

But if anything, she was even more certain now that her hunch was right all along, and Jay-Jay Andrews wasn't their attacker. 'Thanks so much for coming in at such short notice,' Lucy said, getting up and leading the way back out of the incident room with Zack following closely behind her.

'No worries. And by the way, I enjoyed your company at lunch the other day. We should do it again. Maybe dinner some time?'

About to answer, Lucy was relieved when she didn't have to as the main reception door swung open and Holder strode towards them both.

'This looks cosy!' Holder grinned as Lucy ignored the 'told you so' look on his face. 'We just had a call come in from one of the midwives on shift early this morning at the hospital. Katie Farmer. She said that it might be nothing. But that she'd just realised that her uniform cardigan is missing. It had her hospital ID on it and her nurse's fob watch attached to the front. She said that she was with a patient who had been having suspected labour pains. Only she got called away, and when she came back the woman was gone. She finished her shift shortly afterwards and only realised her cardigan was gone now. But get this, she's convinced that the patient's name was Lizzie?'

Lucy pursed her mouth. 'Shit! Holder, do you have your laptop? I'm going to need you to examine that footage again while I go and have another little chat with Jay-Jay Andrews,' Lucy said then with urgency.

'Yeah, I can grab it. Sure,' Holder said. 'Why, what are you thinking?'

'I'm thinking that we have been focusing on the wrong man. In fact, I'd go as far as to say that we've been focusing on the wrong sex entirely,' Lucy said, the realisation that it had been staring them all in the face this entire time hitting her then.

'All this time we've been focusing on Jay-Jay Andrews. What if the attacker was a woman all along?'

CHAPTER FORTY-FIVE

'I thought you could do with something hot to drink.' Sliding the hot cup of tea and the KitKat across the table to where Jay-Jay Andrews sat, Lucy eyed the tape recorder but made a point of not switching it on. 'It's just you and me here, Jay-Jay. I'm not recording our conversation. This is off the record. Just a friendly chat.'

'Oh yeah?' Jay-Jay scoffed doubtfully, unimpressed so far with the good-cop routine that DC Murphy was putting on for his benefit.

He knew how manipulative and fake these coppers could be when they were desperate to get a result. And they were desperate, that much was clear. Because this lot really didn't have a clue what they were dealing with here. Desperate to pin Shelby Cooke's attack on him and the abduction of her baby. And the murder over in Richmond Park. They wanted to lock him up and throw away the key. Well, Jay-Jay wasn't playing any more. Why should he make it easy for them, when all they seemed to do was want to make his life harder?

'I know that you were there the night that Shelby Cooke was attacked.'

'No comment,' Jay-Jay said defiantly.

'I mean, you can't dispute it. Shelby described her attacker so accurately to the Facial Imaging Officer that the E-fit is almost an exact likeness. How do you think Shelby could have done that, if the attacker wasn't you?'

'No comment.'

Lucy sat back in her chair, taking a long hard look at the man before her. She took in the sight of the bleeding, bandaged wound on his head from where Ashley Cooke had struck him with the metal bar.

Jay-Jay's eyes were black, puffy circles. His skin was sallow, his sharp cheekbones jutting through his skin, giving him the look of someone who was suffering from malnutrition. And he probably was given the hovel that Lucy had found him hiding out in.

'The last few days can't have been easy for you. Hiding away while a manhunt was being pursued all around you and everyone was looking for you, Jay-Jay. This vicious, deranged man who butchers pregnant women…' Lucy said, purposely trying to get a rise from the man.

Only Jay-Jay was astute, prepared for her tactics. He'd been the other side of the table here many times before.

'Only I don't think that's who you are at all,' Lucy said. 'Here's the thing: I don't think you attacked Shelby Cooke and I don't think you abducted Riley. And I certainly don't believe you murdered Liza Fitzgerald over in Richmond Park.'

Jay-Jay raised his eyes then, eyeing Lucy as he tried to work out what tactics she was using now, and more importantly why. Reverse psychology? Is that what she was doing? Telling him all the things that he was desperate to hear, in a bid to get him to finally break his silence, just so that he would say something. Anything at all.

'Let me tell you what I think happened that night,' Lucy said, keeping eye contact with the man as she continued, trying to read his reaction to her words.

'I think you were there, on the Griffin Estate, and I think you were there for Shelby. That you were working for the Boland brothers, and they'd sent you there to collect Ashley Cooke's debt, or to give Shelby Cooke a warning. Give her a bit of a scare… Or both.'

Lucy could see that she had Jay-Jay's full attention now. His eyes were boring into hers.

'Shelby saw you. She remembers you.' Lucy nodded down to the E-fit to confirm that fact. 'Only I think someone else got to her first. Before you.'

Jay-Jay remained silent, not interrupting Lucy or correcting her, so she took it that she was either right, or at least close to the truth.

'Only I know that the attacker fled the scene. Leaving the knife and the rucksack with surgical implements behind. Shelby Cooke said in her statement that someone shouted. Alerting the attacker that they'd been seen. Someone disturbed them. But no other witness has come forward to identify or eliminate themselves from our enquiries. Because I think that someone was you. I think you saw the attacker. That you caught them in the act, and you were the one who shouted and warned them off, so that they panicked and ran.'

Lucy pulled out the photos of Shelby's injuries.

'When Shelby Cooke described you to me, she told me that she looked behind her and you were about twenty feet away. That she briefly saw your face, before she turned in a bid to get away. She was attacked from behind shortly afterwards. There are several gaps along that particular walkway. The attacker could have joined the pathway at any point. And maybe they hadn't seen you so far back, walking behind Shelby. Maybe they'd been too preoccupied with what they were about to do. Shelby didn't get another look at her attacker after that. Not throughout her ordeal, or afterwards. The only time she saw your face was when she turned and saw you when she first entered the path. It wasn't you, was it? Someone else got to her first?'

Jay-Jay hung his head in his hands then, relieved that DC Murphy had finally sussed it out. She wasn't just messing with his head. She was being genuine and really didn't believe that it was him.

'I didn't do it,' he said, his voice quiet then, cracked. 'I didn't attack Shelby Cooke, and I didn't murder that other woman in Richmond Park. And I certainly didn't take anyone's kid.' Jay-Jay shook his head, glad to get this all over with, finally. 'I couldn't tell the Boland brothers that I hadn't gone through with the job, because I knew if I did that, I wouldn't get paid. So, I kept my mouth shut and let them believe what they wanted. Only they didn't pay me anyway once they saw my mugshot all over the TV. They didn't want to be associated with me.'

'The only thing I can't work out is why you were caught on the security cameras outside the hospital. After Riley was taken. That bit doesn't make sense to me. So, you're going to have to enlighten me, Jay-Jay.'

Jay-Jay nodded and took a deep breath. 'I had the stupid brainwave of fleecing the old boy, Pete, Shelby's dad. Russ Boland told me that he was good for the money. And that Shelby was his most prized possession. That he'd do anything for the girl. And well, I need the money.' He scoffed then, realising how stupid he had been to get involved any further than he already was. He'd only made things worse.

'That's why you saw me on the camera. Hiding in the car park. I didn't know his address, but I knew he'd be visiting his daughter. So, I waited. I got there stupidly early, but I figured camping out there was better than going back to the shithole of a squat anyway. I was hoping to catch him on his own. I was going to cut him a deal. Exchange some information that I had. For a fee, of course.'

Jay-Jay shrugged; he knew how calculating it sounded. 'I was counting on that job with the Bolands. I've got fuck all to my name. No food, no money. Christ, you saw the cesspit of a place I'm dossing down in. I'm sleeping on the floor of a hovel, surrounded by wine bottles full of strangers' piss. I was desperate...'

Lucy didn't interrupt. She waited, allowing Jay-Jay to speak.

'I knew something was up almost straight away. Pete Baker turned up with his wife and son-in-law. I knew what they looked like, because I'd done my research. That's where I'd been all night, looking the family up at the internet café beforehand. Shelby likes to put it all out there, doesn't she?' Jay-Jay said, raising his eyes, his hands clasped together tight now.

His expression was solemn, Lucy noticed. As if he was ashamed and that he wished he'd never got involved with any of this in the first place.

'I watched as the three of them tore into the hospital car park and ran from their motor, and straight away I knew. I pieced it together and I knew what had happened. At first, I didn't link it. But earlier, I saw someone come out of the side of the hospital fire exit a short while before that. Holding what looked like a rolled-up blanket. I dunno, it was still dark, and I wasn't sure... I mean, she was dressed like a nurse, so I didn't twig at first. But then all hell let loose a bit later, and suddenly you lot were everywhere. Blue lights flashing, sirens. Cops crawling all over the place. And I just wanted to get the fuck out of there before I had that pinned on me too.'

'Wait a minute, you saw someone leaving from the side entrance? Someone who you thought was a nurse?' Lucy said, narrowing her eyes. 'And when did you find out that Riley had been taken?'

'A little while after that. Later that morning. I saw Shelby and Ashley, and yourself, on the news. And that's when I knew for sure.'

'And you didn't think to say anything? You didn't think that if you came to us, that we would be able to eliminate you from our enquires?'

'You are joking? You lot were out for blood, dead set at pinning all this shit on me. I had no alibi, and the prime witness has had all but a fucking oil painting made up of me. The Boland brothers have fucked me over and don't give a flying shit about the repercussions of a job that they sent me on. They've washed their hands of me. And I'd just got out of prison for GBH and assault. I've got previous. Who was going to believe me?'

'I was,' Lucy said with complete conviction. 'Because if there's one thing I know, it's that things are not always how they first appear. And my job isn't just to lock up anyone who fits the bill, Jay-Jay. That's not how I work. My job is to catch the person responsible for committing the crime. And I believe that all of this wasn't you. It doesn't fit. But you haven't made any of this easy for yourself,' Lucy added honestly. 'You ran and you hid, and you made yourself appear like a guilty man.'

But despite her words, she knew Jay-Jay was right. He was their main focus, and all their attention had been on him. All the while blinded to what was blatantly obvious to Lucy now.

'What was the information you were going to offer Pete Baker?' Lucy said, eyeing Jay-Jay and praying her hunch about the attacker was right. That Jay-Jay knew much more than he was letting on.

Jay-Jay raised his head. Trusting Lucy now. Believing that if he told her everything he knew, if he was finally honest with her, then she might just help him out of this mess that he'd found himself caught up in. She was the only chance he had at making any of this right.

'I was going to tell him that I knew who attacked Shelby Cooke,' Jay-Jay said finally. 'It was the same person who came out of the fire exit holding what looked like a rolled-up blanket. Only now I know that she wasn't a nurse and it wasn't a rolled-up blanket she was carrying. It was Riley Cooke.'

CHAPTER FORTY-SIX

'Janey?' Lucy asked as a voice at the other end of the phone answered after just one ring, guessing that the family hadn't moved from the phone, eager to hear of any news about Riley and the ransom. 'It's DC Murphy,' she said, holding on to the dashboard as she spoke, as Holder flew around a bend onto Wandsworth High Street. The sirens were blaring loudly and the blue lights flashing across the dark night sky, so that the other vehicles knew to move out of their way, and fast.

'Have you got him? Have you got our Riley back?' Janey asked with bated breath.

'No. Not yet. I'm so sorry,' Lucy said honestly, recognising the hope and anticipation in the woman's tone and wishing that she had better news.

She heard the loud cry then, away from the phone, and somewhere way off in the background, Lucy could hear Pete Baker soothing his wife before he took the phone from her.

'Lucy?' Pete said, coming to the phone, having only just arrived back home.

The police had no evidence against him that he'd committed a crime and given the circumstances, they'd decided to let him go, pending further enquiries. Only Lucy hadn't had a chance to speak to Pete before he'd left the station.

'We made an arrest, Pete. A couple actually. And I'm sorry to tell you that your son-in-law is currently at St George's Hospital.

There was an incident and, unfortunately, he's suffered a bad break to his wrist. He's going to need surgery. He's got a mild concussion too.'

'Ashley? What happened to him?'

'He attacked Jay-Jay Andrews. Only by the time we found them both, Jay-Jay Andrews was fighting back. We don't have all the facts right now, but I'm guessing from what I do know, that Ashley asked for the ransom money. I think he had good intentions in doing so. He believed that it would get Riley back. He believed he knew Riley's kidnappers.'

'He thought that the Boland brothers took him, didn't he? Only it was this Jay-Jay, wasn't it? The same man that attacked my daughter?' Pete said, wondering how they could have Jay-Jay Andrews in custody but still have no news on Riley's whereabouts.

'We have arrested Jay-Jay Andrews and he's currently in our custody, yes. But, Mr Baker, we don't believe he is involved in Riley's abduction or that he attacked Shelby either. We do have a new lead, and we are heading to the suspect's home right now. So, I thought I'd give you a call, so you could let Shelby know the situation. I wanted to keep you all in the loop. I think we are close,' Lucy said, knowing how important it was to Shelby to know that they were doing everything in their power to get her son back to her.

Lucy had told her that she'd personally see to it, that she'd inform her of every new development. 'I also told the doctor at St George's that I would inform Shelby of Ashley's hospital admittance. She's listed as his next of kin.'

'Shelby?' Pete called, and Lucy heard him marching up the stairs towards his daughter's bedroom. 'DC Murphy is on the… Shelby?' The phone went quiet for a few seconds.

'Pete? Is everything okay?' Lucy said as Holder made a sharp left onto the Griffin Estate, pulling up outside the two tower blocks and cutting the engine.

'She's not here. She's not in her room. She must have gone out.'

'Do you know where she might have gone, Pete?' Lucy said, a bad feeling growing in her stomach. Shelby would have been waiting for their call too, surely. So, where was she?

'We need to move,' Holder said, opening Lucy's door and waiting as she ended the call.

'Okay. Pete. I'm sorry but I'm going to have to call you back. If you find Shelby, keep her with you. I will hopefully have some news for you all soon.'

Hanging up the phone, Lucy got out of the car and stared up at the bright, twinkling lights of the two towers. She shivered, hoping the information that Jay-Jay Andrews had given her was correct. And that the person who had Riley was here, at the Griffin Estate. The baby's life depended on it.

CHAPTER FORTY-SEVEN

Glancing behind her as she made her way along the pathway that led to the Griffin Estate, Shelby Cooke shuddered. She was paranoid that someone might be following her again, though she knew that she was just being stupid. There was no one there. This time, she'd stuck to the main road; deciding against taking the shortcut over the common like the previous night, she'd stayed on the pathway where it was lit up by streetlamps.

She was glad to be out of the house, away from her parents. Because as much as she loved them both dearly and knew that they meant well, they were driving her crazy with all their constant fussing over her. She just needed some space and fresh air. Now that she was here, though, staring up at the two towers that loomed above her, Shelby realised how much she'd grown to hate this place.

The Griffin Estate had been bad enough before her attack. Slumming it with Ashley in this hovel they'd called home for the past few months, had only ever been meant to be temporary. Though how long temporary was, Shelby would never know.

Hearing a noise behind her, she jumped, turning abruptly with fright then feeling stupid as she recognised the sound to be a little old lady pulling her shopping trolley behind her, the wheels whirring loudly on the concrete. Stepping aside, Shelby let the lady pass, closing her eyes briefly for a second as she tried to steady her beating heart.

Was this how it was going to be from now on? Was every little sound, every strange noise going to startle her and make her fear that someone was going to hurt her? It didn't help that she didn't have Riley right now either. She knew that. She was completely and utterly lost without her newborn son, desolate and bereft. Part of her felt so numb and disconnected that the fact that he'd been snatched almost didn't feel real. It was like a bad dream that she just couldn't seem to wake up from. As if she was outside of her body, floating aimlessly, trying to find her way again. But she knew that until she had her boy back, she'd remain lost completely.

Pulling the door to the first tower block open, Shelby took the stairs, turning her nose up at the acrid smell of piss. The graffiti splashed all up the walls, the rubbish at her feet. Reaching her floor, she turned towards the flat and stopped. Unable to move, her feet planted to the ground as she stared at her front door, surprised to see the place in complete darkness. Ashley wasn't here.

She felt the rage inside her start to surge then as she wrapped her hand tightly around the door key in her jeans pocket, the tip of the metal pressing into her flesh.

What was she thinking? That Ashley would comfort her, that he'd alleviate some of the agony that she was in? Why? Just because he was Riley's parent too. Because he'd understand how she felt. What a joke!

Ashley wasn't even home. That's how much he cared. Because if he did, he'd be sitting by the phone just as she had been. Praying for a call to tell her that Riley was all right. That they'd found him, and he was coming home.

She shouldn't have come here, she realised, crying now.

She shouldn't have given in to the moment of weakness that had swept over her when she'd talked herself in to coming to see him. Because Ashley was her closest link to Riley, and for some stupid reason she'd thought that seeing him would make her feel better. When the reality was that this was all his fault. All of this had been because of him.

Staring at the front door with contempt, she knew now that she couldn't go back inside the flat that had once been home. Not even for a second. She was done. Done with Ashley and done with this estate for good. Because when she got Riley back – and she would get him back – this wasn't the place where she wanted to bring her child up. And maybe Ashley wasn't the person she wanted to raise her son with any more either.

Wiping her tears, resolute then, Shelby turned to leave. And as she did, she caught the tiniest movement from Imelda's front window. The slight twitch of a curtain. As if someone was behind there, watching her. Remembering how shaken Ashley had said her friend had been about Shelby's ordeal, how worried she'd sounded, and the fact that she'd been in hospital too, Shelby decided to knock on her door. She could do with seeing a friendly face right now.

Standing back, she waited, eyeing the shadow that danced across the strip of light at the bottom of the door, hearing the sound of numerous locks being dragged from their bolts. Finally, the door opened.

'Shelby?' Imelda said, her eyes wide with shock at seeing her friend standing there. 'My god, Shelby? Are you okay? I heard what happened. And about your baby being taken. I'm so sorry. I didn't expect to see you… I thought you'd still be in the hospital.'

'Riley. I called him Riley,' Shelby said, her voice suddenly full of emotion once more, unable to bring herself to talk about her son. She shook her head. What was she doing? She shouldn't have knocked. She shouldn't have come here.

'I'm sorry. It's late, isn't it? I just had to get out of the house. My parents are driving me insane. I just needed some air and to clear my head for a bit.' Shelby tried to explain, noticing how

Imelda didn't move from the doorway, huddled inside, the door only slightly ajar as she stared out past Shelby. Her eyes were scanning the balcony, as if to check that there was no one lurking about out there. Shelby could see that she was scared, and she could understand why. Because they hadn't caught him yet. Her attacker was still out there.

'Ashley told me that you were worried about me. He said you seemed pretty shaken up by what happened to me,' Shelby said, putting the fact that Imelda's front door had more locks on it than Fort Knox and why she seemed so on edge down to that. She could tell by the panicked look on Imelda's face that the attack that had been carried out here had really got to her too. 'Apparently, the estate's been like a circus the past few days with all the journalists hanging about.' Seeing Imelda still hovering behind her half-closed front door, she forgot her own fears for a few seconds as she tried to reassure her friend. 'He'd be stupid to do it again when there's so much media attention on him. I don't think you need to be so worried,' Shelby said, before deciding to change the subject and nodding down at Imelda's bump.

'How's the baby doing?'

Imelda narrowed her eyes. Her hand protectively going to her stomach. She seemed awkward. As if talking about her own baby would only upset Shelby further.

'The police said that they'd seen you go in for a check-up. I know that we are due the same time… I thought maybe…' Shelby said, seeing the strained look on Imelda's face and worrying she'd said something she shouldn't. That perhaps the baby wasn't okay.

'Why would the police know that I was at the hospital? Why would they tell you that?' Imelda said, looking suddenly stricken then. Put out, as if her privacy had been invaded.

'They went through all the security footage,' Shelby said. 'They were eliminating people from their enquiries.'

'It was nothing. I had a few twinges that's all, and I haven't been feeling well. I just wanted to get checked out, but then I felt bad, you know. I thought I was probably just wasting the midwife's time. So, I left…'

Shelby frowned, eyeing Imelda suspiciously. Her friend was lying. Diverting her eyes and stuttering her words ever so slightly as she spoke. She narrowed her eyes then before saying what she'd suspected all along.

'You made it up, didn't you? You made up that you thought you were in labour.'

Imelda's cheeks flushed a hot red in answer to being caught out.

'You don't have to lie, Imelda. I know what you did… I get it.'

Imelda scanned the balcony once more. As if she was checking that Shelby was truly alone. Convinced that she wouldn't be. Convinced that someone else was out there hiding too.

'Hey, chill out. I won't tell!' Shelby laughed then, seeing Imelda's look of alarm. 'You came to see how I was doing, didn't you? Only what? They wouldn't let you in?' Shelby rolled her eyes. 'It's a strict family only policy… which is a shame because I could have done with them not letting Ashley in. That man…' Shelby spat, unable to hide the bitterness from her tone.

'Ashley. Why? Is he okay? Are you two okay?'

'Not really, no. It's a long story,' Shelby said, shivering as the cold swept over her then. 'I should have brought a coat, only I left in such a hurry,' she said, hinting for Imelda to invite her inside. Only Imelda didn't move and she didn't offer.

'I snuck out when Mum and Dad were distracted, having another one of their "animated discussions" as they like to call them. To you and me, it's a full-on row. My dad paid a ransom to get Riley back. Can you believe it? He didn't even tell me. God, they're doing my head in. I mean I know that they are suffering too. Riley is their grandchild but…'

'Look, I'm sorry, Shelby. Really, I am. For everything you're going through, but I was just off to bed. And like I said, I'm still not feeling great.' Imelda placed her hand over her mouth and feigned a cough. 'I don't want to pass anything on…'

Shelby nodded, realising that she was unwelcome here. 'Oh right. Well, I just thought I'd check on you while I was here. Say hi!' Shelby thought that she wouldn't bother again. Imelda clearly wasn't the friend that Shelby thought she was.

'I'll see you around some time.' She turned to leave – and caught the sound of a tiny sneeze and a murmur.

'What was that?' Shelby laughed, thinking at first Imelda had made the strange noise as she feigned another coughing fit. Only she didn't manage to cover the sound up, and the look of horror that spread over the woman's face made Shelby realise that maybe there was more to why Imelda wasn't inviting her in.

'Oh! You've got company?' Shelby said, raising her eye and giving Imelda a curious smirk, thinking that maybe Imelda had patched things up with her ex. And that was why she was so eager to get rid of Shelby. She'd caught them both at a bad time.

'No. It's the telly. I'm watching *One Born Every Minute*. Though I shouldn't really. It's like a form of torture, isn't it? When I'll have to go through it soon too …' Imelda said, babbling now.

Which made Shelby suspect that the woman was still lying. And for some reason she really didn't want Shelby to know who she had in there.

'Right, well, I'll see you around,' Imelda said quickly as they both heard the faint sound of a baby's cry.

Not from the telly, Shelby realised. The noise was coming from the little room just off the hallway. The nursery?

Imelda closed the front door quickly then; only she wasn't quick enough. Shelby managed to wedge her foot in the gap between the frame and the door. Every instinct in her body screaming at her that something wasn't right. That the noise couldn't be what she thought. What she hoped.

'What was that?' Shelby said, glaring at the woman incredulously before shaking her head as the terrifying realisation dawned on her.

'No. No! That can't be…' Shelby said, pushing her way into the flat now and not taking no for an answer.

Imelda was hiding something. Or more importantly someone. Riley?

CHAPTER FORTY-EIGHT

Pushing her way into the room, Shelby's eyes scanned the beautifully decorated nursery, her gaze going immediately to the cot, where the cooing noises were coming from.

'Riley?' she said in complete disbelief as she stared down at her beautiful baby son. Dressed in clothes that she didn't recognise. Wrapped in a blanket that wasn't his. But she knew those eyes. She knew that little face.

'Riley, darling!' she said again, a strange animalistic screech coming from her mouth, a mix of horror and relief, as she lunged for the cot, ready to scoop her son back up into her arms.

'No!' Imelda shouted, her mouth twisted, her expression feral as she stepped in front of the cot, a knife flashing in her hand. The jagged silver blade was pointed directly at Shelby.

'That is my son, Jason. He is not Riley. And if you take one more step anywhere near him, I'll kill you.'

Shelby stepped back, knowing instinctively by the woman's deranged, possessed expression that Imelda would do it, too. That she wasn't just making empty threats. She'd taken Riley. She'd snatched him from the hospital. And she was still claiming that it wasn't him. That it wasn't Riley, when Shelby knew that it was.

'I don't understand,' Shelby said, trying to make sense of the madness she'd stumbled into. If she hadn't come here tonight, if she hadn't knocked, she'd never have found him. 'You've got your own baby, why take mine?'

'This?' Imelda said, turning the knife and plunging it into her stomach. Shelby screamed out in horror as the knife penetrated her bump.

But Imelda didn't flinch in pain and there wasn't any blood. There was no reaction at all, except laughter as Imelda's cackle filled the room.

'Had you fooled, didn't I?' she smirked. 'It's good, isn't it? So realistic. Even the midwife at the hospital didn't realise.'

She had only shoved the fake bump that she'd bought online back on again when Shelby had knocked at the door. She didn't need it any more now that she had Jason, but it would have come in handy until she'd been able to claim that she'd given birth, in a few days' time. When she'd presented the world with her newborn son, Jason. And no one would have suspected. No one would have questioned her. Only Shelby had fucked that all up now.

'Why?'

'Why?' Imelda laughed then. A nasty, vindictive snigger. 'WHY?'

She edged towards Shelby, the knife between them. The sharp edge of the blade aimed towards Shelby. One false move and she'd lunge at her. Because Jason was hers, and this bitch was not going to show up here and just take him.

'Why should you be the one to get everything handed to you on a plate?' Imelda spat, furious now. 'Because you're the pretty one? The skinny one? Because you're mummy and daddy's little rich girl? Why should you get a man like Ashley who you don't even appreciate?' Imelda narrowed her eyes. 'All you do is bitch and moan and gripe about him. It's no wonder he never wants to go home to you...' Imelda had heard Shelby's countless snipes and comments about Ashley's infidelities, fed to her in rage on the few occasions that they'd stopped and chatted since she'd moved in to the flat. As well as having to endure the couple's numerous arguments like the rest of the neighbours on this floor. 'Why not? Why don't I deserve some happiness too?'

'You do, Imelda,' Shelby said. 'Of course, you do. But this isn't the way to go about it. Riley needs his mum. He needs me.'

Calling Imelda's bluff then, Shelby went for her child, her hands sinking down into the cot to pick him up and hold him. Just as a horrific pain penetrated her side. Like a punch. Winding her. And as she moved her hand to question the pain, she saw the blood.

'You stabbed me?' Shelby said, suddenly light-headed. Realising she'd underestimated Imelda's determination to keep her child.

'Put him down. Now. I told you. You're not taking him from me,' Imelda spat. Her eyes flashed malice. 'I should have killed you the first time I had the opportunity.'

'It was you?' Shelby said, doing as she was told and placing Riley back down in the cot. She could feel the blood dripping through her fingers as she put pressure on her wound, like they did on TV. To stop people from bleeding out. 'You attacked me? You killed that other pregnant woman? That was all you?'

Shelby braced herself for another attack, just as the room was filled with the sound of police sirens floating up from the road. The dark sky outside the window lit up with a bright flashing blue. From the noise it sounded like several patrol cars had just pulled up downstairs. Shelby didn't know if they were here for her or not, but it didn't matter. Because Imelda believed that they were. That Shelby had somehow led the police to her.

'I told you, no one's taking him from me. He's mine!' Imelda cried, snatching Riley up and making her way out of the door in a panic. Ready to run. The knife still in her hand.

All Shelby could do was scream.

CHAPTER FORTY-NINE

Lucy and Holder ran up the stairs towards the flat where Jay-Jay Andrews had told them he'd followed the woman back to, after he'd watched from the shadows while she'd attacked Shelby. The same woman he'd since seen leaving the hospital with Riley Cooke. And the very same woman whom Shelby Cooke had already unwittingly identified from the hospital footage as Imelda George, her neighbour and friend.

But when they reached the floor and flung the stairwell door open, both rushing out on to the balcony, the last person they expected to see was Shelby Cooke, standing there, doubled over as if she was in pain. Tears were streaked down her face, but much worse, blood was pumping out from a wound on her side that she was covering with her hand.

Lucy stared over to the balcony, where Imelda George sat perched on the concrete wall. Her legs were dangling over the edge, and in her arms was a crying baby Riley.

'Don't come another step closer,' Imelda screeched, wild with panic and fury at being cornered by these people. These people wanted to take her baby from her. They wanted to make her suffer for all that she'd done in order to be with him.

'Imelda. You don't have to do this,' Lucy said, holding out a hand for Holder to step back and go downstairs and alert their colleagues of the situation. Shelby was going to need an ambulance. And they were going to need a fire crew here, too, to prepare the ground, in case Imelda went through with her threat and jumped. Lucy just hoped that it didn't come to that. She prayed that, somehow, she could get through to the woman.

Imelda teetered dangerously on the ledge, glancing frantically down to the ground, where the police units surrounded the front entrance of the Griffin Estate.

'You're not taking him from me. I won't let you,' Imelda said, leaning over and looking down at the people who were gathering below.

She could hear more sirens in the distance. An ambulance and a fire engine were pelting towards the estate. She was trapped now, surrounded. She couldn't let them take Jason from her. No matter what.

'Imelda, I know what you did. To Shelby. And I know what you did to Liza Fitzgerald in Richmond Park. If you give Riley to Shelby, we can talk. Properly, just you and me. I promise you that I'll listen. Because I know that none of this has been easy for you, either,' Lucy said, trying to gauge whether or not Imelda was just calling their bluff.

Surely there was no way she would jump. Not with Riley. Only so far, everything Imelda had done had shocked and horrified Lucy. The woman was capable of murder and kidnap. There was no telling what she would do.

'You don't understand. You're just like her,' Imelda said, eyeing Lucy with the same disdain as she'd looked at Shelby earlier. 'You can't know what it's like for me. Look at me, I'm invisible. Fat and ugly. No one gives a shit about me. All I've ever wanted was someone to call my own. Someone to love me no matter what. And I have that now. I have Jason…'

'But that isn't Jason, Imelda,' Lucy said, watching as Imelda stared down at the crying baby in a trance. 'That's Riley and I'm sure you've done a fantastic job of looking after him, but he needs his mum.'

'I'm his mum!' Imelda shouted. Her voice coming out so forcefully that she lurched forward. The arm that was holding Riley jolted, causing Shelby to scream and run forward.

Stopping when Imelda stared at her; Imelda steadying herself as she warned the woman with her eyes not to come any closer.

'Please, Imelda. Please? Give him to me. He's scared, Imelda. He's scared and cold. That's why he's crying. He needs to be fed. He needs my milk,' Shelby said, begging then, aware the pain was getting worse, radiating through her side and into her stomach.

But all she could think about right now was getting her son back safely.

'All I wanted was a baby of my own,' Imelda said to no one in particular, her eyes down, looking on Riley. 'I can't have kids,' she continued. 'So much for there being a God, huh. He made me fat and invisible and then took away my ability to have a baby. I'm ugly on the inside and the outside. But you!' Imelda looked up and stared at Shelby in disgust. 'You've always got everything you wanted, haven't you? You even took him from me.'

Shelby narrowed her eyes as Imelda nodded towards the flat.

'Ashley?' she said, confused. Thinking of all the times that they'd joked about Imelda having a crush on him. When really it had been an infatuation. An obsession.

'You're deluded,' Shelby said, shaking her head. Realising what she needed to do. 'We used to laugh about you, do you know that?'

Imelda was silenced then, her expression physically crumbling, as if she'd just been punched.

'You wouldn't stand a chance with him. Me and Ashley, we used to lie in bed together and cry with laughter about the pathetic crush you had on him,' Shelby said, on a roll now. Seeing the rage spread across Imelda's face. The humiliation. The indignity of what she was being told. It was all she could think about. All she could absorb. And Shelby had to keep talking. She had to distract Imelda.

She could see Lucy gradually edging her way towards her. So slowly, as she inched her way forward, that it was almost as if she wasn't moving at all. And Shelby was revelling in this, wanting to hurt this bitch who had attacked her and taken her child.

'It was the funniest thing, had us both in stiches, because Ashley would never have looked twice at you. Why would he when he had me?'

Shelby expected to see the wild rage in Imelda's eyes. She braced herself for the woman to jump from the wall and pound her with her chunky fists. Anything, anything as long as she got her and Riley off that ledge. But Imelda wasn't as stupid as Shelby thought. She looked at Shelby and her eyes shone with triumph. She held Shelby's whole life in her hands. She had all the power. And in a flash, she could destroy her. Imelda lunged from the balcony.

CHAPTER FIFTY

Imelda had stopped focusing on Lucy. Lost in her own anger, it was as if she'd forgotten that Lucy was even there. All she could see was Shelby and Riley. And she knew that there would be no going back for her now. Not after everything she'd done. She couldn't keep Jason. And the police knew what she'd done. There was no way out for her, nowhere left for her to go. So, she jumped. Leaning forward and releasing the one hand that had been gripping on tightly to the wall, she let go.

Only Lucy was on her in a fraction of a second. Her feet leaping from the floor, hooking one arm around both Riley and Imelda, as her other hand grabbed Imelda's top and yanked her backwards. Fuelled with adrenaline, it was like a surge of strength that Lucy didn't even know she possessed had taken over as she slammed Imelda onto the floor of the balcony. Her plump frame cushioned the fall for Riley, who she still clung to awkwardly as she landed with a thump on her back, her head smacking against the floor.

Pain exploded inside Imelda's skull, leaving her dizzy and confused.

Shelby took her moment. Grabbing her little boy from the woman's clutches, she scooped Riley up into her arms, barely having time to even look at him, when Imelda grabbed at her leg. Shelby kicked out, catching the woman hard in the ribs with her foot and sending her back down into a heap on the floor.

She had no intention of ever letting this woman anywhere near her child again.

'Go!' Lucy ordered her, nodding towards the stairwell.

Shelby did as she was told.

'He's mine. You can't take him…' Imelda screamed and lashed out, writhing around in fury. But Lucy was on her, straddling the woman as she pinned her arms down. Seconds later Holder and a couple of her other colleagues came bursting through the door to her aid.

'Imelda George, I am arresting you for the murder of Liza Fitzgerald. The assault on Shelby Cooke and the abduction of Riley Cooke. You do not have to say anything, but it may harm your defence if do not mention when questioned something which you later rely on in court. Anything you do say may be given in evidence.'

'Fuck you!' Imelda spat as Lucy slapped the handcuffs on the woman and finished reading her her rights.

'Charming!' Lucy said, stepping aside and letting her colleagues take the woman to the awaiting patrol car downstairs.

'You got her!' Holder grinned, seeing how flustered and emotional Lucy looked.

'No. *We* got her!' Lucy said, taking a deep breath. She could relax at last.

CHAPTER FIFTY-ONE

'You did a great job, Lucy!' DS Morgan said, closing his office door, and hoping to speak to Lucy now that they both had a spare five minutes. 'To say that spirits are high is an understatement,' he quipped, knowing how ecstatic his entire team were now that Imelda George had been arrested. The cases were solved. It was a great feeling, no matter how short-lived until the inevitable next big case came in.

'No, Sarge, we did a great job. All of us. Holder included,' Lucy said earnestly, knowing that she couldn't have done all that she had without the backup of her team around her.

She'd acted on a hunch, and Jay-Jay Andrews had given her the information she needed. It had been a team effort bringing Imelda George in. Though Lucy was glad that her superior was pleased with how she'd handled the job. Riley Cooke was safely back with his mother. That was the best result any of them could have wished for.

'What do you think will happen to her, Sarge?' Lucy asked, wondering about Imelda George's fate now that she had been arrested.

'They've detained her under the Mental Health Act, so I'd hazard a guess that it won't go to court. It's clear to everyone involved that the woman isn't of sound mind. It's certainly no surprise to me,' DS Morgan said simply, as if he hadn't expected the outcome to be any different. It had been clear that they'd been dealing with a very messed-up, depraved individual from the very start of the investigation. He'd suspected that this might be the case all along. 'I think she'll be detained indefinitely. Still, it's a great result. She's off the street and we found her before she caused Riley Cooke any harm.'

'I know, thank God we got there when we did. I dread to think what could have happened otherwise. Things could have been so much worse,' Lucy said. 'I've just heard back from the hospital; Shelby Cooke was lucky. She only suffered a minor flesh wound. They've let her go home.'

'That's great news,' DS Morgan said, relieved that Imelda hadn't managed to do any more damage than she'd already inflicted upon the Cooke family.

'Are you coming for a quick celebratory drink then?' DS Morgan said, grabbing his coat as he spotted his colleagues starting to pile out of the office.

'I can't, Sarge. I said I'd pop round and see how Shelby's doing. I just want to make sure that she's okay, you know. After everything that happened.' Lucy knew it sounded silly, but she wanted to see with her own eyes that Shelby and Riley Cooke were okay. Until she did, it still felt like unfinished business.

'Sarge, before you go…' Lucy said, glad that they had a few minutes to talk away from the rest of the team. 'I just wanted to tell you that I've decided I don't want my mother's case reopened.'

'You're sure about that?' DS Morgan perched against his desk, knowing full well that a decision like that wouldn't have come lightly. 'Because I meant what I said, you know. Whatever resources you need, however many officers you need, if you say the word, I'll reopen it. And it's not guaranteed, of course, but there's always a chance that we can solve it this time.'

'I know that, Sarge. And I'm grateful for that. But I'm certain. And trust me when I say, I gave it a lot of thought. I spoke to

Zack, and he said he'd be happy to do the profiling, and I had the E-fit drawn up. But, I dunno…' Lucy sighed.

She knew how much this case had affected her boss, how he'd spent so much time over the years tormenting himself for not catching her mother's killer. There was no one else in the world, aside from herself, who would like to see her mother's killer brought to justice as much as DS Morgan. But she also knew that her boss respected her decision, too, and that he wasn't going to talk her into doing something that she wasn't ready to do.

'I thought about doing it. Dragging it all up again, reopening the case. But part of me thinks that it just wouldn't be the right thing to do. Not now. Not with the way things are with my nan's health. I don't know how much time she has left, Sarge, but the time she does have, well, I want to be here for it. In the present. Spending it with her. Not trapped in the past, consumed with this case, driving myself crazy while we wait for a breakthrough with any forensic evidence it throws up. Because cold cases rely so heavily on forensics, don't they? And I can't help but feel that the odds will be against us. It was two decades ago.'

Lucy paused, gearing herself up to say what else was on her mind.

'And what if it brought other things to light, too?' she said finally, hinting at the real reason behind her decision. 'I mean, the press would get hold of this, wouldn't they? And, of course, they'd run with it. The police officer whose mother got murdered, the case that never got solved, and what about my mother's privacy? What if they found out things that she wouldn't want the whole world to know about her? Because we all have secrets, don't we?' Lucy said, unable to divulge any more details.

But she didn't have to.

DS Morgan nodded in understanding, his silence speaking volumes. Which told Lucy what she'd already suspected. DS

Morgan knew her mum's secrets. He hadn't said anything to Lucy for fear of hurting her further.

'I know that it's not the decision that you hoped for, but I just want to move on. I can't bring her back, Sarge. But I can make sure that she keeps her dignity in death. And that's all she has left.'

'Of course, Lucy. I do understand. Really. And I not only support your decision, but I respect it too,' DS Morgan said finally. 'I learned a very long time ago that you can't win them all. Sometimes you have to walk away from things in order to keep your own sanity. So, I get it, I really do!'

DS Morgan smiled, seeing the relief on Lucy's face now that they'd finally had this conversation and she knew what she wanted to do.

'Right, well, if you're off to see Shelby Cooke, then I better get my arse across the road to the pub. You know what that lot are like. I've never seen that lot move so quickly, bunch of tight arses. Holder's the bloody worst of them. "Last one in buys the round." "First one in buys the round." "The one wearing the blue coat buys the round."' DS Morgan chuckled, pulling his arms through the sleeves of his blue coat and knowing he was going to get stumped with the bill one way or another. 'He makes up the rules as he goes along that one. And I fall for it every single bloody time.'

Following her boss out of the office, Lucy couldn't help but laugh at that.

CHAPTER FIFTY-TWO

Ringing the bell at Janey and Pete Baker's house, Lucy took a step back, admiring the wisteria that twisted up the brickwork of the picture-perfect house, before taking in the immaculately manicured front garden.

The place really was worlds away from the Griffin Estate, and Lucy could see instantly why Shelby would prefer to bring Riley back home here. She clearly just wanted the best for him.

She smiled then, hearing the sound of Riley's gentle cries coming from somewhere inside the house. Guessing that he was alerting his parents that he needed a feed or a nappy change.

'Oh, wow! Ashley, you look awful!' Lucy exclaimed as Ashley opened the front door and she eyed his battered and swollen face. His right arm was set in a cast and sling. She couldn't help but feel sorry for the man. One thing was for sure, he'd certainly been through the wars this week. More than once.

'Why thanks!' Ashley grinned, knowing full well that Lucy was only voicing her concern for him. He knew it looked bad. 'It looks a lot worse than it actually is. Apart from my arm. That's royally fucked!' He stepped back, inviting Lucy inside the house.

'Are you staying here too?' Lucy asked as she stepped inside and wiped her feet on the mat, curious as to whether all had been forgiven and Shelby had taken Ashley back. Knowing how hard it must be for Ashley to be back here, constantly scrutinised under

Pete Baker's watchful eye. The man wouldn't be making it easy for Ashley, that was for certain.

'No. I'm back at the flat. But Shelby wants me here as much as possible to help with Riley. Co-parenting she calls it.' He shrugged. 'Secretly, a small part of me thinks that it's because she wants me here really. Only she's too proud and angry with me to say it. You know, after everything…'

'Well, it's still early days and at least you're on good terms,' Lucy said, sensing the hope in Ashley's voice as he led her to the lounge.

'Have you heard anything yet? About Imelda George?'

'I have. That's why I'm here. To give you all an update, and of course I was hoping to see little Riley too,' Lucy said, following Ashley through.

'Well, as you can hear, he's letting his presence be known and making himself well and truly at home. Shelby won't let him out of her sight, though that's to be expected I guess.'

'Oh, understandably,' Lucy agreed, unable to even imagine the turmoil Shelby must have felt at being separated from her newborn son.

'Lucy!' Shelby smiled as Lucy entered the room. She was in the armchair in front of the window, nursing a hungry-looking Riley. 'You came!'

'I told you that I'd pop in and see how you're doing,' Lucy said, seeing that Shelby was doing just fine as she breastfed her son. A look of contentment spread across her face as she looked down at the boy so lovingly, before looking back at Lucy once more.

'I'd get up and give you a hug, only I've been told to take it easy. I've got to let the stitches heal. They've padded me up with that many bandages I can barely bend over. I feel like something off *The Mummy*. And this lot keep trying to take Riley from me, so that I don't have to keep lifting him,' Shelby said, rolling her eyes playfully. 'Honestly! Even wild horses couldn't keep me away from my son after everything we've been through. A few stitches certainly aren't going to stop me.'

'We told her to rest and let us look after Riley, but she won't have it,' Janey quipped, getting up from the sofa and muting the TV programme that Pete had been watching.

'I'm glad you're doing okay,' Lucy said, genuinely relieved to see Shelby back home and making a quick and full recovery.

'Well, is there any news? Please tell me that you lot have locked that bloody mental case up and thrown away the bloody key?'

'Well...' Lucy started, only Pete was already on a roll.

'The woman is a bloody psychopath. She's sick in the bloody head, that's what she is,' he said, his anger steadily building, ready for a full-on rant about the woman who attacked his daughter and abducted his grandchild.

'Dad!' Shelby said, rolling her eyes then. 'Give Lucy a chance to speak.' She was eager to hear the fate of the woman who had abducted her child.

'Imelda George is being detained under the Mental Health Act. She's going to be transferred to a secure unit, where she'll be placed, I suspect, indefinitely. Going on her heinous crimes, and the rapidly deteriorating state of her mental well-being, it's highly unlikely that she'll be rejoining society for a very long time. If ever again.'

'A secure unit? What? So, she's not going to prison? You're sending her to some sort of hospital instead? How does that work? She murdered someone. She would have murdered again, too, no doubt. You saw that she was capable of it, and what? You're letting her off the hook?' Pete said, raising his voice now, incensed with what he was hearing. 'What is wrong with you people? Why is she getting special treatment? She's not right in the head.'

'Which is exactly why they won't place her in prison, Pete. You're right, Imelda George is a very sick individual. But please, trust me when I say the secure unit that she's going to is no better than a prison. It's very much the same system. And I can assure you that she will be kept away from the public for a very long time to come. She won't be hurting anyone else again.'

'I don't care where they keep her, as long as she's as far away from Riley as possible,' Shelby said, accepting the news that Lucy was delivering to them without question.

Because the truth was, she'd suspected as much. She'd seen with her own eyes how sick and deluded Imelda George was. The woman had been so obsessed with taking a child that didn't belong to her. With trying to make Riley her own. And nobody in their right mind did that. No one would be stupid enough or crazy enough to think that they could get away with it.

'As long as she is off the streets and can't get her filthy mitts near Riley ever again, then that's good enough for me,' Shelby said, eyeing her father now in the hope that if she could accept Imelda's fate, then he could too. And maybe now he would calm down. Though she knew that her dad wouldn't find any form of punishment fitting enough for the woman, after everything Imelda George had put his family through.

'The main thing is that Riley is home and safe. Imelda George will never come anywhere near him again,' Lucy said, wanting Shelby to know that for certain, so that she could move on properly in her life and not worry about looking over her shoulder.

Imelda George had almost destroyed Shelby. She'd taken the one thing she dearly loved the most and she'd snatched him right from under her nose. But in the end, it was Shelby who had won.

'Well, it's something I guess,' Janey said. 'Oh, how rude of me, Lucy. I didn't even ask if you'd like a cup of tea. Do you have time, or are you rushing back to work?' She smiled as Lucy nodded.

'Do you know what, I'd love one, Janey. Besides, it will give me a chance to stay for a few extra minutes and see how this little one's doing.'

'Oh, he's doing just fine. He's already got his belongings scattered all over the place. Cribs and buggies and teddies everywhere,' Pete grumbled, getting up, before casting a look over to where his daughter was now breastfeeding Riley and suppressing a grin. 'But we wouldn't have it any other way. God knows what it will be like by the time he's toddling around. He'll have well and truly taken over the place.'

Lucy laughed then, seeing the excitement in Pete's and Janey's faces at the prospect.

'I'll give you a hand, Janey.' Pete followed his wife from the room, to give Lucy some time alone with Shelby and Ashley.

'Looks as if Riley's going to have big scary Grandad Pete completely wrapped around his finger then. He's going to be super spoiled by his grandparents, isn't he?' Lucy said, once they were alone.

'Don't!' Shelby chuckled. 'The pair of them are both practically falling over each other to look after him. What with me recovering from being stabbed, and Ashley's broken wrist. We're a right old pair. They've got a full house again. And between us, I think that they secretly love it!'

'Not so much me being here though,' Ashley muttered, knowing that Pete couldn't be overly impressed with Shelby insisting that he be allowed around here. Though in fairness to Pete, he'd kept any gripes he still had to himself, putting Riley first and respecting Shelby's wishes.

'Well, like I said, this is about Riley now. We all need to do our best by him,' Shelby said again, reminding Ashley that this wasn't a free pass.

He was only back here because of Riley. Nothing else mattered right now, other than their son. Shelby didn't even want to think about anything else right now.

But Lucy could tell by the way the couple were united together for the sake of their son that there was definitely hope. She could still see a lot of love there.

'How has this little one been?' Lucy said, glancing down at Riley, swaddled tightly against his mother's bosom as he finished his feed.

'He's been great, hasn't he, Ashley? It's like he's never been away from me,' Shelby said, pulling her top across her and looking at her husband as he nodded in agreement.

'He's just perfect! They both are,' Ashley said, his voice swelling with pride as his gaze rested on his wife and child, as if he was the proudest man alive. 'Is there any news on the Boland brothers and Jay-Jay Andrews?'

'We're still working on the Boland brothers. According to their lawyer, they are squeaky clean. They're claiming that they never employed Jay-Jay Andrews, and we've no way to prove that they did, other than Jay-Jay's word. Which unfortunately for him, doesn't amount to much given his record,' Lucy said, wishing she could give Ashley better news. Because men like the Boland brothers always managed to somehow stay out of trouble, and it was always the scapegoats like Jay-Jay Andrews who ended up taking the fall for them in the end. 'But we did manage to find a few illegal firearms in their possession, so they won't be getting away completely scot-free. The rest will depend on you, Ashley. If you are prepared to make a statement about the money that you borrowed from them, they could be prosecuted for operating as illegal unauthorised lenders. We could also pursue them for battery, only the club's security footage has gone missing.'

Ashley shook his head.

Recalling the security disc that Kate had brought around to the flat when Shelby had been in hospital, and the fact that he didn't want to spend the rest of his life looking over his shoulders for the likes of the Boland brothers coming for their revenge if he was the reason that they both ended up getting sent down.

'I don't want any more drama. I just want to be here, looking after my family. Riley is my focus now.'

Lucy nodded, understandingly.

Then remembering her sergeant's words. 'Sometimes, you can't win them all,' she added.

'We managed to get the one that mattered. We got Imelda George.'

'And thank God you did!' Shelby said, moving Riley to her shoulder and rubbing his back gently in an effort to wind the boy. Then seeing the look of sheer adoration on Lucy's face, Shelby smiled.

'Do you want to hold him?'

'Bloody hell, that is special treatment, isn't it?! She's barely let us hold him.' Ashley laughed, raising his eyebrows at Lucy.

'Well, it's the least I can do. And I'm sure that Riley would love to have a cuddle with the detective constable who helped to bring him home safely.'

'Can I?' Lucy said, realising that she would like to hold Riley.

He had been all she had thought about for days, and just seeing him here, home and safe with his family, reminded Lucy why she did this job.

Sometimes it was beyond hard work. The hours, the people they dealt with, the injustice of the system. And then there were times like this, when suddenly it all seemed worth it.

'Course you can,' Shelby said, sitting forward and helping to guide the child into Lucy's arms.

'Ahh look at him,' Lucy cooed, taking in his neat head of hair, his plump little cheeks.

Leaning down, Lucy couldn't help herself but give Riley a small kiss on the top of his head.

'He really is just perfect!'

CHAPTER FIFTY-THREE

'Well, that was a week!' Holder said, scooping up the last bite of his sirloin steak and shoving it into his mouth, watching as Lucy drank back her glass of wine.

'You could say that again!' Lucy said. 'Thank God it's over!'

'Well, I'm not surprised one bit that they locked her up, are you?' Holder said, referring to Imelda George being sectioned under the Mental Health Act. 'I mean, you'd have to be off your rocker to believe that you could get away with cutting babies from their mother's stomachs?'

'Mental or desperate,' Lucy said with a sigh. 'Imelda George was certainly a combination of both. I don't think I've ever seen such vacant eyes.' She shivered, recalling how Imelda had stared at her when Lucy had read her her rights.

It wasn't just evil or malice staring out from behind her eyes, but it wasn't pure madness either. It had been a mixture of all three. Imelda George had been aware that she had committed a crime. And as much as her lawyer would love to argue insanity, it was premeditated. She'd planned it. Every step of the way. Lucy was just glad that she was in the right place now, and that she'd finally receive the right care. And she doubted that the woman would ever be allowed to live as part of normal society again. Though it didn't make it any easier for the victims. A woman and her baby had lost their lives in the hands of Imelda's madness, and Shelby Cooke had had a lucky escape.

'Thank God we got Riley back.' Lucy smiled, recalling how happy Shelby had been when she'd called in on her earlier today, after she'd finished her shift, before coming here to meet Holder for something to eat.

'How are they doing?' Holder said, raising his brow. 'I take it she didn't go back to the estate?'

'No. She's still at her parents' place. She said that they are both driving her crazy but that she wouldn't have it any other way.'

'She couldn't face going back to the Griffin Estate then?'

'No. And I can see why. I guess that place just holds a lot of bad memories for her now. Like it's tainted,' Lucy reasoned, knowing that feeling better than anyone. 'And she said that she wants to bring Riley up in a safer environment. Give him the best start that she can.' Lucy smiled as Holder filled up her glass, before topping up his.

'Well, that will be away from his old man then,' Holder said, referring to Ashley Cooke. The investigation had revealed everything the man had been involved in. Despite his best intentions of tricking his father-in-law into paying the ransom, so that he could clear his debt with the Boland brothers, thinking he'd get Riley back, too, there was still the cheating and gambling to account for.

'Yeah, well. Shelby's pretty adamant that she's going to just focus on her and Riley now, but Ashley looks as though he is really trying. And I could tell by the way she was looking at him that she still loves him. So, I guess, who knows? You can't help who you fall for, huh!'

'That you can't,' Holder said, coughing and clearing his throat, as if he was about to say something else. Only Lucy beat him to it, changing the subject as she glanced around the pub.

'It's nice in here,' she said, eyeing the log burner in the corner of the room. The people scattered about on the wooden tables. The place had an ambience about it; it felt warm and cosy.

'Well, you know. I like to keep it real. I'm not really into pretentious places that sell all that fancy French stuff that I can barely pronounce.'

Lucy laughed then, knowing that Holder was only messing, but finding it amusing that he still couldn't let her lunch with Zack go.

'Well, as it happens, between us, I have to agree. I'm more of a burger and glass of Pinot kinda girl. And this place is definitely more my thing. I can relax here; it feels homely.' Lucy had been glad at the unexpected invite of dinner from Holder when they'd finished shift today. 'And this certainly beats a microwave meal I have waiting for me at home. This is probably the best burger I've ever eaten.'

'Told you!' Holder grinned. Glad that he'd brought Lucy to his favourite pub rather than trying to impress her with a fancy restaurant. Though to say he hadn't been tempted to compete with the likes of Zack Lownrey would have been a lie. 'We should do this more often. Go out for a bite to eat every now and again. It's nice.' He laughed, trying to hide the awkwardness of sounding too forward.

'Did you sort out all that business with the sarge?' Holder said, changing the subject before shifting slightly in his seat, worried that he was bringing up something uncomfortable for his colleague when he saw a fleeting look of surprise on Lucy's face. Though she did a good job at quickly composing herself.

'Yeah. Kind of.' Lucy smiled but didn't offer anything more than that.

Holder knew that Lucy was very private about her personal life and her past, and whatever it was that she had going on in her life right now, she was keeping very close to her chest. She hadn't mentioned the E-fit that he'd found in her house, or the numerous meetings she'd had with their boss. But Holder knew that something was up. Only he didn't want to appear as if he was prying. 'I'm only asking because, well... you do know you can talk to me. I mean, I know I take the piss sometimes and that I like to have a laugh and a mess about, but I can be serious too.'

'Thanks.' Lucy nodded, grateful at Holder's gesture. 'I know you can. And it's not that I don't want to talk about it, it's just...'

She was staring into her glass now. Deep in thought about her own predicament. She'd thought about nothing else since they'd arrested Imelda George. Finally able to put the focus on her own life for a short while, until she threw herself in to the next case that got thrown their way.

'Let's just say that it's complicated,' she sighed, seeing the way that Holder was looking at her.

As if he was trying to read her thoughts. Trying to work her out. But she knew he wasn't prying. That he was genuine. The fact that he actually cared and wanted to know if she was okay made her feel weird inside. Warm? Or that could be the wine.

'Maybe I'll tell you about it one day,' Lucy said finally, not wanting to get into any of that right now. The week had been a long one; the last thing she wanted was for tonight to feel heavy too.

Holder nodded, knowing that whatever it was, it would keep until Lucy was ready to share it with him.

'One day is good enough for me,' he said. 'Right, finish that last glug of wine, Balboa. And I'll drop you home. Sarge wants me in at the crack of dawn tomorrow. Unlike some of us who are lucky enough to have a day off.'

'Balboa? What's that? My new nickname?' Lucy couldn't help but laugh at her new nickname. 'It's better than Lewis Hamilton, I guess. Which we won't go over again, because obviously we both know that women can indeed drive...' Despite herself she was unable to help but bring up the very first argument she'd had with Holder when they'd first met. Which she'd won, of course. 'And now what? Balboa? As in Rocky? Because I took Imelda George down.'

'Yeah, because of your almighty left hook!' Holder laughed. 'Even though you landed yourself a punch too from that drunk driver. Hey, it's been a busy week!' Holder grinned, before adding cheekily, 'or maybe it's because I think you're a bit of a knockout.'

'A bit of a knockout! Woah, Steady on.' Lucy couldn't help but laugh then as Holder turned bright red at his sudden admission. 'I'll have to start dishing out the nicknames too. Cheddar.'

'Cheddar?' Holder said, rolling his eyes at Lucy's weak attempt of a nickname, secretly mortified that he'd said anything at all. 'Jesus, that's lame. What, because I'm dishing out the cheesy chat-up lines?'

'Is that what you're doing? Chatting me up?' Lucy giggled, thoroughly enjoying winding the man up. Normally she was on the receiving end of his teasing. 'Wow, how long has it been since you flirted with a woman if this is the best you've got? I thought you had way more game than this?' Her eyes sparkled, laced with challenge.

'Well. I do actually,' Holder began, trying to think of a good comeback. Only he was fumbling his words. Suddenly feeling vulnerable now that he'd let slip to Lucy how he really felt.

'Fuck it. I've started this now, so I may as well be honest,' he said finally, looking Lucy in the eyes. 'I really do like you.' He shrugged then, feeling as if he was about fourteen years old again and confessing his love to his first crush. 'And I know it isn't ideal, us working together, and I don't know, you probably don't feel the same about me, and that's fine...'

'Ben!' Lucy said, her eyes searching his. Her laughter halted to a genuine smile.

'I do actually.'

'You do what?'

Holder narrowed his eyes. Not sure if he just misheard.

'I do like you too,' Lucy said, reiterating her words. Before draining the last mouthful of wine from her glass.

'Now are you going to sit there jabbering all bloody night, or are you going to take me home?'

CHAPTER FIFTY-FOUR

Walking through the main entrance of Wandsworth Cemetery, Lucy smiled when Winnie linked her arm with hers as they both walked in silence towards her mother's grave. The sun shone down on their faces. It was good for her nan to get out and get some fresh air.

'I wouldn't want to live there, would you?' Winnie said, nodding over towards the lodge that they passed which sat at the cemetery's main entrance.

'Oh, I don't know. It looks like a pretty house,' Lucy said, eyeing the gleaming windows, adorned with pretty floral window boxes. A row of horse chestnut trees lined the border behind the house. 'There're worse places to live out there, Nan, trust me. That place looks pretty idyllic to me.'

'What, with a garden full of death and ghosts. I'd have to sleep with the lights on and a baseball bat next to my bed.'

'A baseball bat? For the ghosts?' Lucy said, shaking her head and suppressing her chuckle, happy that her nan was in such good spirits today, light-hearted and feisty. She seemed like her old self again. Though Lucy knew from experience that could change at any time. 'I don't think a bat would get you very far, Nan!'

'Well, at least they'd know that I meant business. It's got to be better than nothing, hasn't it? What else would I do, leave them a note saying please don't haunt me, my granddaughter's a police lady?' Winnie scoffed as Lucy laughed again. Her nan's theory clearly made perfect sense to her.

The two women made their way over to the far corner of the cemetery, to Jennifer Murphy's grave.

'These places aren't the nicest places in the world to visit.' Lucy shrugged. 'But I always feel, I don't know… peaceful when I come here. Like there's a sense of calm around me. Maybe I just feel closer to Mum when I'm here,' she said, trying to make sense of why she felt better when she came here. When like her nan said, the place was full of death and ghosts. Only for her it meant so much more than that.

Lucy had come here religiously from the age of five. Visiting this same green space whenever she'd missed or needed her mum, she'd sat at her graveside and talked to her mother, as if she was still here. And as sad as it sometimes made her, mainly it helped. It made her feel as if her mum wasn't too far away. As if there was a place she could go when she really needed her.

'We'll come here more often, Nan,' Lucy said, making a silent promise to herself, too, to come here more. Realising it had been ages since she was here last. Winnie too. Work had been so busy lately and life just had a way of taking over. And Lucy knew that it wouldn't be long until Winnie wouldn't be able to remember any of this. Why they were here. Who Jennifer was. Who Lucy was. She was on borrowed time. She had to make every minute count.

'We don't visit her enough.'

'Well, I can see that. When was the last time you cut the grass?' Winnie said, having another of her moments as she eyed some of the more overgrown, neglected graves that they passed.

'We don't cut the grass, Nan. That man over there, the care-taker, he tends to the grounds.'

'Well, he wants to pull his finger out then. Because this is not acceptable. Someone should be cutting the grass. And what about a nice pond. This place could do with one. And a café…'

'No, Nan. Honestly, it's fine…' Lucy said, realising that her nan was on a mission now. but it was too late. Winnie had already taken it upon herself to shout out to the caretaker.

'Cooee! Hello…'

The man turned and nodded at Winnie in answer. Only Winnie pursed her mouth, forgetting then what she'd been about to say. Instead, she threw the man a wink and shouted, 'I'm not too old to catch you, you know, and you're not too young to enjoy it.'

'Nan!' Lucy said, seeing the man laugh and take her nan's comment in good humour, guessing by Lucy's horrified expression that Winnie didn't mean any harm.

'Why did you say that?' Lucy said, holding Winnie's arm and guiding her off in the other direction, hoping to keep her out of trouble, as she started cackling.

'He's my boyfriend, isn't he?'

'No, Nan. He's the caretaker.'

'Well that's a real shame for him. I bet he wishes he was my boyfriend.'

'Oh Nan!' Lucy said, laughing then too.

Reaching the grave, Lucy placed the white roses that she'd brought her mother in the vase next to the headstone and stepped back to read the writing scripted upon it, even though she knew the words off by heart by now.

JENNIFER MURPHY – GREATLY LOVED AND SADLY MISSED

'Twenty-five. She was the same age that I am now,' Lucy said, noting her mother's date of birth and death. Wondering once again how different her and her nan's lives would be if her mother was still alive.

'Nan. If you had the chance to find out what happened to her, to catch her killer, would you do it?'

Winnie narrowed her eyes then, a pained look across her face that Lucy took to mean she didn't understand the question. Maybe it was futile even asking her, because she seemed so confused. Her words and thoughts so disjointed. But Lucy needed to say it. She needed to get this off her chest. Because even though she knew in her heart that she'd made the decision already, she'd never want her nan to think that she hadn't consulted her first.

'Would you want him brought to justice? Even if it dragged everything up again,' Lucy said, not sure who she was trying to convince of the enormity of what she'd told Morgan that she was going to do. That she was really going to walk away from this. That she was really going to let it go.

Winnie held Lucy's hand then. Gripping it tightly and looking her granddaughter dead in the eyes. 'I'm not long for this world, Lucy,' Winnie said, shaking her head sadly.

'Nan, don't say that,' Lucy said, not even wanting to think for a second about a time when her nan wouldn't be here either.

'It's true.' Winnie waved her hand, dismissing her grand-daughter. 'Look at me, I'm an old lady who's barely in charge of her own faculties any more. If you want to dig deeper, then you dig. If you want to let it be, then let it be. But you have to promise me something, Lucy. Whatever you decide to do, do it wholeheartedly. Because you are going to let this eat you up inside.'

Lucy nodded, knowing that her nan spoke the truth.

'Whatever you do, you need to do it and then move on. It's been twenty years now. It's time.'

Wiping the tears that fell from her eyes, Lucy felt the emotion of her nan's advice. This woman who, despite everything, in the midst of her illness, was still in there somewhere. Hiding away. And the times when Lucy really needed her, for short bursts of time, she was right there.

'You're right, Nan,' Lucy said, already knowing deep down that she'd made the right decision. Despite the guilt of knowing that her mother's murderer was still out there somewhere, that he'd never been brought to justice. Her nan was right. Twenty years was a lifetime. If she didn't finally let it go, it wouldn't just eat her up inside, it would devour her whole.

'Nothing's going to bring her back, is it?' Lucy said, knowing that she couldn't keep coming back to this point. If she kept doing this, she'd never get past it. It was time to lay it to rest. To move on.

'Come here,' Winnie said, taking Lucy in her arms and giving her a big hug.

Lucy relished the moment. Standing in her grandmother's arms and breathing in the familiar smell of her musky perfume.

'I love you, Nan!'

'And I love you too, my Lucy-loo,' Winnie said, before staring down at her daughter's grave and blowing Jennifer a kiss.

'Come on, Nan, let's get going. Vivian's over at the gate,' Lucy said, stepping back from her nan and giving Vivian a wave, where she waited patiently at the gates to let them have their moment alone to pay their respects.

'Are we going for tea and cake?' Winnie said, excitedly then, remembering that Lucy had told her that they would.

'We are indeed, Nan,' Lucy said as they made their way back towards the entrance, and Vivian walked to meet them.

'Lucy, darling! Winnie!' Vivian said, taking it in turns to hug the two ladies. 'Are you both ready to devour the best chocolate brownies in the whole of London?' She knew that they were Winnie's favourite. Vivian often brought her a few when she visited her at Treetops. 'They do a lovely strawberry tart there too.' Vivian winked, knowing that Winnie would more than likely pick a couple of cakes. And why not?

'Goodbye, ladies,' the caretaker from earlier said with a smile as they passed him.

'You been making friends, Winnie?' Vivian smirked, seeing the vague, amused look cross Lucy's face.

'You could say that!' Lucy laughed. 'She's on top form today, Vivian! Thought he was her boyfriend.'

'Ohh!' Vivian shrieked playfully.

'Oi! "She" is standing right here. And "she" can hear you,' Winnie said tartly, as the two women exchanged a knowing look, recognising the fiery mood that Winnie was in, and another of her mischievous moods.

'And I'll have you know, he's not my boyfriend. He's the caretaker,' Winnie said, mimicking Lucy's voice and repeating word for word what her granddaughter had said to her.

Then turning to Vivian, Winnie shot the woman a cheeky wink.

'And let me tell you, he can take care of me any day!'

'Oh, Nan!' Lucy said, rolling her eyes in despair and laughing again at her nan's brazenness.

'Oh, Winnie my love!' Vivian roared with laughter then too. 'I don't think he'd be able to handle you, my darling!'

A LETTER FROM CASEY

Dear reader,

I want to say a huge thank you for choosing to read *No Going Back*, the third book in the DC Lucy Murphy series. If you did enjoy it, and want to keep up to date with all my latest releases, just sign up at the following link. Your email address will never be shared and you can unsubscribe at any time.

www.bookouture.com/casey-kelleher

The crime genre holds a lot of darkness, but for me it's characters like Lucy Murphy and her beloved nan, Winnie, that really shine through. They are the people that we readers root for. The true champions. The real survivors. So, I'm so thrilled to have brought Lucy and Winnie back for a third time. Back at the Griffin Estate, with new characters around them causing mayhem and a whole new set of problems to overcome. And I'm equally thrilled to know that you love them both as much as I do!

If you loved *No Going Back* and you'd like to leave me a review, I'd love to hear what you think. I read every single one. I also love hearing from my readers – your messages and photos of the books always make my day! So, please feel free to get in touch on my Facebook page, or through Instagram, Twitter or my website.

Thank you
Casey Kelleher

OfficialCaseyKelleher

@CaseyKelleher

caseykelleher

www.caseykelleher.co.uk

ACKNOWLEDGEMENTS

Many thanks to my brilliant editor, Therese Keating. It's been an absolute pleasure working alongside you once again, on this third Lucy Murphy book! I've loved writing this series, and I'm already looking forward to our next exciting project together.

Special thanks to Noelle Holten and Sarah Hardy – PR extraordinaires! And to the rest of the Bookouture team, you guys are the best!

Biggest shout out to my fellow Bookouture authors, too, who I've been so lucky to meet along the way. For all the giggles, and for keeping me sane! Special mention to Emma Graham Tallon, Angela Marsons, Helen Phifer, Susie Lynes, Barbara Copperthwaite and Alex Kane.

Huge thanks also to all of those at the Scene of the Crime. And to the Savvys for all your fantastic advice and support. And to all the lovely NotRights.

Special mention to the real-life Lucy Murphy, my bestie! Who has always been so super supportive of everything I do. Will there be a gin festival in 2021? Maybe a socially distanced one. We can live in hope ;)

Thank you to Graham Bartlett and Neil Lancaster for all your help and advice when it came to police procedures. And to Katie Farmer for her help with midwife terminology. You may spot a familiar name in here. Though the fictional character is far less sweary! As always, creative licence does come into play when writing fiction, so any discrepancies on both counts will, of course, be mine.

As always I'd like to thank my extremely supportive friends and family for all the encouragement that they give me along the way. The Coopers, the Kellehers, the Ellises, and all my lovely friends.

A big thank you to my husband Danny. My rock! Much love to Ben, Danny and Kyle. Not forgetting our two little fur-babies/writer's assistants Sassy and Miska.

And finally to you, my lovely reader. You are the very reason I write: without you, none of this would have been possible. I love receiving your reviews, feedback and messages, so please do keep them coming!

Casey x

Printed in Great Britain
by Amazon